"Do you know wh[ ] another piece of bread [ ] through the heart. I wa[ ] like that. He never saw [ ]

"No, I'm sure he didn't," I said. [ ] people talking about it."

"Do you really think Bridges put them there?"

"He must have done."

Then we talked about Bridges. He was always known as Bridges, and nothing else. I'd only ever seen him from a distance. He was stout and wore the same old long coat no matter what. If we spotted him in the fields, we didn't go in. I'd never come across him at the shops or walking through the village. Sam said he was supposed to go to the inn sometimes, but we didn't know if that was true.

"Do you think it was him that scared Judy and Susan?" Sam questioned.

"I expect so," I said.

"Is he old?" Sam asked.

"I think so," I said.

"Is there a Mrs. Bridges?" he asked.

"I don't think so. He lives on his own."

"Do you think he killed the birds, or were they dead already?"

"I don't know," I said. "But why would they be dead already?"

The Five Things

by

Beth Merwood

This is a work of fiction. Names, characters, places, and incidents are either the product of the author's imagination or are used fictitiously, and any resemblance to actual persons living or dead, business establishments, events, or locales, is entirely coincidental.

The Five Things

COPYRIGHT © 2021 by Beth Merwood

All rights reserved. No part of this book may be used or reproduced in any manner whatsoever without written permission of the author or The Wild Rose Press, Inc. except in the case of brief quotations embodied in critical articles or reviews.
Contact Information: info@thewildrosepress.com

Cover Art by *Diana Carlile*

The Wild Rose Press, Inc.
PO Box 708
Adams Basin, NY 14410-0708
Visit us at www.thewildrosepress.com

Publishing History
First Edition, 2021
Trade Paperback ISBN 978-1-5092-3499-8
Digital ISBN 978-1-5092-3500-1

Published in the United States of America

Dedication

For Mum and Dad

Acknowledgements

So many thanks to my editor, Melanie Billings, and all at The Wild Rose Press, Inc. Also to Ed Handyside, Vicky Blunden, Alex Hammond, to author Linda Green, and to Brendan.

Prologue

I can explain what Tommy meant when he described himself as one of the birds. Most of the local kids knew about them. Not everyone had seen them, but I was one of the ones who had.

A while ago, when I was out on my bike and there was no one else around to play with, I cycled up to the top of the village on my own. I'd been to the lower field before, but it was the first time I'd ever been to the upper field. I walked across the grass—I remember it was soaked with dew—and came to the edge of the wood.

I'd heard about this place, and I was curious. You could see the wood from the lanes and footpaths. It wasn't all that big. It was almost round in shape and dense; people said you could never see far through it, even in winter when the leaves had fallen. Up close, the first thing that struck me was that most of the trees were very old. I'd come on a morning in early springtime. The surrounding land was beginning to burst with new foliage, and everything was full of bud. There was a cool sharpness to the air. I found the path, but it was as if it hadn't been walked on for some time. I hesitated, but then pushed past a tangle of spindly, spiky branches to where the way was a little clearer. Here the atmosphere changed; it was dark and dank, and the more so the farther into the wood I went. The path was sticky with mud and soft with layers of old leaves; ancient-looking ferns and networks of twisting ivy grew at the sides. I continued on. I came to another tangle and a fallen tree. I ducked down to clamber under a thick, moss-covered branch. Thorns stabbed at the top of my head through my hair and tore into my arms, even through my anorak. I pulled myself up on the other side and looked up.

What I saw was probably the most disturbing thing I'd ever seen: a huge black bird, hanging by a string from a higher branch, dead. The string went through the center of its back. It was hanging horizontally. I'd emerged right beside it; I'd almost touched it. The smell was rancid; the bird was decomposing, eyes gone and feathers dull. Its wings were outstretched as if it were flying. Some wing feathers were missing. Congealed blood clotted at the sides of its beak. I was startled and jerked back, cracking my head against the branch with some force. At that moment, I saw that deeper into the wood, more birds were hanging in a similar way, all dead, all decaying. The whole place had a deathly air. I was aware of the stench, the stillness, and the silence.

My heart was thumping. I pushed my way back along the path as quickly as I could, ran to my bike, and rode home at top speed. I went up to my room and lay on my bed for a long time, staring at the ceiling. You must never kill a living thing—unless it is for food. That's the way of the countryside.

"What's the matter?" my mum had asked later. "Something's the matter," she'd said.

In the coming days, I couldn't get the birds out of my head. I told a few friends about what I'd seen, but I never told a grown-up. We weren't really allowed in those fields, and I felt sure I would get into trouble.

The image of the birds stayed with me. I was frightened, and besides, I couldn't understand how someone could do a thing like that to such beautiful creatures. As children, we were taught to love and care for and cherish the land that surrounded us and all living things. It came naturally to us. We sang about it. We wrote essays about it. Seeing the birds was an abrupt wake-up call; not everyone lived that way.

I found out that a couple of the older boys had also seen the birds, and like me, they couldn't work it out. The only thing I could think was that they'd been put there deliberately to scare us, to keep us away, as some sort of grotesque warning.

Chapter 1
The First Week of the Holidays, The Birds

Late July 1969

What follows is the story of a group of children and the events of the summer in a small coastal village in the south of England. The year was 1969, and one of the children was me.

"Someone else is coming."
"Who?" said Anna.
"I think it's Naomi," I said.
It was the beginning of the holidays, and Anna and I had gone to the top of the village on our bikes. We'd left them at the gate to the lower field and climbed over. We were on our way up the steep path beside the tangled hedge to the upper field. I started walking backward.
"Look, I can see them coming," I said.
"I believe you," said Anna.
There were no cows that day and no farm vehicles. No gate separated the two fields, just a wide gap big enough for a tractor. The grass was long and brushed against our shins, and we had to avoid the stinging nettles and the brambles; everything grew so quickly at that time of the year. We walked across the upper field to the wood.

"I wish I wasn't wearing bare legs," I said.

We went on through the path between the trees, over the fallen trunk, beneath the low branches, and along until we emerged on the far side. Back out in the open, the sun was throwing down heat. Anna did some cartwheels and handstands. She was good at all that. I climbed onto the tree stump and looked down across the never-ending farmland.

"So?" said Anna.

"It is Naomi, and she's with Tommy," I said.

I carried on standing on the stump, squinting into the distance. Anna did more handstands.

"Tommy has a handkerchief on his head or something," I told her.

"Sounds like him all right!" she said.

Naomi and Tommy finally arrived. Naomi was wearing a summer dress and certainly wasn't planning on physical exertion. She sat down. Tommy ran into the wood shouting and hitting out at the cow parsley with a huge stick he'd picked up. He was being a pirate with a sword. He was Naomi's little brother, but he'd been out to play with us on plenty of occasions. We didn't mind him. He was young, but he had some funny things to say and a lot of suggestions about things to do.

"How long have you been up here?" Naomi asked, in the way she had of appearing completely disinterested.

"We only just came," I said.

We sat amongst the grass: Anna and me in our shorts and T-shirts, and Naomi in her dress, her arms covered by puffy, flower-patterned sleeves.

"I know a joke," Anna said.

"Go on then," I encouraged her.

"What's black and white and red all over?"

"Don't know."

She gave me an exasperated look. "Wendy! You have to guess. You have to think about it."

"Ummm…"

Anna attempted a headstand but toppled over, landing beside me in a heap. She sat again. "Come on, guess."

"Ummm…can't think of anything," I said.

"It's so hot today," said Naomi.

"I love it when it's hot," I told her.

"Me too," agreed Anna. "I hope it stays like this forever."

"Aaaaaaaargh…" Tommy rushed out of the wood with his stick, heading straight for us and yelling. He pretended to turn the sword on himself, pushing it between his arm and his side, and fell facedown. We all ignored him. Naomi was picking the small, trumpet-shaped flowers of the field bindweed that grew up through the grass and making chains with them, like daisy-chains. After some minutes, Tommy hadn't moved, so Anna, still sitting, her hands on the ground behind her propping herself up, started to kick at the sole of his shoe. She kicked for a while, one kick every so often. We carried on chatting.

"You still haven't got the joke," Anna said.

"Give me a clue," I said.

"Okay…think about the word *red…read.*"

"Ummm…"

"Well?"

"A zebra? With a coat on?"

There was no movement. Anna found a lump of dry soil and threw it so that it hit Tommy's back. He didn't budge. We continued talking, picking flowers. In time, I went over and proceeded to tickle Tommy, but still he didn't move or speak. At this point, Anna came and sat right on top of him.

"Come on Tommy, it's boring now. Sit up!"

Anna took his right arm, and I took his right leg, and we rolled him onto his back. He flopped over and lay there, his eyes closed. We peered down at him. I checked Anna's expression. I could tell she was getting a little worried. I swallowed, my throat was dry, flies were buzzing round my head. I wiped my brow with the palm of my hand. I didn't think he was breathing. A moment later, an almighty roar came out of Tommy's mouth and he jumped up. He grabbed the stick, and swinging it round over his head, he ran back toward the wood to begin another battle amid the trees.

"You didn't really think he was hurt, did you?" asked Naomi, who'd carried on with the flower chain all the while.

Naomi and Tommy were to play a significant part in our lives that school holiday.

****

The summers always seemed long and hot and were a time when we were left alone to dream and live as if in another kind of world. There was no structure. Most of the things we did in term time didn't happen in the holidays. There were no music lessons, and Brownies didn't go on. Even the swimming club didn't meet.

To begin with, it was like any other summer. We met up and roamed the village, making up games to play and hanging out together in days of blissful freedom.

The next morning started in a familiar manner. I fed Poppy, my pet rabbit, ate my breakfast, and asked Mum if I could go out. She rarely stopped me from doing things. I took my bike and pushed it up the rough, unmade road that led to Anna's. I dropped it on the driveway and went to the front door. I could see Anna's mum in the kitchen, and she beckoned me in and through the house. Anna and I were at different schools and that seemed to make our friendship feel more special. We often called at each other's houses unannounced, generally knowing when each other would be in and able to play. I passed Anna's dad in his study. Anna was in the garden. She was lying on her stomach staring into the fishpond, feet waving in the air behind her, flip-flops dangling.

"Hiya," she said, still concentrating on the pond.

I spoke to the freckle-faced girl in the reflection. "Hello, shall we go out somewhere?"

Anna had some watercolor paints and some sheets of thick, white paper beside her on the ground. She'd been painting pictures of the fish and the long, green weed sticking up from the stony bottom.

"It's hard to paint the water," she observed distractedly. Anna thought about things like that.

"My brother says they've built a camp up on the cliff at the end of the beach," I said.

We were soon on our bikes, racing toward the seafront. It was all downhill: through the village, along beside the posh hotel, and down the beach road. We came to the sea wall and carried on cycling. We were on our way to the camp, but before the end of the wall, we met two of the Taylor boys. They'd dug a huge pile of sand and were jumping off the wall onto it. We stopped to watch them. It wasn't that far to jump, perhaps four or five feet, but you also had to jump outwards to make sure you landed safely in the middle of the pile. I took off my plimsolls.

"Can I have a try?"

The older Taylor stood aside. He checked me up and down. He looked skeptical.

"I bet you won't," said the younger one. His name was Mo. He stood on the wall beside his brother, hands on hips.

"I bet I will, you know." I really wanted to jump. Anna stayed back. I put one foot on the edge of the wall and leant back on the other, ready to spring.

"Go on then!" said Mo.

I weighed it up again. Somehow, I found the courage and pushed off, not knowing if I was going to land in the right place, but almost as soon as I'd leapt, I was in the sand.

"Hey, good jump," the older Taylor shouted. "Now, your turn," he said to Anna and nodded toward the pit.

"Push the sand back," Mo ordered. I tidied it up. Anna jumped too, and we stayed there jumping for a while.

The boys finally tired of the game and headed off toward the pier to look for crabs.

The road brought you to the pier end of the beach. Then you could walk or cycle on the path, which ran along the top of the wall and continued most of the way round the bay. Near the pier, the beach was covered in steep banks of pebbles, but farther on round it was sandy. Dotted along, there were steps from the wall down to the beach, and there were a few places where you could climb steep wooden or concrete steps from the wall back up to the outskirts of the village.

"Shall we go?" I said.

"Let's leave the bikes here," said Anna.

We walked along to the end to see if we could spot the camp. Where the wall ended you could climb up onto the cliff. It was only really us, the kids from the village, who did this. You could get up partway onto the shallow lower level of the rock face, then walk and walk along sort of half paths, created over the years by a few humans like ourselves, but mainly by the families of wild rabbits whose white tails you might spot bobbing quickly out of sight if you encountered them. You had to pick your way carefully through the trees and plants that grew there. Sometimes you'd come to an area with no trees or shrubs at all, little chalky clearings, where you could look down to the sea below and along the tiny crescent-shaped bays that went on and on round the coast, too many to count.

We looked up into the trees, but we could tell there were bigger kids up there, and we knew they might not want us with them. Instead, we found some sticks of driftwood on the shore. The tide was low, and we wrote our names in giant letters in the sand. *Anna, Wendy; ANNA, WENDY; Anna + Wendy; WENDY + ANNA WOZ HERE!*

****

I had my own piece of garden where I grew tomatoes and nasturtiums. I was watering it when Mum called me in.

"Who were you playing with today?"

"Anna."

"Anyone else?"

"Some of the Taylors for a while."

"Where did you get to?"

"The beach. Why?"

She looked at me in a way that meant I mustn't hold anything back.

"Why, Mum?"

She knew there was no more to tell. She kept a gentle eye on things, but somehow mums knew everything without needing to ask at all.

"All right, quickly go and wash your hands while I put the tea out."

Philip, my brother, was watching TV, and my dad was getting home late because he had a meeting. After tea, Philip and I played French cricket on the lawn until it was too dark to see the ball.

Chapter 2

The holidays were broken up by a string of events. On Saturday, the village fete was on. Mum was helping out on one of the stalls in the afternoon and she left the house early. Dad was in charge of us. We walked along the road to the playing field.

There was already a crowd by the time we arrived. Nobody wanted to miss the fete. There were stalls with things to buy and also stalls where you could compete for prizes. It was hard to know where to start, Dad said. We passed the tombola and the coconut shy.

"Shall we go to see Mum first?" suggested Philip.

Mum's stall was selling cakes, made and donated by the women of the village. Mum was one of four women looking after it. They'd laid everything out on a row of cloth-covered trestle tables.

"Busy?" Dad asked her.

"I've never made so many cups of tea!"

Customers could buy cakes to take home, or buy a slice of cake and a cup of tea and sit at another trestle table to have them. The stall also sold jars of homemade jams and pickles and sweets wrapped in cellophane and tied with ribbon. Later, I spent time examining these: toffee apples, different types of fudge and honeycomb, green and white peppermints, pink and white coconut ice.

We worked our way around, stopping to say hello

to our friends and their parents and to other grown-ups, but we stuck with Dad. We followed him from stall to stall, asking for goes-on things and watching him trying to win stuff.

Anna was there with her cousin Bea. They ran over.

"Hey, look, do you like it?" Anna said. She showed me a necklace made from wooden beads.

"Where did you get it?" I asked.

"There's a lady selling them," said Bea. She showed me a similar necklace.

"We're going to watch Mal now," said Anna. Her brother, Mal, was doing tug-of-war, so they went off again to cheer him on. My brother wanted to throw darts at the stall where, if you got a bullseye, you could win a prize. He wanted the transistor radio. Dad took him over to have a go.

I went back to Mum's stall, and she gave me a job collecting the used crockery from the tables. It was even busier now. Naomi saw me and came over. She wore a pale blue summer dress, and although it was an extremely warm day, she had on a long-sleeved cardigan of a similar color. I always thought her old-fashioned: the way she dressed, and something about her quiet demeanor that I couldn't define. She was pretty, though. She was slender with long, dark hair and dark eyes. Naomi was with her mum and Tommy. Tommy's fair hair had been cut short. He looked very young and was holding his mum's hand. Their dad wasn't there. Mum asked after him.

"How is Mr. Williams?"

Everybody knew Mr. Williams wasn't that well. The family hadn't lived in the area for long. They'd moved because of Mr. Williams' health; he wanted to be nearer to the coast. I'd seen him a few times. He was tall and very thin, and his face had deep craggy wrinkles. Mrs. Williams sat down at one of the tables. I thought she looked tired. Mum brought over a tray with a cup of tea and two orange drinks; also, a plate with three small, iced cakes, each a different color and decorated with a flower made from hard sugar.

"These are with the compliments of the stall," she told them. "I hope you enjoy your afternoon."

"Thank you," said Mrs. Williams. "Say thank you, Tommy."

Naomi gave her one of her smiles.

"I must get back to the counter," Mum said. "The queue isn't getting any shorter!" She went back to make more tea. "That poor family," she said to me later, when they were out of earshot. "We are very lucky, you know, and we don't always appreciate it."

There was a loudspeaker announcement, and everyone stopped to listen. I was carrying a stack of plates and they were quite heavy.

"Last chance to buy your raffle tickets, Ladies and Gentlemen."

Dad bought us all some raffle tickets, and one of his won a bottle of sweet sherry. He was really pleased, though we all knew he'd never care to drink it.

****

Sam called for me. Sam was my other best friend. I'd asked him to my party earlier in the year, and after that, we started sitting next to each other in class and being partners when you had to work in pairs. We went outside. We took Poppy out of her hutch and let her lollop round on the lawn. Sam really liked Poppy.

"My granddad might let us have a boat later in the afternoon, when the visitors start going back to the hotel," he told me.

Sam lived with his granddad who was a fisherman. He kept lobster pots out in the bay, and in the summer, he hired out boats to the holidaymakers on the beach. There were rowing boats, rafts, and pedalos.

"The hotel people won't be able to stop us?"

"No. It's up to Granddad."

The hotel was both good and bad. There were some perks. I was in the tennis club and we were allowed to use the courts, but locals weren't allowed in for the entertainment. Sam and I had already been thrown out of the roller skating, which went on in the large hall in the mornings.

We picked armfuls of dandelion leaves for Poppy. We were always trying to train her, but she didn't really understand. Usually, she went off to the end of the flower bed where the plants were tallest and hid. Sometimes she went through the picket fence that divided our garden from the house next door, where the undergrowth was thick and there was lots for her to eat. She would stay until we missed her, found her, and brought her back again.

"I wonder what Poppy is thinking about?" Sam said.

"Maybe she's wishing we'd give her a huge lettuce," I suggested.

Poppy looked at us for a moment, then hopped to a new position and carried on grazing.

"I think Poppy might have special powers," Sam said.

"She knows what you're saying," I said.

"She can speak but she doesn't want to."

"She can run really fast."

"She could escape to the downs, but she's decided not to."

"Poppy's like a superhero."

"Poppy is Super Rabbit!"

****

The following day Anna, Sam, and I went to look for the camp on the beach. It was a cooler day and a little misty. The sea lapped against the shore, otherwise everything was quiet and still. We went to the end of the wall and climbed the first steep section of rock to the level area. We couldn't hear anyone else up on the cliff. The pine trees were giving off their pungent smell. We walked along, holding on to branches to steady ourselves, up a little hill and down again. We didn't need to walk far. In a gap between the trees, we found the camp. There was definitely no one else there.

"Wow!" I said.

"It's a really good place," said Sam.

"It's really fab!" said Anna.

"How did they get all the stuff up here?" I said.

We admired the work that had gone into it. There was actually a sort of building made from pieces of corrugated iron.

"Those crates must be for sitting on," said Sam.

"There's even a carpet!" Anna said.

Sam went to the corner and took three crates from the pile. We arranged them on the sack matting and sat looking out.

"No one would ever find you here," said Sam.

"Oi!" We heard a shout, the cracking of vegetation breaking underfoot, and the swishing of branches.

The Five Things

Someone rapidly approached. It was Robbo.

"What are you doing in the camp?" He pretended to be annoyed with us but soon forgot and started to show us around. "Look," he said, "we put up a swing." He pulled a long, thick length of rope down from an upper branch of the tree opposite. It was tied to the branch at one end and there was a knot in the other, so you could sit astride it and go for a ride. You could swing quite a long way to and fro. He demonstrated. "Not only that," he said, "we can also make tea." He scrambled over and revealed an old kettle, pushed into a hole in the cliff face behind. "There's water, and I have matches." He pulled over another wooden crate, which had been camouflaged under some foliage, and took off the makeshift lid. It contained a box of tea and some enamel mugs. He uncovered a jerry can filled with water. He set about gathering some sticks and trying to light a fire.

Robbo was older than we were. He had a reputation for being a bit of a tough guy, but we knew that in fact he was quite friendly. He was a big, strong-looking boy with lots of curly, dark hair and already had the first signs of a dark hair growing on his chin. We watched him in admiration.

"Shall I help you?" I asked.

"I might have messed up," he admitted. "I think the matches have got a bit damp." He smiled at me, a warm-hearted sort of smile. We all liked Robbo and we trusted him.

"You won't tell the others we were here? They might be mad," I said.

"Nah," he confirmed. "You know I always look out for you lot."

"Shall we go now…and ask Granddad if he'll give us a boat?" Sam said.

The tea didn't materialize. The four of us went along to see Sam's granddad, and a little while later he found the time to take us out himself, in a dingy with an outboard motor, for a ride around the bay.

Chapter 3

August 1969

Philip had been invited to a party at the Taylors'. To me, the party marked the change. I see it as the point when everything started.

There were four Taylor brothers and one sister, so instead of lots of birthday parties during the year, their parents were giving them one big party. It was going to be a fancy-dress party, and it was going to be at their house. Over the next few days, there was a lot of talk about what Philip would wear and what everyone else would be wearing, whether Mum would make a costume like she did for school plays, or if something would have to be bought.

Philip was a good bit older than me, so our social lives didn't coincide that often. He was at the grammar school and traveled to school on a bus. Most of his friends lived farther away but he knew the Taylors and sometimes went over to see them. Even Mo, the youngest Taylor, was older than me, so I was surprised when, much later in the week, Mum met his mum at the shops, and I was invited along to the party too. Mum accepted on my behalf. It was short notice, an afterthought. I didn't have a costume and I said I wouldn't go. Eventually, on the day, Mum persuaded me, as Mrs. Taylor had said you didn't have to come in fancy dress if you didn't want to.

I put on my new trousers, which were slim fitting and dark with a blue zigzag pattern. I put on my pale blue top. It was made from quite a thin material but had a polo neck and a pouch pocket on the front that you could put your hands into from both sides. I'd decided to wear it because although it was summer, this party was to be in the evening, and I thought it would be a good choice. I put on my new white plimsolls that were really meant for tennis.

I'd never been to a house party before, or a party that happened in the evening. I didn't know what to expect. My brother hadn't wanted to walk with me. He'd gone on ahead a while beforehand. It was only just along the road, so I was allowed to walk over on my own. I arrived at the front door, which was wide open. Nobody greeted me. The house was a Victorian red-brick property with a giant garden. Inside, I could see the wide hallway and the tall staircase. The balustrade disappeared upward, a shiny wooden handrail above white painted posts. It was dimly lit inside. I saw a few people going in and out of the doorways of the downstairs rooms. I stepped in and peered into the first room on the left. At that point, Mrs. Taylor suddenly materialized on the stairs.

"Ah…hello, Wendy. I'm so pleased to see you. I see you've come as a skier."

I could imagine I looked sporty. I was tanned and my hair was bleached from the sun.

"Yes," I said.

"If you have a coat, you can leave it in Jonathan's room upstairs." With that she whisked away to tend to other guests, and though I didn't have a coat, I decided to make my way up. A few others passed me.

"What are you?"

"A skier." No one seemed to question it.

I found the room with the coats. The doors of the other rooms were open, but nothing was going on in those. I went back downstairs and walked along the corridor. I stopped at another doorway. Inside was a group of older boys, including Peter Clay, who was very good at football, and his friend, Max. Some of the boys were sitting, some standing around a long, bendy racetrack. They were racing model cars. The track went all over, looped across itself, and weaved under chairs. They were making a huge amount of noise: shouting and cheering. I carried on and found a room where a record player was going, and some girls were dancing. Farther along, I found the kitchen, which was the only room where the lights were on brightly. There was party food laid out on the plastic-cloth-covered table. A few adults stood around.

"What would you like? Have a jelly? A cold sausage?"

I thanked them and selected a red jelly in a waxed paper dish. The nearest grown-up smiled widely and handed me a teaspoon to eat it with. I was ushered through the open French windows to the verandah. Beyond, the garden was lit with strings of hanging colored lights. Garden tables and all sorts of chairs were dotted around. I sat on the steps at the end of the verandah and ate the jelly.

There were quite a few guests in the garden. I analyzed each of their costumes, trying to work out what they'd come as. I didn't recognize all of them; they were mostly older than me—quite a lot older in some cases. I couldn't see my brother, who was a cowboy. He might have been in the room racing cars. It was muggy. I felt too warm in my polo neck. Moths were flying noisily into the bulbs on the verandah, and high-pitched buzzing insects you couldn't really see were biting at my ankles and ears. Then I heard a familiar voice.

"Hello, Wendy."

I turned to see a small figure with a large, orange cone shape on his face. He pushed the cone, which was held in place by thin elastic, up on top of his head like a hat. It was Tommy.

"Hello, Tommy. How come you're here? Where's Naomi?"

"Naomi's not here. She didn't want to come, but I did. My mum brought me, and she's in the kitchen."

I studied him. "Are you a crow?"

He had black shorts and plimsolls on and a black T-shirt. He pulled the hand-painted cone back over his nose. It was made from paper glued together along the side and with holes to tie the elastic. He stretched his arms out in a cross shape, then leaned forward.

"I'm one of the birds," he said.

****

Dad asked if I'd enjoyed the party.

"It was okay."

"Your brother had a good time," he said.

"It was fun, I suppose."

He stopped for a moment, pondering over my response, before getting on with the household tasks that would carry on whatever. I just kept thinking about Tommy's costume.

****

I'd written a poem about the birds after I'd seen them in the wood. I was keeping it in the tin under my bed where I kept special things. It was entitled *Poor Birds* and began *Poor, poor birds, I feel so sorry for you and hope you are now free.* It was quite long.

I asked Philip if he'd help me dig up the jam jar from behind the garage. I didn't want to tell him about what I'd seen, but I thought it would be good to put the poem in the jar. It would be like some kind of burial, in remembrance of the beautiful creatures.

"It's supposed to be discovered by people in hundreds of years' time," he said.

"They won't mind," I said. "They won't even know."

"Why do you want to dig it up?"

"I want to see what's in it, then we can bury it again."

"You know what's in it."

"I want to have another look."

"Maybe later."

We'd buried the jar a few months earlier. We'd put things in it that we thought represented our life and times: a coin with the date on, a toy that came free with the cornflakes, a newspaper article, various things. We'd watched the presenters do something similar on a TV show.

Finding the birds had really disturbed me, and for a while, I kept well away from the wood. But one day, at the playground, Sam said that the bigger kids were going there again. Not long after, Adam Smart, who lived near Sam, told us that he'd been going and that the birds weren't there anymore. I wasn't sure. I caught up with Robbo who was walking in front of us on the way home.

"Robbo, Adam says he's been back to the wood," I said.

"There's nothing there now," said Robbo. "It's okay to go."

"Have you been?"

"Yeah…bin a few times."

So we started going again too, even though it had a mysterious sort of past.

****

The next day Anna and I rode our bikes to the beach. The tide was high, and the sea was calm. We didn't ride to the camp; we stayed at the pebbly end, a little way along from where Sam's granddad hired out the boats. We left our bikes on the wall and jumped down. We threw in a few stones. Then we walked up and down hunting for flat stones, skimmers, and tried to make them jump across the water.

"If you skim three in a row, it's lucky," I said.

We managed that.

"Another three would be very lucky…and then three more means all your dreams will come true," Anna told me.

"Who said that?" I asked her.

"I made it up," she said.

"I don't think there are enough stones," I concluded.

Anna was convinced she could walk right along a breakwater without falling off. The breakwaters stretched out from the wall and into the sea. There was one every so many yards, right around the bay. That day, due to the tide, there were five wooden sections that it might be possible to walk along. If you fell off on the first three sections, you'd fall onto the shingle, and if you fell off on the next two, you'd land in the sea; after that, you'd be under the water altogether. The sections were divided by metal posts. Anna kicked off her flip-flops and climbed up. It was easier to walk them in bare feet; you could curl your toes around the edges of the wooden planks to help stay on. I went to the next breakwater and got up to have a go. It wasn't that easy. I could keep my balance for a few steps, but then I would waver and have to try to run to the next post and grab ahold before I fell.

We did this for some time. Then we went to watch some of the boys who'd gathered at the end of the pier and were leaping off into the water. Some were jumping, some bombing—their arms wrapped around bent knees on the way down—and some were diving in. I think only Peter Clay and Max were actually diving. It was exciting to watch them, and I was amazed at how long they stayed beneath the surface before they came up.

Chapter 4
The Rabbit, Bridges

Tommy had us lying on our backs in the grass at the far side of the upper field. It was really just a game of hide and seek that he'd slightly embellished.

"Count to a hundred," he said, and we heard him running off.

We had to lie on our backs so that he knew we would keep our eyes shut. The sun was blazing down, and I put my arm over my face because it was so bright it seemed it could burn right through my eyelids.

Anna, Naomi, Sam, and I were all there.

Sam was moaning. "I'm so hot."

"Thirty-four, thirty-five, thirty-six..." Anna counted.

"I feel weird," I said.

Naomi never said very much. She was joining in the game, though, so that was something.

"Fifty-one, fifty, forty-eight," Anna said.

"Fif-ifty-fi-i-ive, fiiiiiifteeee-siiiiix, fty-svn," said Sam. He was saying the numbers slowly, or quickly, or in a funny voice to make it more interesting.

Anna started to giggle. It's hard to stop giggling when you're lying on your back, and soon we were all giggling, and no one was counting. Sam stood up.

"Give it a bit longer, then we'll go and search," he said.

We waited. He lay down again. I was trying to look at him through gaps in my fingers without being blinded.

"One hundred!" Naomi said. We weren't sure if she was guessing or if she'd continued counting the whole time.

We got up and headed to the wood to hunt for Tommy. Anna said we had to split up. I was sent on the normal path, while Sam was to go to the left of the path and Anna to the right of the path. Naomi was to walk round the outside of the wood looking in.

I had the easiest route, but I was finding it hard to adjust my eyes after coming out of the sunlight, and I felt dizzy. It seemed so dark, but it was lovely and cool. A piece of ivy, hanging down, brushed my bare shoulder and made me jump. Then, as I climbed over the fallen tree, I thought I spotted something moving. I sat on the trunk for a while, watching and listening. All I could hear was the sound of the others in the undergrowth, the swishing sounds as they thrashed their way through. I went on. Eventually, I thought I'd been in the wood long enough and came out the other side without finding Tommy. I headed back to where we'd been sitting. As I walked round, I saw Tommy and Naomi lounging on the grass in full view. Tommy put his finger to his lips to silence me. I strode over.

"You're supposed to be hiding," I whispered loudly.

He whispered back, "I waited until I saw you all come into the wood, and then I came back here."

"Tommy, that's cheating!" I told him. Naomi probably knew he would do something like that.

He shrugged.

"Well, the others won't be too pleased, they're searching high and low for you."

"Shhhhh…" he said.

The others were anything but pleased when they finally returned. In fact, they told Naomi and me we were as much to blame because we hadn't called off the hunt. Sam had torn his T-shirt, and both Sam and Anna had been scratched by brambles and stung by nettles.

"You're in for it this time, squirt," Sam said.

"Little brothers can be very annoying," Naomi confirmed.

"I love it up here," Tommy told us. "I love it so much that when I get married, I'm gonna live up here."

He could make us laugh and was usually easily forgiven.

"No one will ever want to marry you, Tommy," I said. "You're far too irritating."

He thought about that. "And I s'pose the farmer wouldn't let me live here either."

The farmer was called Bridges. He was the strangest man in the whole village. He lived in a huge house on his own. You couldn't really see the house because it was so grown in. I'd seen glimpses of it, but there were wide-trunked oak trees, yews, and tall pines at its boundaries that blocked it from view. On one side, a track led down to it. The track led off from a rough road that was really only used by the various farmers to access their land. There was another entrance to the house from a footpath, which was part of a network of paths that meandered between the fields and the different areas of the village. On that side, there were old, once grand, stone gateposts with high, wooden gates that had the look of never being opened. You had to climb up to see over.

Inside, it wasn't like a garden. Beyond the gates, there was what was probably a neglected orchard. Everything was overgrown, and there was a damp smell. Robbo had once climbed over for a dare. He was meant to look for apples. He was in there a few minutes, and then we heard Bridges shouting. He was shouting in an alarming kind of way, and he was coming after Robbo. We heard Robbo running back toward the gate. He pulled himself over and we all ran, faster than we even thought we could, back along the path until we were completely out of breath. We were genuinely scared.

Bridges, of course, was the one who must have hung the dead birds in the trees.

****

The next afternoon, Philip and I were at home. He asked if I wanted to go shrimping. We gathered up the nets, found a large bucket, and set off for the rock pools that appeared at the far end of the beach at low tide. We walked to the end of the sea wall, beyond the breakwaters, and past the camp on the cliff.

"Do you think there's anyone up there?" I said.

"Can't hear anyone."

"It's a good camp, isn't it?"

"Not bad."

I knew Philip admired it, but being older meant he had to be a little dismissive too. We took off our plimsolls and paddled through the shallow water to the first stranded rocks. We began sweeping our nets beneath their overhangs, under the weed, and into the pools that had formed between them.

"I suppose you kids are going to Bridges' fields?"

Philip said.

"Sometimes."

"There's a lot of stories about those fields, you know."

"I know. I've heard some stories."

"And some people say the wood is haunted."

"Haunted?"

"Yeah." Philip's net came up jumping with glistening shrimps. "Look, there's tons here! Come and help me." We knelt on the sand and carefully sorted them out. Most went into the bucket, but we'd been taught to return the small ones and also any females that were carrying eggs.

Philip was soon striding on ahead toward the next cluster of rocks. I followed, almost having to run to keep up.

"What stories do you know?" I asked, keen to hear some tales I could pass on.

"About the fields? I can't really tell you."

"Why not?" I said.

"I'll tell you when you're older."

"Tell me now!"

"Look, there's a hermit crab!"

"Let me see." The tiny creature was scuttling across the drying sand.

Philip selected a large rock covered with brown weed and swept his net around its base.

"There's a whole other world under there," he said.

"Last year we found a starfish, remember?" I said.

"Yeah, I caught it in the net."

"We put it back, though."

The large rock had only delivered a small number of shrimps. Even so, they hopped about energetically until they were deposited into the bucket. We walked on again. Shrimping was somewhat mesmerizing. We went from pool to pool, rock to rock.

"One day, I'm going to find a seahorse," I said.

Philip finally announced we should be going home. We'd caught a bucketful, and the tide was on the turn.

"You take the nets, and I'll carry the bucket," he said. "Mum will be pleased with this catch, I think."

We made our way back along the shore barefoot, searching for the shoes we'd left behind some time before.

****

"What's your favorite thing about the countryside?" Anna said. "My dad asked me that this morning." Anna's dad was a teacher. He was probably preparing some new lesson for unsuspecting pupils.

"My favorite thing," Sam said, "is the cowpats." He kept a serious expression.

Anna and I giggled. We were on the lawn watching Poppy, who was mooching about nibbling at the grass. Now and then, she stopped and sat up on her hind legs, twitching her nose.

"No, really though, what's your most favorite thing?"

"I don't know," said Sam. "I like everything about it."

"All the animals," I said. "What did you say?"

"I said the animals, too," Anna told us.

We decided to go to the camp on the beach again. Sam's bike was broken, so we'd walk. We went down through the village, past the shops, and round the path above the bay. We went as far as the last set of steps and ran down them, walked to the end of the wall, and pulled ourselves up to the level part of the cliff. The camp was empty, so we took our chance to have a go on the rope swing.

Soon we heard voices, and a crowd of the older boys arrived: Robbo, Peter Clay, Max, and Adam. Judy and Susan, two of the girls from the top class at school, were with them. Max was smoking a cigarette.

"Hiya," we said somewhat hesitantly, unsure if we were welcome.

"Wotcha," they said. They seemed friendly enough. Judy had brought some cushions. She said her mum was about to throw them out.

The older boys took turns on the rope swing, aiming to impress. They were swinging as high as they could and jumping off. Robbo didn't join in. He was trying to make tea. He started to talk about the wood and then about Bridges. Judy said she wouldn't go anywhere near the wood or the farmer, and she focused on the three of us and told us we should be careful if we were going to the fields. She said to make sure Bridges didn't see us there.

"Susan and me were up there once last summer. It was quite late in the day."

"We heard noises," Susan said.

"We heard odd noises," said Judy. "Screeching sounds coming from the wood. We tried to hide in the grass. We kept really still, and we waited."

Susan nodded in agreement.

"We were lying facedown. We were petrified." She had everyone's attention. We gathered round; the rope became still. "We lay in the grass for ages. We kept looking toward the wood. The noises were sort of eerie. We were sure we weren't alone up there."

"We didn't dare speak," said Susan.

"We didn't dare make a sound," Judy said. "We were waiting for someone or something to come out of the trees."

"We were almost too scared to breathe," Susan said.

"It got later and later." Judy looked up and around at each of our faces. "And then it got so late that we knew we'd have to do something. We had to get home."

Robbo shifted his weight, and a stick under his foot cracked loudly.

"We whispered to each other. We'd count to three, then jump up and run for our lives across the field. We picked our moment and made our move. We leapt to our feet and ran really, really fast over to the hedge by the lookout stump. We climbed over. Then we just kept running down. Down the hill, down and down until we came to the road. We managed to get away, but we'll never forget it…and we've never been back there. We're never going to go back."

A tense atmosphere pervaded the camp.

"That wood's creepy," Susan said.

****

"Mum, I'm going to the playing field!" I shouted.

"Don't be late home!"

I was meeting Sam there. It wasn't far. It only took a few minutes to walk over. I found him sitting at the end of the slide. There was a slide, a seesaw, and three swings. They were at one end of the field, and there were football goal posts at the other end. Apart from that, it was just a big grassy space; it was the place where the fete was held.

Sam smiled and waved when he saw me coming.

Sam was good looking, I suppose. He had tightly curled, light brown hair and big blue eyes. He was a normal height and of slim build, but strong, not weedy. He had a neat, tidy way of doing things. I was aware of all that, but they weren't the reasons I hung around with him. The main reason was simply that I liked being with him. He wasn't aggressive or loud like some of the other boys, and he wasn't a show-off. He was iron-willed, though, and he was always thinking. He was funny, and he was considerate. He would help if you needed help, and he would think of a way to make something seem better if he thought you were upset.

Sam had brought a ball, and we stayed on the field for a while, throwing it to each other. We rolled it down the slide a few times, and Sam showed me some of his football skills. I had a few to show him as well.

"I'm George Best!" said Sam, kicking the ball to me.

"So am I," I said, side-footing it back.

"Okay"—he sent it out to me—"see if you can get it past me." He crouched, his hands held out in front of him, ready to make the stop. I kicked it as hard as I could to the right of him. He dived down athletically and caught it in outstretched fingers.

"I'm Gordon Banks!" he said.

After quite a lengthy game, we walked down to the beach to see Sam's granddad. We sat on the edge of the sea wall, swinging our legs. Sam was wearing brown leather sandals, and I had last year's tatty plimsolls on; my big toes were sticking out of them. Sam's granddad brought us two plastic beakers of lemon squash. He was too busy to pay us much attention, but he said if we wanted, we could take some old bread he had and feed the gulls. He told us to go along the beach, though, and not to throw it near the holidaymakers he was trying to hire boats to.

We took the bread and walked farther on round. The gulls were crying. Sometimes they sounded as if they were laughing, and sometimes they sounded as if they were crying; sometimes they sounded like cats meowing. They soon found us. We waited until a gull flew quite close and threw a piece of bread up toward it. We were up on the wall, and the birds were a few yards away, flying low over the sea, landing and floating, flying off again. After a couple of throws, one gull caught on and swooped to get the food. Within minutes, we had attracted a large flock that could expertly pluck the pieces out of the air.

"You know Tommy is always talking about the birds in the wood," Sam said.

"I know, and I told you he dressed up as a bird at that fancy dress party I went to."

"Do you know what he said to me?" Sam threw another piece of bread. "He said the birds were strung through the heart. I was sort of surprised when he said it like that. He never saw them, did he?"

"No, I'm sure he didn't," I said. "He's just heard people talking about it."

"Do you really think Bridges put them there?"

"He must have done."

Then we talked about Bridges. He was always known as Bridges, and nothing else. I'd only ever seen him from a distance. He was stout and wore the same old long coat no matter what. If we spotted him in the fields, we didn't go in. I'd never come across him at the shops or walking through the village. Sam said he was supposed to go to the inn sometimes, but we didn't know if that was true.

"Do you think it was him that scared Judy and Susan?" Sam questioned.

"I expect so," I said.

"Is he old?" Sam asked.

"I think so," I said.

"Is there a Mrs. Bridges?" he asked.

"I don't think so. He lives on his own."

"Do you think he killed the birds, or were they dead already?"

"I don't know," I said. "But why would they be dead already?"

Chapter 5

It was raining, and I was bored. Mum was cooking. I'd helped for a while and then gone up to my room. I took Piggy, my gonk, to the window, and we looked out. Poppy had gone into the covered part of her hutch. I took my tin from under the bed, opened the lid, and studied the contents. Piggy sat on the bed beside me. He'd been knitted from blue wool and had gray woolen hair that stuck up on top of his head in a tuft.

I took out my jewel collection. The jewels were kept in a container that had previously been for a typewriter ribbon. I tipped them out onto the bedspread. All the girls had a box of jewels. We took them to school and swapped them. Mine were mostly made from glass and had probably once been parts of old necklaces or bracelets. It was soothing to sort through them, turn them over in my fingers, and study them. I had a big, pale blue stone, which was my best one. Everyone knew I'd never swap it, and they didn't ask about it. I had a few clear ones. We called those diamonds. I had a dark ruby, and various others in green and pink and yellow. I arranged them in rows in front of me. A little snail-like fossil had also found its way into the container as well as a tiny brooch—a silver sailing ship with a painted sail. The ship had belonged to my grandmother, and again, that would never be swapped.

Also in my tin, I had a small leather purse with an old bun penny inside. Dad had given it to me. I think it came from the house of another old relative. It was important enough to be in the tin, and I liked to look at it every now and then. The poem was in the tin too, folded up but not very well protected. I went to ask Mum for an envelope, and she got out the big envelope full of all sorts of other envelopes and said I could choose whichever one I liked. I chose a small brown one, made from thick paper. I put the poem in the envelope and back into the tin with the other things. I put the tin away. Then I put Piggy to bed.

****

I had a tennis lesson the next morning. I met Sam on the playing field afterward, and we sat on the swings, not swinging.

At the bottom of the field, Peter Clay, Max, Adam Smart, and Mark Wade were having a serious game of football. I'd seen Peter play for the school team a few times. He scored all the goals, and he'd had his photo in the local paper because he also played for the county.

I had to go home for lunch. Sam was going back to the beach to see his granddad, and then he would call for me. It often seemed Sam spent more time on the beach than at home in the summer. He and his granddad lived in the oldest part of the village, close to the river. His granddad traveled to and from the house in a boat. He moored the boat beside the nearby bridge, which was only a few steps from their front door. In the old part of the village, there was just the lane they lived on. The area was pretty. There were two other houses, a church, and the tiny inn, which was quite popular.

Sam called and we went to Anna's. The three of us

then went up to the fields; Judy's story hadn't put us off. We took the bikes; we had my bike and Anna's and took turns in giving each other a saddle.

Naomi and Tommy were in the upper field when we arrived. We were anticipating one of Tommy's games, but both he and Naomi had grave looks on their faces. They had something to tell us, but first, we had to swear not to tell anyone else. We all swore solemnly.

"There are no birds, but there's a rabbit," Tommy said.

"How do you mean?" I said.

"There's a dead rabbit in the wood," said Naomi. She sat in her long-sleeved dress and long white socks and sandals, her legs stretched out in front of her.

"It's lying there, dead," Tommy said. "Somebody killed it."

"It might have just died from old age," Sam suggested.

"It's got blood on it," said Tommy. "D'you wanna see it?"

Naomi didn't want to come because it was horrible, she said. The rest of us went to the wood and walked tentatively along the path to the fallen tree. The rabbit was lying there on its side, one eye staring up at us. It seemed perfect at first, but then you noticed the blood at its neck. It hadn't been dead for long.

I bent and stroked its head. I felt angry and sad, and then I closed my eyes and turned away because, like Naomi, I didn't want to see it anymore. We went back out to the grass and sat down in a circle. Tommy made himself into a ball, drawing his knees up to his chin and winding his arms tightly around his legs. We needed to have a long discussion: what had happened to the rabbit; why was it there; should we move it; should we bury it?

"Bridges killed it," said Tommy, "and put it there for us to find."

I think we all thought that, but there were other possibilities.

"Perhaps it was killed by a fox?" Naomi suggested.

"I don't think so. A fox wouldn't leave it there like that," said Sam. "It didn't look sick either," he added.

"What if the fox was scared by something and dropped it?" said Anna.

"Perhaps it's been left as bait by someone for some reason," I said. "Maybe they were trying to lure a fox."

"Or it could have been injured somehow," said Anna, "and then died because of its injury."

We wondered about moving it, but Sam said there was no point unless we actually buried it. To bury it, we'd need to go and get a spade. We'd have to do it straight away because otherwise it would just become food for another animal: a fox, the crows, the flies, the maggots.

In the end, we left it, and we left the field and walked around the footpaths toward the part of the village where Naomi and Tommy lived. We were pushing the bikes. One of us would hop on now and then, if the path allowed it, riding or freewheeling, standing on one peddle as we traveled downhill. We passed by the back of Bridges' house.

"We hate you! We hate you!" Tommy sang loudly.

"Shut up, squirt! Are you mad?" said Sam.

"Be quiet!" Anna said.

We walked a bit faster until we were a good way farther on, Tommy with his hand over his mouth.

"Anyway, it's wrong to hate anyone," I said, "even Bridges, I suppose."

****

Later, Dad was helping me change Poppy's bedding.

"People kill the wild rabbits, don't they, Dad?" I said to him.

I could tell he thought carefully before he replied. "They shoot them sometimes if there are too many. Then, I'm afraid, they might end up in a pie."

The one we'd found that day was just left there, though.

Dad saw I'd been able to deal with his answer, so he told me something else. He told me that shooting wasn't good but that it was perhaps a better way to control the rabbits than some other means. He said that when he'd been my age, he'd sometimes found traps left out. They were nasty things, like metal jaws that would snap closed if an animal touched them. The animal may not die straight away. Thank the Lord they didn't use those anymore, he said. He said that if he and his friends found a trap, they would push a stick into it to set it off. They'd leave it that way, and then no animal would be caught.

****

The rabbit was a bad thing but nothing like as bad as the birds. It wasn't to be approved of, but it was possible that the death of the rabbit could be explained. Nonetheless, Sam wasn't happy, and he'd been back to investigate on his own.

"The rabbit's not there now," he said.

"We knew it wouldn't be," I reminded him.

"You realize it had been trapped?"

"They don't use traps nowadays."

"Well, someone does. Its neck was broken."

"How d'you know?"

"I looked when we found it. So, the birds were strung through the heart, and the rabbit had a broken neck."

"Maybe it was shot, and then they broke its neck."

"It wasn't shot."

Sam and I were lying on the lawn under the late afternoon sky. I knew the conversation wasn't over. Sam was still thinking about the meaning behind the rabbit. We both thought Bridges was to blame for everything, and that he'd left the rabbit to frighten us. Bridges wanted us to stay away from his fields and the wood. There was no real reason; he just didn't like kids. He didn't like anyone.

"Maybe you should stop thinking about it, Sam," I said.

"How can I?"

I rolled over and lay on my front, resting my chin on my hands. "Well, I don't want to go there anymore," I told him.

"You don't want to go to the fields?"

"No."

"Then Bridges gets his own way."

"It *is* his land."

"But we don't do any harm there, not really, and the kids have always gone up there. There has to be something we can do."

Chapter 6
The Tent, Surveillance

Anna and I were playing at her house. We had an extremely bouncy ball and were bouncing it on the paving stones and trying to catch it. The ball went over the wall a couple of times, which was okay because that was where our mums' friend Maggie lived, and we could hop over and get it back. Maggie was out at work, but she wouldn't have minded. It was really hard to control the ball, and it did go into the fishpond once. We got it out with a net and apologized to the fish for the disturbance.

We tired of that and sat by the pond on the garden bench. We were wondering what to do.

"I'm going to look in the shed," Anna said.

"What's in there?"

"Loads."

We went to the garden shed. Like our own shed, various old toys and games were kept in there, as well as garden tools, wire, string, and so on. Anna stepped in, and I followed her.

"It's a bit cobwebby," I said.

"No one ever clears it out."

"What's that?"

"I think it's something my dad uses in the garden." It was long with a hook at one end and a wooden handle at the other. We prodded it. Anna stepped in a little farther. I looked up and inspected the various things hanging high up on nails along the sides.

"Is that a tennis game?" I asked.

"Yeah, but it's broken."

Anna then spotted the canvas bag in the corner, and her eyes lit up.

"It's the tent!" she pretty much screamed. We were both genuinely excited.

We brought the tent out into the garden. Anna's garden was narrow but very long. We took it down to the far end where there was a level grassy section with bushes all around and took it out of the bag. Both being Brownies, we were sure we could set it up. We laid it out, assembled the poles, and found the pegs. This took some time.

"Bring it over this way," I said.

"Stretch it out more," said Anna.

We got it ready, then tried to pull the cords to make it stand up. Every time we pulled one way, another part collapsed. We persevered. Several times we ended up lying in a heap on the grass. I was laughing so much that I was actually in pain.

"What if I do this?" Anna suggested.

"Don't, I can't stop laughing."

"You have to help me!"

"I can't. I can't even breathe. Just let me lie here for a bit."

Eventually, we managed a saggy version of a normal tent. It didn't look as we'd hoped.

Unbeknown to us, Anna's mum and brother, Mal, had been watching from an upstairs window. They had also been quite amused. Mal finally took pity on us and came out to take charge. He was older, a similar age to my own brother, and well capable of the task. He had us help him, methodically explaining the process as we worked. Soon the tent was pitched, splendidly upright. He tied back the flap at the opening. He went to the shed and found some groundsheets. Anna's mum came out with some travel rugs and some old pillows, then some cold drinks, and after that, we were left alone to enjoy our pad, as Mal had decided to call it. Somehow even just sitting in the tent was fun.

A little later, Anna's mum came and said they were planning to have a barbecue in the garden in the evening, and why didn't I pop home and ask if I could eat with them? We would be allowed to have ours in the tent and stay out until it was dark.

Mal built the barbecue out of bricks. He put wood and charcoal inside and a metal grill over the top. There were sausages, some chicken, and some fish cooked on skewers. There were homegrown tomatoes and little onions. Mal also cooked potatoes in foil amongst the coals. He toasted bread on a stick over the heat.

"The food smells so nice," I said to Anna.

"Everything tastes much better in the tent than it does indoors," she said.

"It tastes really special, like the Queen would eat."

As it grew darker, Mal brought out some blankets for us to wrap around ourselves and set up an oil lamp, which he hung from a pole pushed into the ground outside the tent.

"Anna," I said, "I think this is going to be the best night of the whole summer."

It seemed magical. The air was beginning to cool, the grasshoppers were chirruping, and a soft breeze passed through the trees making a calming, whispering sound. Anna's mum, dad, and brother ate at an outdoor table nearer to the house; the murmur of their voices was gentle and reassuring. We were too far away to hear what was being said, but we could tell from the tone that they were cheerful, and we heard plenty of laughter.

Dad drove the car to collect me, even though we lived only a few minutes away. I think I was all but asleep by the time we arrived home.

****

The tent was our new favorite place to be, and Anna, Sam, and I were inside. It was big enough for all three of us to lie down, and we were stretched out horizontally across it, next to each other. By now, we had stocked up with books and a pack of cards for entertainment. We lay on the rugs with our heads on the pillows, looking up at the roof.

"It's better than the camp on the beach," I said.

"It's our pad," Anna told Sam.

"You should sleep in it," he said.

"Maybe, but I'm not sure I'd like to be out in it all night…not on my own anyway."

"You'd need a sleeping bag. Then you'd be really warm, and you can close up the door. I'll close it." Sam went over to the entrance on his knees, clambering over me on the way because he'd been lying in the middle. He unfurled the flap and tied it down, came back, and lay down again. "I've had an idea about the fields," he told us then. "I think we should keep watch up there."

"Keep watch?" I couldn't believe my ears.

"Yeah, so we can find out what's happening," he said.

"I'm happy here now, now that we've got the tent,"

The Five Things

I said.

"Me too," said Anna.

"You know Philip says the wood is haunted," I told them.

"I don't believe that," said Sam.

"They say our school is haunted," said Anna. "I've never seen the ghost, though."

"So, Sam, if the wood isn't haunted, would you sleep out up there...in the dark?" I asked.

"You could borrow the tent," Anna told him.

"Would you?" I pressed him.

He smiled. "Maybe not."

"You see!" said Anna.

There was a pause and we continued to stare at the roof of the tent for a few moments. I was first to speak.

"Let's forget the fields," I said, "and the wood."

"I agree," said Anna.

"Well, I don't think I can." It appeared Sam wasn't going to be put off. "I like it up there, and I want to find out what's going on."

Anna pretended to start snoring and we all had a fit of the giggles.

Sam grabbed one of the blankets and threw it over his head, "Wooowooo," he said. "I'm a ghost. I'm really scary."

After that, we had a massive fight with the pillows.

****

At home, Philip was becoming less likely to want to play French cricket and more likely to want to listen to music. He'd started buying records and borrowing records from other people. He studied the words, which he said were called lyrics.

There'd been a record player built into the top of

the old television cabinet, but Dad had acquired a better television. Luckily, my uncle, who listened to a lot of music, decided to buy us a new record player as a present. It was small enough to carry around, so Philip sometimes took it to his room, and I'd hear the music, but muffled. I liked some of the songs, and Philip was well informed. If I took an interest, he'd talk to me about the bands. Some of the records were LPs, long players, with fascinating covers.

"They're The Rolling Stones," said Philip, showing me the latest one he'd come by.

"That's a funny name."

He turned it over. There were pictures on the back. He pointed to them. "He's the singer. He's the drummer."

"Tell me about the fields," I said.

Philip grinned. "I'll tell you when you're older."

"Stop teasing me…I'll tell Mum!"

"Then I'll tell her you're going to Bridges' fields."

"You're a moo!" It was the best insult I could think of on the spur of the moment. Philip could really wind me up. He'd made me too angry to come up with a winning response. "Who's that?"

"He plays the guitar," he said.

"Anyway, I don't think you know any stories," I told him.

"Well, I do," he said.

"Tell me!" I said.

He spoke with a softer voice. "Okay, I'll tell you one of them, but you better not tell anyone else."

"I won't. I promise." Lately, there seemed to be a lot of secrets to keep.

"I was in the wood with Jonathan one time," Philip

began. "We were a bit older than you, probably. We saw some of the girls coming. They were on their way across the fields. We decided to play a trick on them, so we hid behind the trees. I hid on one side of the path, and Jonathan went to the other side. We were going to wait for them to come into the wood, then jump out in front of them. We got into position and watched for them. It was really, really quiet and the girls were just coming…but then we heard someone shout…'Get out of here! Get out of here, you good-for-nothing little nippers. Get out now!' The voice was put on, but straight away I knew it was Jonathan. I yelled back, 'Get out yourself, you weirdo!' Then Jonathan shouted, 'Shut up, you idiot, the girls will hear you.' It was too late. The girls had already sussed us. We came out and I went over to Jonathan. 'You ruined it, you complete wally!' I told him. 'You mean *you* ruined it!' he said. He swore he hadn't shouted out at all. He thought it was me, I thought it was him."

"So who was it?" I pressed him.

"I don't know," he said.

"Bridges?" I asked.

"Maybe," he said.

"But you didn't see anyone?" I checked.

"No." He shook his head.

I thought for a moment. "Perhaps it was a ghost?" I said.

"Could have been," said Philip.

"Were you frightened?" I asked him.

"Yeah, a bit…there's something strange about that wood."

I took the record sleeve from him and studied the picture on the front. "You're just saying that."

"No. Jon wanted to look around, but the rest of us wanted to go. He yelled back into the trees, 'Who are you? Come out, you big fat coward.' But there was just silence. Then we got the shivers, and we left pretty quick…and all came back to the village."

I tried to convince myself it was Jonathan who did the shouting. I was beginning to wish I hadn't asked Philip to tell me any of his stories.

Chapter 7

We were at Anna's again. We'd been playing Patience with the cards, then Sam arrived. His granddad finally found time to mend his bike. He tried to persuade us to ride up to the fields, but we didn't want to go. He said he'd go anyway, and then he'd come back.

"You shouldn't go up there on your own, Sam," I said.

"Well, if you won't come, I'll have to."

After that, we didn't see him until quite a lot later, and by that time he had plenty to tell us. He'd been talking to Adam Smart, who lived near him, about finding the rabbit. I reminded him that we'd sworn not to speak about the rabbit, but he said he thought it was okay if he was speaking to someone who already knew about the birds, because it was kind of the same thing. Adam then told Robbo.

"We're going to take it in turns," said Sam, "to keep an eye on the wood, see who's going up there."

"I don't think that's a very good idea," I said.

"Nor do I," said Anna. "It sounds kind of risky."

"There's all sorts of stories," I said.

"We'll be careful," Sam told us. "We're going to think it through properly. Adam is clever; we all know that. We'll make sure we don't do anything stupid."

"I don't want to take a turn," I said.

"Me neither," said Anna.

"I know. We're going to do it. Just me, Adam, and Robbo."

****

A few days went by. Anna and I were given frequent feedback about the surveillance of the fields. Sam was riding by a couple of times a day. Adam took that route whenever he went anywhere, and Robbo was trying to go first thing in the morning because he thought that's when things were happening. Our minds were on other matters.

"Shall we go for a walk through the footpaths and see if there are any blackberries to pick?" I suggested.

We went blackberrying every year. We'd spotted a few ripe ones recently and had been thinking about having a proper look. Anna told her mum where we were going and collected a plastic food container from the kitchen cupboard. We walked up the rough road to the start of the footpaths. It was warm, and the road was so dry that dust puffed up as we stepped on it. We turned left onto the path known simply as *The Way*. There were a couple of houses on the left-hand side and then it ran alongside fields. There were brambles in amongst the other plants—hawthorn, blackthorn, elder—that made up the hedgerows. We soon found there weren't many berries ready to be picked. We ate the few that were, then carried on nevertheless. Sparrows were darting in and out of the bushes; they almost seemed to be accompanying us as we walked. We came to the point where we could choose to go in any of four directions and set off to the right where the path ran between more fields. On one side it was hedged, and on the other was barbed wire fencing.

The Five Things

There were three rows of wire: one at the top, one in the middle, and one at the bottom. You could easily climb in between the lines of wire if you wished to for any reason. The fence was there to keep the animals in rather than the people out. A herd of cattle watched as we passed. They continued to chew, flicking their tails to deter the flies.

"Hello, cows," I said.

"Hello, flies as well," said Anna, swatting a few from round her head.

"Hello, ladybird," I said.

"Where?" said Anna.

"It's on my arm." I showed her.

"Oh yeah. Good afternoon, Mr. Ladybird."

"Do you think it can be a mister?"

We came to the high fence that ran alongside The Hall. The Hall was the building that intrigued us most. No one seemed to live there, though it was very hard to tell. There were a few tiny gaps in the fence that you could try to peep through. If you moved your head from right to left you could see a little bit more, but you would probably graze your nose on the wood, which had quite a rough surface. The building was large, and old, and built from yellow brick with a tower at one end. It had an important look about it, but it wasn't very well looked after. We'd seen dusty-looking furniture in the rooms and faded curtains hanging at the windows. We peered through the gaps. There was no entrance to The Hall from the path. In fact, we weren't even sure where the entrance was.

"No one's in," said Anna.

"As usual," I said.

"Unless they're asleep."

"Or in the back garden."

"If there is a back garden."

Farther along, just before you reached the next houses, there was an opening where you could get into even more fields. You were allowed into them. There were stiles at the corners to make it easy, and everyone knew that it was okay to walk there so long as you kept to the edges. This was where the best blackberries grew. The fields were planted with wheat. It had grown since we were last there and looked amazing. We already knew the blackberries weren't yet ripe, but we still walked round the path because it was nice to be beside the waist-high yellow blanket as it stood proudly in the midafternoon heat. The land was high up at that point, and where it dipped down ahead of us, the road was visible at the bottom. After that, the land rose again, and where it rose, that was the lower field. From where we were, we could see the lower field, the upper field, and the wood.

"We can tell Sam we came and did some lookout work," I said.

We shielded our eyes from the sun with our hands and checked to see if we could spot anything moving. We couldn't see a thing, not a person, not a car on the road, nothing.

We decided to walk back a different way and ended up taking the path over toward Naomi's house. We hadn't seen her for a few days. We wondered if we should call in, but we'd never called for Naomi.

"Do you play with Naomi at school?" asked Anna.

"Sometimes," I said.

"Only sometimes?"

"She doesn't like ball games or anything like that.

She hardly ever does P.E."

"She's quite new at your school, I suppose."

"Yeah, and some of the girls were nasty to her first of all."

"It's hard to be new at school."

We came to the beginning of the road where the Williamses lived. On the left, there was a farmhouse set back from the road, and after that, a little triangular green with a bench seat, a tiny stream running beside it.

"Who's Naomi's best friend?" Anna said.

"She sits next to a girl called Isobel," I told her.

"You do like Naomi, don't you?"

"Yeah."

"But you don't play with her much."

"She's really quiet at school."

"She's really quiet anyway…not like you!"

"Not like you either!"

Anna pulled a face.

"Right, I'm not speaking anymore," I said.

"Bet you do, though."

Wide grass banks lined each side of the road. The bank on the left bordered pastureland, while the bank on the right provided the forefront to a row of semi-detached brick cottages with pretty names: Rose Cottage, Primrose Cottage, Myrtle Cottage, and so on. Mr. and Mrs. Johnson lived in the first cottage. Mr. Johnson worked on the farm and had a collie dog called Meg. A few doors along was where old Mr. Morris lived and he, as usual, was out leaning on his gate. He gave us a wave, and we crossed to say hello.

"Hello, Mr. Morris," we said.

"Hello, girls. Are you enjoying your holidays?"

"Yes."

"What have you been doing with yourselves?"

"We went to look for blackberries, but there weren't any," Anna told him.

"Too early?"

"We think so," I said.

"How are your parents, Wendy?"

"They're well, thank you."

"And yours, Anna?"

"Very well, thank you, Mr. Morris."

Everyone liked Mr. Morris.

Naomi lived in the last cottage but one, Lavender Cottage. We walked up to the gate. She saw us from the window and came out. She told us that her dad was very bad and that he was in bed. She told us Tommy was in the back garden. We said that Sam and some of the others were keeping watch on the fields and the wood and were trying to find out if someone really was trying to scare us, but Naomi knew this already, and Tommy had also found out. He couldn't stop talking about it and wanted to be part of it.

"Wotcha, wotcha!" Tommy heard us and came to greet us. "I was up the tree." He smiled.

"Wotcha, Tommy," I said. "It's very nice of you to come down from your tree to see us."

"I can always go back up later," he said.

Naomi was obviously concerned about Tommy, and she gave him a warning, probably hoping that we'd back her up.

"Anna and Wendy aren't going to the wood at the moment, or the fields. They're leaving it to the big boys. You might be a boy, but you are not old enough for anything like that."

"I am," he said, "and I told them I'll help. When

they need me, they're gonna come and get me, and I'm gonna go." He had a determined expression on his face. I put my hands up in fists as if I was ready for a fight, and he took me on. We pretended to box.

"You have to leave it to them, Tommy," I said.

"They're probably going to get themselves into trouble," said Anna.

"I won't go until they say," Tommy said, dropping his hands.

Naomi frowned at him. She told us she couldn't ask anyone in because of her dad. We said goodbye but told her we'd try to come again in a day or so.

****

At the weekend, we had one of my favorite kinds of day. The sun was shining, and a powerful breeze was whirling and twisting amongst the trees. Puffy, white clouds raced across the sky; I couldn't wait to go swimming.

Dad drove us to the beach: Mum, Philip, and me. We found a spot beside a breakwater so that we wouldn't get blown away. We laid out the beach mats and secured them with large stones. Mum had brought sandwiches to eat afterward. We put the basket in the shade and were soon in our costumes, hurrying into the sea. We were at the mercy of the water, thrown about by the current, but at that time of year, there was no real danger. Philip and I dived through the waves and threw ourselves onto them so that they carried us back to the shore. Several times I found myself under the water and had to hold my breath and wait until I'd been spun around a number of times and deposited back on solid ground. I loved this kind of sea. It was warm, frothy, and roared deafeningly. The gulls were crying out above us, and we could hear the shrieks of other bathers either side of us along the bay. On calmer days, we could recognize other villagers by their stroke, but that day it was hard to actually swim, and everyone was really just frolicking in the swirling surf.

We held our towels by two corners and let them fly out like flags in the wind, almost taking us with them. We lay down behind the breakwater, so that we were beautifully warm in the sun as the breeze hummed over us. The waves carried on smashing onto the shore and growled as they retreated back across the sand.

****

Sam called for me. He came to find me in the garden. I'd picked one of my own tomatoes and was offering it to Poppy, but she wasn't that keen. I told Sam about the wheat fields and how you could see the wood from them. He thought that was really interesting and might be useful. He had nothing to report in terms of any activity.

"How long are you going to keep investigating?" I asked.

"Until we find out what's going on," he said.

"Then what?"

"I don't know. We'll have to decide."

"I think you should stop," I said. "Have you told your granddad what you're doing?"

"Of course not!"

"You know who's found out?"

"Who?" He scowled at me.

I waited for him to think about it for a moment before telling him, "Tommy Williams."

"Oh, Robbo must have told them, the Williams."

"He shouldn't have told Tommy."

"Why not?" said Sam.

"Robbo's such a big mouth!" I said.

"He probably thought it was fair enough to tell them, because it was them that found the rabbit in the first place."

"It would be good if he used his brain sometimes!"

"Well, it doesn't really matter does it?"

"It does. Because Tommy wants to help now. He wants to join in. He's too little for that, Sam."

"We're not really gonna bring him with us. We just said it."

"Well, he's expecting one of you to come and get him. He thinks he's going to be doing surveillance."

"I'll talk to Robbo about it," Sam said.

"Tell Robbo he has to be more careful about what he says…and who he says stuff to."

Philip and his friend, Mike, came out into the garden. We quickly changed the subject. Philip was holding some golf clubs, and he and Mike were going to practice putting. They had both just enrolled at the local course, where Dad was also a member, and were taking it extremely seriously. They laid flowerpots on their sides in various places on the lawn, then tried to putt balls into them.

Mum was busy indoors. She had a sewing machine in her bedroom and made some of my clothes and a lot of her own. She was making a dress for me. She'd found some unusual material, which she knew I would like, with red squirrels, nuts, and fir cones in the pattern. Every now and then she summoned me for a fitting, and the new garment was gradually taking shape.

****

The next day I asked Anna if she thought we should go to visit Naomi again, because she couldn't be having a very nice time. Anna agreed that we should. She'd been making biscuits with a biscuit machine her mum had bought from a catalog. She'd made rather a lot, butter ones and chocolate ones. With the machine, you could choose different shapes for the biscuits, and it seemed Anna had tried out every possible option. I sampled a chocolate one in a wavy pattern, a bit like a shell, also a heart-shaped buttery one. Anna found some grease-proof paper and chose a number of biscuits to wrap up as a gift.

We set off toward the path. We would take the quickest route to Naomi's house. We turned the corner by the farmhouse and walked toward the cottages. Mr. Johnson was walking along with Meg and we stopped to pat her. Old Mr. Morris called us over. He wondered what Anna had in the packet, and she told him it was a present for Naomi. He told us he had been feeding cat food to a hedgehog that had been coming into his garden.

It was almost as if Naomi had been waiting for us, she was out to meet us the minute she saw us. We walked across the road to the green and sat on the bench so that we could talk.

"These are for you," said Anna. She handed the parcel to Naomi.

Naomi lowered her dark eyes and examined the grease-proof paper packet, tied with a bow of blue wool. She took it tentatively, looked at Anna, at me, then back to the parcel; it was as if she'd never been given a present before. She didn't rush; she pulled the bow, then folded back the paper to reveal the biscuits.

Her face lit up. I couldn't remember ever seeing her smile so much.

"Thank you. Thank you, Anna. They're so pretty," she said. She marveled at them. "I'm not sure I'll want to eat them, because that would spoil them." She admired the biscuits for a little longer, then wrapped them carefully again, wound the wool back around the paper, and held them on her lap.

We told Naomi about the tent and how we'd been spending so much time in it. She told us her dad was a little better, but that his illness would never go away altogether. Her mum was working part-time at the grocery shop, so she had to help in the house and help take care of Tommy.

"I don't really mind," she said. "Tommy will see you're here soon, and he'll come over."

Even though there were eight cottages in the row, there weren't any other children of Naomi's or Tommy's age. Mr. and Mrs. Johnson had a grown-up son who no longer lived with them, and there was a young couple called Mr. and Mrs. Barclay who had a small baby and a toddler. Otherwise, the cottages only housed adults.

"Wendy! Anna!" Tommy hurried along the bank opposite, jumped down to the road, and ran across to greet us.

"You're late," I teased him.

"I didn't hear you come. What's in the packet?"

Naomi looked at him in a big sisterly way. She knew how to tease him, and enjoying his suspense, she slowly unwound the wool and opened up the paper to reveal the biscuits.

"Wow! Can I have one?"

We all laughed, and Naomi, who'd not yet sampled one herself, pushed them toward him so that he could take one. Tommy chose a smooth, round chocolate biscuit, and without another word, he sat down cross-legged on the grass in front of us and took a small bite. He concentrated on the biscuit for some time, chewing it thoughtfully, getting maximum enjoyment from the delicious chocolatey-ness.

The biscuits were wrapped up once more, and Naomi said she would save them until teatime and share them with her mum and dad, and it would cheer them all up.

"Anna, you are a very good cook," Tommy concluded on finishing the final mouthful.

"Why thank you, kind sir," Anna replied.

Tommy seemed to have forgotten about the investigation, at least for the time being.

Chapter 8
Following Bridges, Looking for Tommy

Anna had gone to stay with her cousin Bea for a few days. I was at home consulting the encyclopedias about hedgehogs. We had a set of twelve encyclopedias. They had previously belonged to one of our parents, but now we used them, Philip and I. The index was in Book Number Twelve. Then you had to work out which book contained the page number you were looking for. Things would drop out of the encyclopedias because we also used them to press flowers and keep favorite birthday cards, postcards, and so on.

We'd had hedgehogs come into the garden before, but I'd never read up on them. The books were informative. There were a number of entries. There was some information on page 351, and a picture on page 357, both in the first encyclopedia of the twelve. Then on page 4520—that was in a much later volume—there was information about how to attract and take care of a hedgehog. Apparently, they ate all kinds of meat and vegetables. You could feed them the same as a cat or a dog: raw meat was suggested, bones and eggs, but not milk. You could give them hay or straw to lie in and water to drink. In the winter, they would go off and sleep under a pile of leaves, and you weren't to disturb them. The young ones would squeak like piglets when left alone, it said. It also said that hedgehogs slept in the day and went hunting at night, and that you might be able to find them when they were hunting by listening out for them. I put the books back and decided to go to the beach to look for Sam.

I shouted goodbye to Mum and collected my bike. I rode through the village and down the hill to the pier. I could see Sam sitting on the wall where his granddad had the boats and carried on along to join him. He had his mind on the wood again. We jumped down onto the pebbles to discuss things.

"I'm not sure we're getting anywhere," Sam told me. "Robbo's the only one who's seen anyone at all up near the wood...and that was only Patricia Price's brother."

Patricia used to be at school with us. She was a few years ahead of us. Her older brother, Danny, had left school, and he was now working as a farm laborer.

Sam began combing the pebbles for sausage-shaped stones. If you threw them so that they spun longways over and over, and they landed end on, they made a good sound when they hit the water. There were never that many sausage-shaped pebbles to be found, though, and you generally had to have several goes at throwing before one fell correctly. It was quite a challenge. Sometimes we couldn't manage any at all; other times the sea was too loud, so you couldn't hear the sound they made anyway. That day, the sea was very still, and we went back up onto the wall and tossed the stones in from there.

"Chuck them right up in the air...take a run up," Sam instructed.

"Don't fall over the edge!" I said, as he tested the

technique.

"Yes, yes, what a throw!" Sam shouted. He threw his arms up in celebration.

The successful stones made a satisfying sploosh sound rather than an ordinary splash sound. We both managed one good throw.

Sam's granddad was busy. It was the best weather for hiring out the boats. People would take them for an hour or a half hour. Sometimes they might return a raft and book out a pedalo. The boats belonged to the hotel. There was a storage hut at the back of the path. His granddad took them out in the morning and put them away at night, although when the weather was calm, he kept them chained together on the beach. He also maintained them. Not all the people who hired boats were experts, so he had to be vigilant too. He might have to go to someone's rescue if they perhaps dropped an oar in the water, or if, as sometimes happened, a person couldn't row quite as well as they'd thought they could. Today was such a day. No one was in peril, as the sea was so quiet, but as we sat on the wall, Sam's granddad had to make several journeys out in his dingy with the outboard motor to give assistance. The final time he took Sam along to help. They brought back a couple who were having trouble getting their rowing boat back to shore. Sam jumped in with them and tied the boat so that it could be towed back safely.

"Why don't the two of you take a raft out?" Sam's granddad offered when they returned.

So we pushed a raft out into the shallow water and paddled to and fro for a while, our legs dangling beneath in the warm sea, and the sun beating on our backs.

We were on the beach again later when we heard a shout.

"Oi!" It was Robbo. He came over to talk to us. He agreed they weren't getting far with the investigation. "Time for a change of tactics," he said, nodding his head wisely.

"How do you mean?" Sam asked, keen to hear.

"Let me think. Let me think for a while," Robbo told him.

****

"Can we go up to the fields?" Tommy asked.

Sam and I had cycled over to the green in the evening.

"We've given up going there at the moment, remember?" I said. "What's wrong with playing here?"

"I'm fed up." Tommy had become used to roaming around the countryside, like the rest of us, and having to stay around the house with Naomi wasn't so much fun. The days were long, the weather was good, and he'd had a taste of a wider world.

"Have a go on my bike," Sam suggested.

Tommy didn't have a bike. He was too small for Sam's or mine, but Sam sat him on his saddle and had Tommy hold on to the handlebars. He couldn't reach the pedals, but Sam pushed the bike around the green. Then Sam hopped up in front of him, told him to hold on tight and rode up and down on the grass, Tommy clinging to the back of Sam's T-shirt, giggling.

I cheered them as they went. Naomi sat quietly on the bench, but she must have been happy to see Tommy having a good time.

We played as many games as we could think up, making use of the plentiful resources provided by the little green. We shot at each other with plantain, looping the stalks around the black, spiky flowers and firing them off like pellets. We picked sticky burdock buds and ran around attempting to attach as many as possible to each other's clothing. We selected coarse blades of grass, held them between our thumbs, and blew to produce piercing whistles, like rare birds. Finally, we sat on the grass pulling petals from the clover flowers and sucking the ends that tasted of honey.

It was starting to get dark by the time Sam and I set off for home. We'd only reached the end of the road when Sam came to a standstill. "Stop a minute," he said. "There's something I want to see." He began to wheel his bike down a narrow grass pathway opposite the farmhouse. It ran along the side of the old barn. "Robbo told me about it."

"Where are we going? I'm gonna be late back." I'd never even noticed the little path. It went on for a few yards. "We're definitely not supposed to be here," I told him. "*Trespassers Will Be Prosecuted,* it says."

"Yeah, but it doesn't mean us. Those signs are for the holidaymakers." He carried on beside the black wood-slatted building, left his bike, and went to climb the gate. "Come on," he said. I followed. Sam went to the corner of the barn and peered round. "There's a back entrance. Robbo and that lot come here. They keep stuff here. You know, stuff they can't keep in the house." I supposed he meant to do with smoking. The door was ajar. He pushed it and went in. I was right behind. There was a noise from up in the hayloft. "Must be Robbo," he said. He started up the ladder, but as soon as he reached the top, he was on the way down again. He looked over his shoulder, his face white as a sheet. He put his finger to his lips. "Get down!" he mouthed. He reached the bottom and pulled me back against the wall. A head appeared above us. It was Danny Price. Then we heard a woman's voice.

"What is it? Was someone there?"

"Nah. S'nuthin," said Danny, after looking around. "Just cats."

We heard more noises coming from above us and made a quick exit.

"They were snogging," said Sam when we reached the gate. "They didn't see us."

"No, they mustn't have," I said.

We walked, pushing the bikes. Sam continued to divulge what he'd seen.

"Is it a love nest?" I asked him.

"I reckon."

"Woooo! Danny's love nest. I wonder who he was with?"

"I saw who it was," Sam said.

"Did you know them?" I wasn't sure he wanted to tell me.

"It was…it was Adam Smart's mum."

I could tell he wasn't messing about, but I couldn't believe it. "It can't have been."

"I'm telling you. It was."

"Oh my God!"

"We're gonna have to keep quiet about this. What if Adam found out? It'd kill him." Sam had a strong sense of loyalty. He stopped walking. He kicked abstractedly at his pedal, sending it spinning in circles with a whirr. "Do you think Robbo knows?" he said.

"No, he'd have told us…and if Mr. Morris had

found out, he'd have told the whole village! We're probably the only ones."

"I hope so," said Sam. "Don't even tell Anna."

We'd gone into the barn expecting to find some secret stuff, but we'd come away with a bit more than we'd bargained for.

****

Sometimes I talked to Piggy.

"I said I didn't want to go to the fields anymore, Piggy, but I do sort of miss them. I miss the breeze in the trees and the big, grassy space where there's so much room to play. I miss the teasels and the thistledown. I miss the butterflies that flutter around up there and the giant bumble bees."

"Sam's here!" Mum shouted up to me.

I went down and took Sam out into the garden. It was time to feed Poppy, and Sam could help me.

"Robbo's had an idea."

"What?"

"Well, surveillance of the fields was a good idea, but it's getting us nowhere. We're going to follow Bridges, and then we're sure to catch him at it."

Like everyone else, I thought Bridges was responsible for the birds and the rabbit, but I didn't like the idea of the boys following him. It sounded dangerous.

"You could get into a lot of trouble, Sam. What if he sees you and gets angry? Anyway, we haven't seen him in the fields at all lately. It might be someone else that's doing it."

"They're his fields and he goes there, I know he does. It's him that's trying to scare us."

"Sam, you're crazy," I told him.

"It makes more sense than keeping watch."

"What if he turns on you? I can't imagine what he'd do, but I know it would be bad."

****

I spent the next day with Mum and Dad. I was worried about Sam, but he wouldn't listen to me. He had a mission, and it was to catch Bridges in the wood leaving a dead animal or doing something worse. I was hoping Tommy wouldn't hear about this new development because he would want to be a part of it.

In the evening, I asked mum if I could have some food and water for the hedgehog, and I asked Philip if he'd come out and listen for it with me. Hedgehogs walked about and snuffled around quite noisily, it said in the encyclopedia.

"Is there a hedgehog?" Philip asked.

"I think there will be one nearby. We just need to find him."

"Okay, you go out and start, and I'll come out in a bit."

I took a chair from the patio and placed it over near the shed where the garden was overhung with shrubbery. I went back for the food and some water, which we'd put into an old saucer. I set the offerings down underneath one of the birch trees, sat on the chair, and listened.

I sat for a while but not much happened. It was a quiet night. Once in a while, I heard a car in the distance. I heard the wind blowing gently, and now and then I heard the bell buoys chiming in the bay. Eventually, I abandoned my chair and went in. Philip was in his room playing the muffled music, and Mum and Dad were watching a serial on TV about some

American family. They watched it every week.

****

Anna was home from Bea's, and we were back in the tent. I told her that Sam and the others were planning to follow Bridges.

"He never goes anywhere," she said.

"I know, I think they're nuts, but you can't tell them anything."

"You know what I think we should do?"

"No?"

"Take him some biscuits."

"You're joking."

"No. I'm going to make more tomorrow, ginger ones, and more chocolate ones. We could take him biscuits and ask him if we can go to the wood and see what he says."

"I'm not sure about that either."

****

Robbo would sit outside Bridges' house on one side and Sam would sit outside near the other entrance. They would sit there for a given amount of time, then meet up on the wheat fields to exchange information. If Bridges set off for the fields, they could watch his progress from there. They would alternate which side of the house they covered, so that if someone saw them it wouldn't seem suspicious. If anyone came along, they could pretend to be inspecting their bike tire or something like that, then they could just cycle off. They would start the next day and do an hour in the morning and an hour in the evening. In a couple of days, Adam would take over from Sam. Robbo and Adam would be on duty, after that Sam and Adam. They would rotate until they had success. It seemed quite like waiting for the hedgehog.

****

We were more than halfway through the holidays now, but the days kept on coming. We'd carved out new lifestyles for ourselves. For a time, it was as if this was the new normal, and nothing would ever change.

Chapter 9

I was surprised when Naomi came to the door. I was about to leave for Anna's when Mum called upstairs.

I came down expecting to find Anna, but it was Naomi. Naomi had never been to my house before. She hadn't even come to my party although I'd invited her. I took her out to the garden to introduce her to Poppy and show her my nasturtiums and tomatoes, but she was distracted and obviously had something to tell me.

"Something's the matter, isn't it?" I said.

She took a breath, closed her eyes, and let the breath back out. I could see she was building up courage. The expression on her face made me anxious. Part of me thought it could be a prank, but I also remember thinking that what she had to say was going to be something that was too big for me to deal with.

She opened her eyes and said it. "Tommy's been taken."

Then there was a silence because neither of us knew what to say next.

"How do you mean?" I said eventually.

"Someone's taken Tommy. He's gone, and it's my fault." Her big, dark eyes were now filled with tears; she blinked, and they began to roll slowly down her cheeks. I reached forward and put my arms around her.

I can't remember exactly how the conversation

continued. Naomi was very agitated, and it was hard to make any sense of it, but she said that she and Tommy had been left at home by their parents. Naomi had been watching TV. Tommy was in the garden and then he wasn't in the garden, and she didn't know where he was, and we mustn't tell anyone because she was supposed to be looking after him. I had to help her find him.

I wasn't sure I was going to be very good at the role I was being plunged into, but I thought I should try to keep calm and be practical and logical, the way my mum or dad would act in such a situation.

"I think we need to tell someone else," I said.

"Oh no, please don't tell your mum. I'll be in such trouble," she replied.

So I persuaded Naomi we should go up to Anna's, and the three of us should decide what to do next. I told her to wait by Poppy's hutch. I went to my room, took two handkerchiefs from my drawer, and put them in the pockets of my shorts. I shouted to Mum to let her know where we were going and went back outside. Of course, Naomi didn't have a bike; we'd have to walk. We set off up the rough road. I gave Naomi one of the handkerchiefs and told her to dry her eyes. We needed to make sure everything appeared to be normal, or Anna's mum and dad would soon be onto us. She said very little but went along with it.

We arrived at the house, and fortunately, Anna came to the door. She was typically bouncy and smiling and welcomed us, but she soon picked up that we weren't quite so cheerful. I told her Naomi wanted to see the tent. She knew me well enough to understand we had something to say to her that needed to be said in

The Five Things

private. She gave us a quick signal and led us through the house and outside. Anna's dad was gardening. He was wearing khaki shorts, a white vest, and a large floppy hat to keep the sun off. He looked up for a moment and said hello to us as we passed, but he was too engrossed in his digging to take much notice.

The tent flap was open, and the rugs and pillows were spread out on the groundsheets. We went inside and sat down facing each other. I looked at Naomi and waited for her to speak. She lowered her head and took out the handkerchief, which she had pushed up into the sleeve of her cardigan. She put it up to her eyes and dabbed them.

"It's about Tommy," I said. "Naomi says Tommy's been taken."

"How do you mean, taken?" Anna took over. "Naomi, what do you mean? Tell me exactly what's happened."

Naomi found her voice, and between tears and short jerky intakes of breath, began to tell us in a little more detail what had happened. Her dad had an appointment at the hospital. He and her mum had to go there on the bus. Naomi was left to look after the house, keep an eye on Tommy, and give him his lunch. She told him she was going to watch a cartoon on television, but he had a ball and said he would rather go and play in the back garden. She could hear him bouncing the ball and throwing it against the wall. She couldn't remember how long that went on for. The cartoon ended, and she went upstairs, to the bedroom they shared, to get a book she'd been reading. She saw Tommy from the window. He was at the far end of the garden near the old shed, watching the cows that were grazing in the field beyond. There wasn't anything unusual about that. She went back downstairs and read her book for a while, perhaps half an hour. Then she went to the kitchen to see what her mum had left for lunch. There were sandwiches and some apricots from the grocery store. She went into the garden to call Tommy in, but she couldn't see him. She went upstairs and looked. Then she went downstairs and checked there, even though she knew he couldn't be downstairs. She went to the front gate and looked over to the green. There was no sign of him. She went through the side gate to the back garden and right down to the end near the fence. He wasn't there, and he wasn't in the shed. She called his name a few times. After that, she went back indoors and looked everywhere again.

"Then you went to Wendy's?" Anna checked.

"Yes," Naomi confirmed, in a small voice.

"Well, he must be somewhere," said Anna. "Let's think."

Anna then began to question Naomi. Could he have been hiding somewhere? We knew that he liked to play games. Could he have been visiting a neighbor? Would he have actually gone into the cow field? Naomi seemed a little less distraught. Perhaps there was an explanation.

"When are your parents getting home?" Anna then asked.

"By teatime, five o'clock," Naomi said.

"Right, that means we have the rest of the afternoon. Let's start looking for him," Anna said decisively.

I said we should find Sam so he could help us. He might still be waiting for Bridges, or he might be on the beach. Anna said she'd take her bike, see if she could find Sam, and then come to Naomi's house. Naomi and I were to walk to Naomi's and start a new search. Anyway, by now Tommy might have come back.

****

The Williamses' house seemed dark inside and it had an old kind of smell about it. I was surprised to see that there were a lot of ornaments, some on the mantelpiece and some displayed in a glass cabinet, china animals and figures. There was a framed wall hanging that said, *Home Sweet Home*.

We called Tommy's name but there was no reply. There was no sign of him. I was convinced he would have come out if he'd been hiding. I felt uncomfortable looking around the house. I didn't want to look into other people's rooms or cupboards, so I suggested I go outside and that Naomi should search indoors. I went to the back garden. It was quite overgrown, but it wasn't difficult to see that no one was there. I looked up into the tree, which must have been the one Tommy sometimes climbed. I opened the door of the dilapidated shed. It was very messy, full of disused tools, stacks of soil encrusted flowerpots, and bamboo canes. I went in tentatively; there wasn't much room for me. Toward the back, there were a couple of rusted watering cans and a decrepit wheelbarrow, but no one was in there. It didn't look like the sort of place anyone would want to spend their time. I went right to the back of the garden. There was what seemed to be a neglected vegetable patch, almost completely covered by weeds and grass. Beyond that was the boundary. I looked over the fence to the cow field. You could see every part of the field from where I was standing, and I was sure that only the cows were in there.

I went to the front gate. Old Mr. Morris wasn't outside. I wondered whether it would be a good or a bad idea to ask him if he'd seen Tommy. There was no one in the other front gardens. I stood for a moment, making sure. It was obvious that Naomi had had no success inside the house. My head was swimming with the heat and with the whole situation, which was becoming more and more overwhelming. I stepped out onto the bank, climbed down, and looked up and down the road as far as I could see. When I turned back, I saw Sam cycling like mad around the corner. He arrived right in front of me, braked sharply, and dismounted. He stood astride the bike, hands on the handlebars, eyes wide, out of breath.

"Have you found him?" he asked.

"No. We've searched all over the house and garden, and we've been calling out his name. Where can he have got to?" I said.

Anna arrived and we all went inside to join Naomi. We sat down in a circle on the floor of the living room. I was starting to feel really concerned. Naomi was now sobbing.

Sam asked Naomi to go through what happened once again, and when she finished, he said, "Do you think he could have gone to the wood? He keeps talking about going up there."

The doorbell rang. Naomi leapt up. She thought it was Tommy, but it was Robbo. He'd seen the bikes outside. Naomi went through the happenings of the day again, for Robbo's benefit.

"Your mum's not back 'til five?" he checked.

"No," said Naomi.

The Five Things

"It's three o'clock now. I think one of us should go to the upper field, and if he's not there, we should tell an adult. He's a little kid. We need to find him."

Naomi didn't protest this time. It seemed she didn't have any fight left in her. Sam and Robbo were dispatched to the fields, and then they were to return to the house. Anna, Naomi, and I waited. We weren't feeling too optimistic by that point. Naomi began to sob again, and Anna put an arm around her. I passed her the second handkerchief.

Sam and Robbo returned without Tommy. They'd walked through the wood shouting his name. They'd stood on the stump and looked down through the countryside and walked right across the upper field so that every angle had been covered, but they'd found nothing. So we had to decide who to tell. Anna said we should tell her dad. He was a teacher. He was used to children, and he was at home gardening, which meant we could tell him straight away. Robbo said it was stupid for us all to go. Anna should go and ask her dad to come to Naomi's house.

Naomi, Sam, Robbo, and I were left waiting in the dark living room with the old sort of smell. Robbo soon became restless and said he would have a walk up and down the road just in case he could see anything. Sam held Naomi's hand and tried to convince her that everything was going to be all right.

The time we spent waiting for Anna to return to the house with her dad was in a way the time between the end of one world and the beginning of another. It was increasingly dawning on me how serious the situation was, and I had lost track of time altogether. We could have waited for ten minutes, we could have waited for two hours, the nature of time had changed. Sam sat holding Naomi's hand and it seemed to calm her. I stood up once every so often and went to the window, checking for Tommy, or Anna, or her father. I went to the back garden one more time. I returned to the living room. The events of the day continued to unfold, and we were a part of them.

The familiar big, black family car with the rounded bonnet finally pulled up outside, and I saw Anna's dad get out of the driver's side door and walk round to the bank. Anna climbed out of the passenger side. They stepped up onto the grass and walked toward the gate. Anna's dad was still in his shorts but with a shirt on now and no hat. He walked in front of Anna. The front door was open, and we heard a knock, then Anna's dad came into the room with Anna just behind him.

"Hello Wendy, Sam. And you are Naomi, I understand," he said.

"Hello, Mr. Martin," I said. "Yes, this is Naomi."

"May I?" he asked, before sitting on the edge of the seat of the armchair.

He leaned forward. We were still sitting on the floor and Anna had joined us. We looked at him in anticipation. Anna had filled her dad in as much as she could on the way to the house. Mr. Martin gently asked Naomi a few questions about Tommy; he didn't ask her to go over everything again. He asked exactly how old Tommy was and precisely when and where she'd seen him last. He asked us to wait in the house while he went into the garden.

Robbo arrived back, having found out nothing of any consequence. Anna's dad came inside again and greeted Robbo, who was known as Robert to Anna's dad. He said how pleased he was that Robbo was with us. Mr. Martin gently asked a few more questions. Could Naomi remember what Tommy was wearing? Had he ever gone off on his own before? He asked Robbo if he had his bike with him and instructed him to cycle over to the police house and tell Constable Gordon he would like him to come to Lavender Cottage as soon as was possible. Robbo was to state that it was very important. If he wasn't there, Robbo should stay and wait for the constable. Mr. Martin spoke slowly and made everything clear. He didn't seem angry.

It was four thirty, and if the bus was running on time, Naomi's parents would be getting home soon. Mr. Martin told us we would wait for Mr. and Mrs. Williams, and then we would be going to Anna's house for something to eat.

"Shouldn't we be looking for Tommy?" Sam asked.

"We will," said Anna's dad, "but I think you've all done enough for now…and we need a little help."

It was comforting to have Anna's dad with us and not to have to do any more thinking. He knew what to do, and we just did what he said.

A police motorbike pulled up, and Mr. Martin went to meet Constable Gordon. He spoke to him outside on the bank before they came into the living room together. Constable Gordon was wearing his uniform, and it was as if, when he entered, he brought an extra layer of seriousness. He'd been to the school on one or two occasions to talk about road safety. He had a way of speaking that made me start to feel uncomfortable again.

"Now, Naomi, come and sit here on the sofa. I've

been told about your brother, Tommy. He's been missing for a little while now, hasn't he? I need you to think very carefully, start at the beginning and tell me exactly what happened. There's no need to be frightened."

By that time Naomi appeared almost drained of emotion.

Robbo arrived back and hurried in. "The Williamses are walking across the green!" he yelled.

Anna's dad sat with an arm around Naomi while Constable Gordon went out to speak to her parents. He hadn't forgotten about us. "Anna," he said, "I want you to take Wendy, Sam, and Robert, and get into the car."

****

Anna's mum must have had forewarning about the afternoon's events, as she seemed to have enough food ready to feed an army of people. We were led into the lounge, where Anna and I rarely played, and told to find ourselves a seat. The glass doors through to the dining room were open, and Mrs. Martin had laid out sandwiches and cakes on the table. There was a stack of small plates at the side. She told us to help ourselves.

I'm not sure we knew what we were doing, and we had no idea if we were hungry, but we were pleased to be there. Anna's mum, realizing we were all just sitting, began to pick out food for us and bring it to us. She handed me a plate with two triangular sandwiches on it, one with grated cheese and pickle and the other with egg and cress, also a slice of sponge cake with a layer of jam through the middle. She gave me a plastic cup of orange squash and she brought similar for the others. She said to eat up. Not long after, she arrived with mugs of tea and offered them around. She gave one to

Mr. Martin and sat down to drink one herself.

Mr. Martin spoke to us. "Now children, I am very proud of you and the way you have behaved today. I want you all to stay here and eat your sandwiches while I go and speak to your parents…and your granddad, Sam, and let them know where you are. I don't want you to worry about anything. Constable Gordon is going to start a formal search for Tommy. He will make sure no stone is left unturned. Naomi is with her parents, and that's the best place for her at the moment. We'll collect your bikes later," he added. He put down his mug and went out to the car, and the car disappeared out of the driveway. I felt as if someone had built a wall in my head, and I could only think in the very small space inside the brickwork.

We sat on the large comfortable furniture in Anna's lounge. Mrs. Martin sat with us and talked to us, though I can't remember what about. I recall her asking frequently if we would like more to eat and going to and fro to the kitchen to bring more tea and jugs of squash.

My mind was closing down, engaging less and less in any meaningful way with the situation. The others must have felt the same. We were just sitting while time passed. At some point, Anna's father returned. He came to let us know where he'd been. He pulled over a chair and sat down with us. He spoke slowly, making eye contact with each of us.

"I've seen your mum, Wendy, your granddad, Sam, and your mum, Robert. I've let them know where you are, and that I will drive you home in a short while. I've also seen Constable Gordon again, and he is going to come here to the house shortly because he has a few questions you might be able to help him to answer. There are some other policemen and women assisting him now. They are looking for Tommy. Of course, we hope to have some news soon."

There were so many questions, and I knew that somewhere inside my head I was asking them, but mainly my head just felt as if it had stopped working.

Constable Gordon arrived. He came into the living room.

"Hello again, children. I think Mr. Martin has told you that I'd like to ask you a few questions before you all go home and get some rest."

Mrs. Martin brought him a mug of tea. He asked us to think about the last few times we'd seen Tommy. He asked us if we could remember Tommy talking about running away or going anywhere out of the ordinary. He asked where we had been during the last few days and what we had been doing; if we might have said anything to Tommy that could have made him curious, that may have sparked his imagination. The constable said Tommy was a bright, inquisitive boy and might have been tempted to go off exploring; perhaps he had gone on something of an adventure. The constable was satisfied that Tommy was not at the Williamses' house nor in the garden, so he must have gone somewhere else.

If we'd been asked these questions under different circumstances, I'm not sure we would have answered them so readily. We had our secrets, but today we just said what we knew and were prepared to divulge anything we thought could help.

Robbo began, "We've been going to the upper field and to the wood there. But we haven't been for a few days, except for today when Sam and me went up to check if Tommy was there."

The constable had a notepad and scribbled into it. "So you went there today? Did you already know Tommy was missing at that point?"

"Yes, it was just before Anna went to tell Mr. Martin," Robbo said.

"We were trying to find him," said Sam.

"Have you previously been there with Tommy?"

Anna answered, "Yes, I have. Wendy, and Sam, and I have."

"And with Naomi," I added.

"And when was the last time you went there. Can you remember?"

"Not for quite a few days. Tommy asked us to go, though," I said.

"Do you remember exactly when Tommy last talked about the wood? Do you mean that he wanted to go there with you?" Constable Gordon's questions were very precise.

Sam responded, "It was when Anna was away. That was last weekend. Wendy and me were with Naomi and Tommy on the green by their house. Tommy asked if we could go there but we didn't go."

Constable Gordon wrote some more notes. "Now, is there anywhere else you think Tommy might have gone?"

"We made a camp on the beach," said Robbo, "but he's never been there, I don't think."

I don't know why no one mentioned the surveillance of the fields or the following of Bridges, but nobody did. I don't think we thought about it. Of course, we couldn't know what Naomi had said. She seemed to have been asked a lot of questions.

Constable Gordon told us that he had nothing further to ask, but that if we remembered anything we thought was important, we should tell our parents so that they could let him know. He closed his notebook and stood up. He said he would leave us in the capable hands of the Martins. He thanked Anna's mum for the tea, and Anna's Dad showed him back outside.

Mr. Martin drove me home, and Mum and Dad brought me inside and sat down with me. They wanted to give me more to eat, but I wasn't hungry. Mum came up to my room with me and folded back the bedclothes. I put on my nightdress and climbed in. She made sure Piggy was tucked in beside me underneath the blanket, and she stayed with me. A little later, Dad came with a small cup of warm milk. He told me he'd put a drop of brandy in with it. I swallowed it down.

Chapter 10
The Search

When I woke the next morning, I felt empty. I reached for Piggy, then called for Mum. She arrived quickly. She said it was good that I'd had a long sleep, that she knew I'd had a shock. She said I could get up whenever I felt ready, and we'd spend the day together doing some nice things.

"Have they found Tommy?" I asked. I could tell from her expression that she understood how wretched I felt. Nevertheless, she was matter of fact with her answer.

"We've not heard anything today, but your dad is going to pop up to the Martins' shortly and see if they've been given an update."

I put on my dressing gown and went downstairs. Philip shouted to me that our favorite program was on TV and I might like to watch with him, but I went to the kitchen where Mum was cooking. I sat on the stool beside the kitchen table and watched her instead. She broke off from what she was doing to make some toast for me. She spread it with butter and honey and put it on the table beside me with a cup of milky tea. She carried on stirring her mixture with the big wooden spoon in the big brown basin. The rhythm of the stirring was soothing, and the clunking of the bowl was familiar and comforting. She was making fruitcakes, she told me, and then she would make some pastry and prepare a plum pie for lunch. She swirled around the kitchen opening cupboards and measuring ingredients, breaking eggs, putting items for washing into the kitchen sink. She took the baking tins and cut greaseproof paper to line them. She checked the temperature of the oven.

Dad had gone to the Martins', but in the cozy environment of the kitchen, I could believe, at least for a time, that everything would be all right. Philip came in and began to tell us what happened in the program. He said he would start the washing up. He carried on with his review as the hot tap poured loudly into the sink. He began to clank and clatter the bowls and utensils as he washed them.

At the table, another mixing bowl had been produced. Butter and flour were going into it. Mum started to rub the butter into the flour with her fingers. Water was added, and a lovely yellow ball of pastry was formed.

I heard the car being parked outside and knew Dad was on his way back in. I would often dash out to meet him when I heard the car, but not that day. I had a feeling he wasn't going to be saying what I wanted to hear. Mopping and splashing sounds were still coming from the sink. The plums were sitting in a large colander, washed and shining, waiting to be stoned. Dad opened the door. He smiled, but not in a happy way. He came and stood behind me and put an arm around me. I looked up.

"There's no news at the moment, I'm afraid," he said. He didn't give any details. Then he said he had managed to take the day off and that in the afternoon we would go for a family outing.

The outing ended up being a long drive in the car. We went out of the local area and Dad drove along the north side of the downs. He took us along country lanes and through little villages. It was lulling to sit in the back, next to Philip, and look out of the side window as we traveled by. Mum and Dad talked in the front. Philip joined in with them now and then. Every once in a while, he would spot something that interested him and point it out to us. After some time, we drove down a narrow lane that led to a small beach. We got out of the car and went to sit on a bench from where you could look across the bay and see a lighthouse. Dad and Philip went away and came back with four huge ice cream cornets and we sat and ate them, listening to the waves and the gulls. Later, we drove back along the coast road and cut in through Haverley, where there was a pretty castle.

In the evening, Philip asked us all to take him on at putting in the garden. Dad and I played against Mum and Philip. I was enjoying myself in a way, but things weren't right. No matter what we did, there was one big question and lots of smaller ones battling away somewhere inside my head.

****

Another morning began. I had slept. I'd not had bad dreams, at least not that I could remember. Piggy was next to me and Mum had come in to see if I was awake.

"Have they found Tommy?"

"We don't think so, darling. Dad has gone to see if there's any news."

She asked if I would like to try on my dress. She'd nearly finished it, and this would be the final fitting. We went into her room, and she helped it carefully over my head. She told me to take a step back, to arm's length. She studied me, then knelt in front of me on the rug. She proceeded to take a few pins from a seam, stored some of them by pinning them into the fabric of her own dress and some by holding them in her mouth while she made the adjustments. She re-pinned the seam and smiled at me before turning me around so that I could look at myself in the mirror. She took her brush from the dressing table and ran it through my hair, then stood behind me as if admiring her work in the reflection: my hair, the dress, and me.

"There," she said. "It's just as I imagined."

She helped me get out of it and I went to put on my shorts and T-shirt. I came downstairs and found her scraping a basinful of new potatoes that had been grown in the garden.

Dad was soon back, and I could tell there wasn't any news and that he was disappointed because he hadn't wanted to come back with no information. He put a hand on my shoulder and squeezed. He couldn't stay with us; he had to set off for work. I went into the garden to feed Poppy and look at my tomatoes. All the while, I could feel the watchful presence of my concerned mum and the comfort that it gave me.

A little later, when I was out in the garden again, Mum came to find me. She told me Constable Gordon had come to the door and that he'd like to see me. It was nothing to worry about she said, although I thought she looked uneasy. She said that the constable was in the lounge and she came into the room with me. She showed him to an armchair and sat with me on the sofa.

Constable Gordon began, "I'm sorry to disturb you,

The Five Things

Wendy. It's just that there are a couple of questions I'd like to put to you." He spoke clearly, making sure that I understood. He said that Tommy's sister, Naomi, had told him that when I went to the house with her to look for Tommy, I'd gone to look in the back garden while she searched in the house. He asked if that was the case. I said it was. He then asked if I remembered seeing a ball in the garden. I said that I didn't. He said that Tommy had been playing with a blue ball in the garden that morning, but that the ball had not been found. He asked was I sure I'd not seen the ball. I said I was sure, but that the garden was quite overgrown. He paused, and I could somehow tell the next question was going to be a bigger one. He asked if, when I'd gone to look in the garden, I'd also looked into the field beyond the garden. I said that yes, I had, and that it was full of cows, but Tommy wasn't there.

"Was anyone in the field—someone you recognized—anyone at all?" he asked.

I was surprised by this question.

"Please take time to think," he said. He smiled at me but kept his lips pressed together.

"No one was there. Only cows," I said.

"Now, I'd like you to think carefully one more time. Did Naomi say anything to you, at any point that day, about having seen someone in the field?"

This question surprised me even more. I caught Mum's eye, and she gave me a supportive look in return.

"No, she didn't. She didn't say anything about any other person."

"Thank you, Wendy," said Constable Gordon, "and don't forget to let your mum know if you remember anything else that you'd like to pass on to me—anything, no matter how small or insignificant it might seem."

Mum showed him out and came back to the lounge to talk to me.

"Don't worry about those questions," she said. "It's the constable's job to ask questions." Mum said she thought it best I stay at home for the day, but perhaps the following day I could go to the tennis club if I wanted to; it might do me good. I was happy to stay at home. It seemed the best place to be. I surrounded myself with the familiar patterns of the day. I was aware that there was a lot going on just beyond that sheltered space, but for now, I was pleased not to have to participate.

****

It was the third morning after the event, and I didn't even ask about Tommy because I knew he hadn't been found. For the first time, I started to think about the others. I thought about Naomi, Anna, and Sam, then my mind reverted to the comfortable constraints of the house. I could hear Philip's music and the routine kitchen clatter of breakfast being prepared. It was Saturday, and soon I heard the lawn mower. Dad was cutting the grass.

I was dressed when Mum came in with my tennis skirt and a white T-shirt and reminded me that it might be nice to go and play for an hour or so. Dad would walk me over if I wanted.

I went down for some breakfast then changed into my kit and found my racquet. Dad had finished the lawn. The garden was full of the smell of the cut grass and the dampness it created as the morning sun heated up. He opened the gate and ushered me through. We walked around the corner and down along to the hotel grounds where the tennis club met. We could see a few people gathering. There were four courts and a wooden building, a bit like a giant beach hut, that we used as a clubhouse. We kept the nets in there and balls and it was somewhere to leave our things while we were playing and so on. A quantity of folding chairs was kept in the clubhouse, too, and taken out and unfolded for sitting on between games. I was often given the task of unfolding and folding up the chairs; some club members seemed to prefer sitting on them, on the grass area in front of the building, chatting rather than playing.

It was the first time I'd seen anyone apart from my family and the constable for more than two days. Most of those who'd come to play that morning were adults and almost all from the nearby villages. From our village, there was only Peter Clay's dad and the club captain, Mr. Thornton, who also gave the lessons.

Mr. Thornton saw us arriving and came to meet us. I could tell that he was making sure I didn't have to greet the whole crowd; he called Barbara over straight away. She was about my age and from one of the other villages. We played together relatively often. Mr. Thornton sent us off to the far court to have a game. He carried on speaking to Dad. Soon, he and Dad went over to the other players and they spoke for a few minutes before Dad turned and was quickly on his way. He waved over to me as he departed. He'd told me earlier that he'd come to meet me at midday.

I tried to concentrate but it wasn't easy. Barbara was beating me. After a few games, we took a break for a drink. There was water and squash available in the clubhouse. There was a random collection of china cups and mugs that had collected over the years. A group of the adults stood by the net of another court, talking. I wasn't taking much notice of them. I was trying to concentrate on listening to Barbara who was telling me a long, involved story about her dad and her uncle, but as we passed, although I wasn't sure, I thought I overheard one of them say, "...not another boy." I tried to hear more but they became aware of us and lowered their voices. *Not another boy?* What did they mean?

"...and then my uncle did exactly the same thing!" Barbara's story concluded, and she began to laugh loudly. I had no idea what the story had been about, but I laughed along with her and seemed to get away with it.

Dad collected me and I said I'd enjoyed the tennis, that I'd played against Barbara and Mr. Thornton had given me some tuition on my service.

****

I can't say I was missing my friends, but I was pleased to see Sam when he came to the door after lunch. The sun loungers were out on the patio. Sam and I dragged them across the lawn and put them under the sycamore tree. We lay down on them, looking up through the branches as they swayed in the breeze. Beyond the branches, the sky was blue, and the clouds were broken into small squares, like a puzzle that had fallen apart.

"I never thought it would take them this long to find Tommy, did you?" said Sam.

"First of all, I just kept expecting them to come and say he'd turned up. I thought we'd all be back together again on the green. But this morning, I started thinking that he might not turn up. Where can he be?" I said.

"I'm sure Bridges has something to do with it."

I couldn't believe Sam was still going on about Bridges. "How could he?" I said.

"Think about it, first the birds, then the rabbit…"

I sat up. "What, are you saying? That he's taken Tommy to scare us?" As I said it my heart leapt. Sam saw the look on my face.

"What is it?" he asked.

"I've just thought, the very first time Naomi told me what had happened—it was right here in the garden—she said he'd been taken, not he'd gone missing or gone off somewhere. She said he'd *been taken*. Not only that, Constable Gordon came yesterday and asked me more questions, and one thing he asked was if I'd seen anyone in the field. Do you reckon that they all think someone kidnapped Tommy?"

"We have to tell Constable Gordon about Bridges," said Sam.

"Maybe we should go and talk to Naomi. Have you seen her?" I asked.

"I haven't seen anyone. You're the first. I don't think Naomi's mum and dad will let us see her at the moment, though. I think the adults want to keep us away from everything."

Sam said there'd been a massive search going on. His granddad was making sure they avoided the area, but when they were on the beach with the boats, people kept coming over to talk. Sam had heard bits and pieces, about the searching of all the local land and the riverbank. Apparently, the police spent ages checking the camp at the end of the wall. The coast guards were checking the shoreline and the cliffs, and there was a helicopter searching along the coast. It was a very big operation.

"But if someone has got him somewhere, they'll never find him like that," I said.

"It makes sense to tell the constable about Bridges, doesn't it?" said Sam.

"I'm not sure. What would we say?"

"Just say we get the feeling he didn't like us going to the field. He doesn't like kids, and he might have taken it out on Tommy?"

"I just want Tommy to be found."

"I could tell Granddad."

Philip came across the lawn to talk to us. Dad was going to take us for a swim, and Sam was welcome to come. Sam said he'd better go because he'd promised his granddad he wouldn't be long. He said he'd call in again as soon as he could.

It wasn't until after Sam had left that I remembered about the tennis club and hearing someone say something about another boy going missing.

On the way back from swimming, Dad stopped by at Anna's. He said to wait in the car while he went in. Anna came out, and I asked her if she would come to our house the next day, even just for a short visit. She said that she would.

****

It was Sunday, and I was awake. Piggy was next to me in the bed, and I was listening to the wood pigeons in the trees in the garden. The doorbell rang and I heard voices, my parents talking to a man at the door. I heard them all come into the house and go into the kitchen. They carried on talking for a while, then the man left.

The Five Things

I got out of bed, dressed, and went downstairs. My parents were sitting at the kitchen table. I could tell something had changed. Dad wasn't interested in the newspaper. Mum looked worried. She stood up and poured a drink for me. She sat back down at the table.

"Anna's father came to see us just now," she said. "He's been told something, and he wanted to share it with us straight away."

I already knew what was going to be said. I felt numb and my ears sort of hummed as if they were trying not to hear. Mum was getting ready to speak again, and Dad moved closer to her with a concerned expression on his face. My head was throbbing inside. Adults weren't always good at saying things in the right way. I spoke for them.

"Is Tommy dead?" I said.

Mum came and wrapped her arms around me and squeezed me very tightly. She held on to me for a long time.

****

I was told where Tommy was found and how he was found, but it was unimportant to me. I'd already known he wasn't coming back, or perhaps that was just my head preparing me for the worst. I expected the outcome, but it didn't make it any easier to deal with; it didn't mean I knew what to do or how to feel. Mum and Dad did their best. They said it was an accident and very unusual; it was nobody's fault and not something that was ever going to happen again. They kept me close to them, reassuring me, talking, and inviting me to talk. I stayed near and listened, but I had nothing to say.

Philip seemed to understand that sometimes it wasn't necessary to discuss things. He came and sat with me from time to time. He had some French books, and he read me pieces from them, then translated them for me. It was comforting. Anna had been supposed to come to the house, but our parents decided it was best we stayed home. We stayed home, and somehow, we got through the coming hours.

Chapter 11
After The Happening

"We took the tent down," Anna said. "I didn't feel like sitting out in it anymore."

Anna and Sam had come to tea. It was the first time I'd seen them since Tommy was found. Mum and Dad thought it would be a good idea for us to get together and spend a little time with each other. We went into the garden and sat on the grass.

"I never knew anyone that died," said Anna.

"I never knew anyone young that died," said Sam.

"Do you think he was lying there for ages, hurt?" said Anna.

"In that old quarry? Hurt and frightened?" I said.

"He died straight away," Sam told us. "Well, that's what they said. Mr. Johnson found him. He was walking Meg, and he found Tommy's ball. Then he found Tommy…with his neck broken."

Anna blew upward to prevent her fringe from falling into her eyes.

"They only say nice things about you when you die," I observed.

"I noticed that," said Sam. "Tommy wasn't always good, but it's like everyone can only remember the best things."

"That's on purpose, I suppose," I said.

"He was always pulling girls' hair and stuff like

that. He was always fighting with those Wilson twins," Sam continued.

"Do you think Naomi is all right?" I asked them.

"No, I don't," said Anna. "I don't think she'll know what to do without Tommy."

Dad came over to speak to us. He must have been listening to what we were saying. He told us he didn't think we'd be able to visit the Williamses. It was too soon. But he said that he would go and buy a card, and we could all write in it. We'd send it to them so that they'd know we were thinking about them.

Anna and I had both reverted to the sanctuary of our family lives over recent days; we'd been happy to be sheltered from external events. But Sam's home life was very different. He hadn't switched off from reality. He was much better informed about what had been going on, and he'd done a lot of thinking. Once Dad had returned to the house, Sam took me back to the conversation we'd started a few days earlier, before Tommy was found.

"Do you remember? There was supposed to be someone else?" he said.

I filled Anna in, about the constable asking me if I'd seen anyone in the field or if Naomi had told me she'd seen anyone.

"Who?" asked Anna.

"He didn't say any more," I said. "I don't know who."

"Did you see someone?" she asked.

"No," I said.

"Well, there probably wasn't anyone then," she concluded.

"But," said Sam, "Naomi must have told the police

she'd seen someone. She must have. I think it was Bridges. Bridges might have scared Tommy, chased him or something."

I asked Sam if he'd said anything to his granddad, but he hadn't. We'd had that conversation on Saturday. Sam was going to tell his granddad that we thought Tommy might have been kidnapped. But his granddad had come home late in the evening, and Sam had thought it better to talk to him the next morning. The following morning was Sunday morning, when Tommy was found…and then everything changed.

There was another obvious person, but he was ruled out. Danny Price had an alibi, otherwise Sam and I might have thought of accusing him of chasing Tommy. Danny Price had something to hide. If Tommy had found out what we'd found out, Danny might have wanted to keep him quiet. But Danny spent the night before Tommy went missing in a cell. He was arrested in Binton with a bunch of his friends for being drunk and disorderly. His father told Sam's granddad about it. Mr. Price was devastated. He kept saying how well he'd brought up his son and daughter, Danny and Patricia. He had to go to pick Danny up the next day. He brought him back to the village in the afternoon. Danny wasn't too old for a good telling off apparently, and afterward, his dad had kept him near the house where he could keep an eye on him. Unless he was working, Danny would be at home doing chores for his father—for the rest of the summer.

"Did you ever follow Bridges like you said you were going to?" Anna asked Sam.

"No. Well, there was just one day when we started following him…but we didn't see anything. Then

Tommy went missing and we couldn't really do it after that."

"What about Robbo and Adam?" she said.

"No," said Sam. "We should have kept watch the whole time."

"Have you seen them—Robbo and Adam?" I asked.

Sam said he'd seen Adam, who lived close to him, but not Robbo. Adam didn't want to do any more watching or following, and he didn't even want to talk about it in case he got into trouble. Robbo had apparently been helping the police with the search.

Sam went quiet. He'd exhausted his information, but Anna was having none of it. "Tommy fell into the quarry, they said," she stated matter-of-factly. "It was an accident. I suppose he just went into the field behind the house and found his way onto the track and along by the downs where the quarry is. He probably tripped over something."

"Can we talk about something else?" I asked. I didn't want to keep thinking about Tommy. It was making my head hurt and talking about it like this felt sort of wrong.

"What else?" said Sam quite crossly.

Mum rescued us. She walked across the lawn to see us. "Come and have some tea," she said.

We sat at the garden table on the patio. She'd been busy baking. She'd made scones full of big, fat sultanas and smothered them with jam and cream. She offered us flapjacks and homemade lemonade. Seeing the food, I realized I was hungry. It was the first time I'd felt hungry for days. Mum had an instinct when it came to catering. I adored almost everything she made, and the others seemed equally pleased with the distraction. Mum asked Sam if his granddad was busy with the boats and Anna if her dad was getting ready for a new term. If only for a while, we managed to take part in some other topics of conversation.

****

"Do you think Bridges lured him there? Why would he go to the quarry? Why go to the quarry when he could have gone anywhere? He would have gone to the fields if he was going to go somewhere because he never stopped talking about the fields. I never once heard him talk about the quarry. We didn't talk about the quarry. I can't remember the last time I went there." There was a short pause. "What about that other person? What about the other person the police asked you about?"

"Sam, shut up!" I said. "I'm not going to play with you anymore unless you talk about something else." It was a couple of days later and Sam was sitting on the lawn with Poppy in his arms. Her ears lay flat along her back as he stroked her.

"Sorry, but I can't help it."

"Will you come for a game of tennis with me? I'm allowed to bring a guest every so often, even though I'm a junior. I've got a spare racquet. It's my old one but it's okay."

Sam agreed to come and have a go. We took the racquets and a few balls and walked across the road and along toward the hotel. There was a court available. Club members were allowed to play at any time if there was a court free, although hotel guests would have priority. I went to the reception and booked Court 3 for half an hour. I sent Sam over to one side of the net and told him we'd start by just hitting the ball to each other. Sam was quite good for a beginner.

When our time was up, we walked over to the edge of the hotel grounds from where there were steps down to the beach. We could see Sam's granddad standing on the pebbles farther along. He didn't seem to have hired out many boats that day; there were a lot left on the shingle. It was getting later in the season and the type of holidaymaker had changed. There was more of the older type and less of the adventurous type.

We went down the steps and walked along. Sam's granddad was pleased to see us and particularly pleased to see me. I hadn't seen him in over a week. He came and gave me a hug.

"Hello, Mr. Wells."

"Hello, Wendy. Come and sit down here, both of you."

"There's no boats hired," said Sam.

"No. Well, just the one out there. I should start sorting them out soon, putting them away."

"This one's been bumped into." Sam pointed to a large graze on the side of a hull.

"Yes, I'll look them all over and repair the ones that need it." He would put about half of them away and keep the rest out until the season petered out altogether. He told us that he usually enjoyed the tail end of the season most of all. "Now then, as it's not too busy, I might have time to eat an ice cream."

Sam and I smiled, and his granddad handed us some money and told us to go along and buy three cones from the kiosk by the pier.

"Make sure to hurry back before mine melts!" he said.

We chose three cornets with square-shaped tops. They came with brick-shaped vanilla ice cream slabs, individually wrapped in paper. We rushed back and the three of us sat on the bottom of an upturned rowing boat; we put the vanilla slabs into the cornets and devoured them.

****

Things were a little more normal. Our lives began to be more like they had been before Tommy disappeared, but thoughts of him would frequently come to me and I would feel a deep ache.

Sam and I were on the beach again the next day when we saw Robbo. He was with Peter Clay, Max, and a couple of the Taylors.

"Robbo!" Sam shouted out. When Robbo was with his older friends, he wasn't always so friendly. But he looked over and when he saw us, he left them to come to speak to us.

"Are you okay?" he asked.

"Yeah, we're okay."

"It's hard to believe what happened," he said.

I knew Sam wanted to get Robbo talking about Bridges, but luckily Robbo seemed to have left all that behind. He told us that the police had asked him to help them make a list of the places we'd been going to together and any other places where he thought the village kids might go. He said he actually had to take Constable Gordon to the camp on the cliff. He said he knew Tommy would be found because there was nothing the police and the rescue teams didn't check on, and they looked everywhere in the village.

"Did you tell them about the surveillance?" asked Sam.

"Oh no, that wasn't important. I told them where we were spending our time, the upper field and the wood. I told them we'd been in the wheat fields and that we'd been walking all over the village, down the paths and everything. We'd been on the green, and the playing fields, and the beach, of course." Robbo was quite full of himself. Then he looked at Sam and said, "I even told them about the barn."

"Come on, Rob!" Max shouted.

"I'd better go. I'll see you."

We were pleased to have met him, but I agreed with Sam, that although Robbo had listed the places where we might spend our time, Tommy didn't really go to most of those places, and that it was actually Mr. Johnson who found Tommy in the end rather than the police or the rescue teams.

Chapter 12

Sam rarely spoke about his parents. He'd told me on one or two occasions that he didn't have a dad. My parents said that Sam's mum had him when she was *just a girl*. As far as Sam was concerned his granddad was the only one who mattered; he didn't need anyone else. All of this meant I was quite surprised when he said that his mum was coming to visit.

It was a sunny morning and Sam had called for me. We decided to head up to Anna's. Sam said he couldn't stay long because his mum was coming to the house and he had to be back to meet her. He didn't seem overjoyed about it.

"Is she here from France?" I asked.

"Yeah, she's here for two days. She's not staying with us, though," he said.

Sam's mum had gone to work in France some years before, so I'd been told. I'd never met her.

"How will she get here?"

"On a ferry. Then on the train to Porton."

"Then on the bus to Cherlton?"

"I think so."

It was hard to drag much out of him. "It's quite exciting," I said.

"Yeah," said Sam. He sounded anything but excited.

"Are you looking forward to seeing her?" I asked.

"I'm not sure, but I don't have any choice," he said.

It was hard for me to imagine how Sam could feel unsure about whether or not he wanted to see his mum. I reckoned I'd miss my own mum, even if I spent a single day without seeing her. I supposed they were different sorts of mum; Sam's was almost like a stranger. We walked up to Anna's. Mal was on the driveway washing the car. He greeted us and called in through the open front door to let Anna know we'd arrived. Anna took us into the garden, and we sat on the seat by the fishpond.

"Sam's mum's coming over today, from France," I informed her.

Sam gave her a resigned look.

"Have you been to France?" Anna asked him.

"No. I don't think she has room for guests where she lives," he said.

"It would be fab to go to France," Anna stated. "They eat croissants all the time."

"I'm not bothered about France. I like it here," said Sam.

****

I didn't see Sam again for two days, and when he came round, he still didn't seem happy. He'd been spending time with his mum, but not only his mum. She'd brought a boyfriend with her; she'd wanted Sam to meet him. He was French and he was called Marcel. That was why she wasn't staying at the house. She and Marcel had booked a room in a guesthouse in the next village, and Marcel had hired a car. They'd taken Sam on a drive and gone to one of the beaches farther along the coast.

"Is he nice, Marcel?" I asked.

Sam shrugged. "He's okay. My mum never brought a boyfriend here before, so she must like him."

"Does he speak English?" I asked.

"Yeah," he said. "He has a French accent, but he speaks English. He was trying to be nice. You know, we played football on the sand, and he took us to a cafe and stuff."

I had more questions. "Did your granddad meet him?"

"Yeah," said Sam. "He says he likes him, and that I should be friendly to him."

"But they've gone back to France now?" I checked.

"They're going today. But they said they'd come back to see me again soon."

I could tell Sam was trying to be reasonable but that he'd probably have preferred it if they hadn't come at all. I thought I should try to cheer him up.

"Shall we go to Anna's, or see if there's a tennis court free...or go to the beach?"

"I don't care," he said.

"Let's go to Anna's."

I decided that was the best thing because Anna could keep on talking even if no one else had anything to say, and she could think of something to do in any situation. In fact, it was Anna's dad who came up with an idea to lift our spirits.

"How would you all like to go to the cinema?" he asked.

"Wow! Yes, please!" we shouted.

Mr. Martin said we would go later in the afternoon. The film was a musical we'd all enjoy, and it was on in the nearest town.

"Now," he said, "Wendy and Sam, you'd better go and let your mum and dad know, and Mr. Wells. Tell them we'll get something to eat while we're out, and that I'll drop you both home afterward."

The trip was really good fun. Mr. Martin drove, and Mrs. Martin traveled beside him in the passenger seat. Anna, Sam, and I sat together in the back. As we drove along, Anna's mum told us a bit about the film.

"There are a lot of larger than life characters, and I think it will make us all laugh," she concluded.

When we arrived in the town, Mr. Martin dropped us near the cinema, and we went in to pick up the tickets with Mrs. Martin while he parked.

"We've got really good seats," said Sam. There was a plan of the auditorium on the counter and we could tell which seats were ours.

"They're right in the middle!" Anna said.

"The best seats in the house!" said Mrs. Martin. The lady in the kiosk tore off five tickets and handed them over.

"Can I have my one?" Anna asked.

We joined another queue and Mrs. Martin bought us all popcorn to eat during the showing.

"You're not having popcorn too, are you, Mum?" Anna found that amusing.

"Why ever not? Dad and I will share a box."

We found our row and squeezed past some other customers who'd already taken their seats. Sam was in between Anna and me.

"Shhh," he said as the lights started to lower.

Anna leant back into her chair. We were soon completely engrossed in the picture, almost unaware of the real world for the duration. I knew that we were certainly all laughing, though, and once every so often, the whole auditorium erupted in one collective howl.

There was an interval, and we were bought orange drinks in plastic cartons with straws. Mrs. Martin had been right about the film, and as well as being funny, there were lots of songs, some of which we already knew, even though we didn't know beforehand that they were part of it.

When it finished, we walked to the car park, though Anna danced most of the way.

"Do you remember the bit when the man started dancing on the furniture?" she asked.

"That was so funny," said Sam.

"Then they all danced down the stairs!" I said.

"Or slid down the banisters!" Sam added.

"Or leapt right over them!" said Anna.

"That was the very best bit," I said.

"I hope you're not going to be trying it!" Mrs. Martin joked.

It was early evening and Mr. Martin asked if we all liked fish and chips. We all loved fish and chips, so he said we would go to Haverley where there was a great place to buy some, and we'd take them up beside the castle to eat them. We stayed in the car while he went into the shop and returned with a huge bag of food.

"It smells delicious," Mrs. Martin said.

The aroma filled the car, and by the time we reached the parking area, we were ravenous. We sat out on the grass looking over the spectacular view of the castle, shared out the food, and ate it with our fingers.

We could remember the words to some of the songs, and we sang them on the journey home. Anna's mum and dad joined in.

"Thank you, Mr. and Mrs. Martin," I said, as they dropped me off. "I had a really, really good time."

"You're very welcome, Wendy," said Mr. Martin.

"We've enjoyed ourselves very much too!" Mrs. Martin smiled.

I said goodbye to Anna and Sam and went indoors to tell Mum, Dad, and Philip all about it.

In a way, the cinema trip marked the end of the holidays. There were a couple of days left, but those were mainly to be spent at home getting ready to go back to school. We were to be in the third class when we returned. We'd be in the third class for two years before we moved on to the next school. Sam and I would be together. Anna would be back at the school where her dad was a teacher. My brother would be going off on the bus to the grammar school. Our days would seem different. Robbo and the others of his age would be starting at St. Mary's in Porton; so this term, we wouldn't be seeing Robbo, Peter Clay, Max, or Mo, the youngest of the Taylors, at the playground anymore. Susan and Judy wouldn't be there. We would see Adam Smart; he'd be in our class; he would be in the top year of Class 3.

I always felt a little sad when the holidays came to an end, and I tried to remind myself that once you actually started back you soon began to enjoy the lessons, and it was always nice to see all your classmates again. This year, going back might be especially hard. I had a few chats with Piggy about it.

Chapter 13
Going Back to School

September 1969

On the first day back at school, the teachers were at the main entrance to greet us. They made sure we headed to the correct classrooms. Sam had called for me and we'd walked together along the main street, past the shops, and on through the lane to the school. Sam wore a smart, white shirt and a new sweater. Our school sweaters were royal blue and had the school badge stitched onto them. He wore long, gray trousers and new black leather shoes. I was in my new dress with the squirrels and the nuts; the weather was still mild, and Mum thought it too early for me to have to start wearing my pinafore dress. She was knitting me another school cardigan, but for the moment I was wearing last term's. We carried our anoraks and our school bags with our packed lunches inside them. We went to find our new desks, put our pencil cases into them, and our bags beneath them at our feet. Our class sat in groups of four or six. The new pupils in the third class took up two groups of desks, and the pupils who were now at the top of the third class sat at two other clusters of desks behind us. Sam and I took our seats. We knew all the others; there were no fresh faces.

Sam cast his eyes around the room. "Where's

Naomi?" he said.

I turned to look. "Not here yet. Not in the classroom anyway."

We waited, watching the doorway to see who else was coming in. Sam put up his hand and Miss Charlton came over and stood between us.

"Can we keep a desk for Naomi?"

Miss Charlton studied us with a kind and thoughtful expression, then she spoke softly. "I'm not sure when Naomi will be coming back to school. But don't worry, we'll find room for her. Thank you, Sam, for thinking of her." She paused before continuing. "Mrs. Marshall is going to talk to the school in assembly today about the very sad loss of Tommy."

Mrs. Marshall was the head teacher, and the assembly was to be in a few minutes' time. As it was the autumn term, Mrs. Marshall would welcome the new children and tell us of her expectations for the year ahead.

"Hello, you two," Adam said as he passed us on the way to his new seat at the back of the class.

"Wotcha."

"Hi, Isobel."

"Quiet please!" Miss Charlton said, with a commanding voice. "Quiet! I'm going to take the register."

She called our names, and we all replied with a "Yes, Miss" or a "Here, Miss." I listened to the names. Williams would be one of the last to be called but it wasn't. Naomi Williams wasn't in class, but her name wasn't read out, so no one had to say, "She's not here, Miss."

We were each issued with a new exercise book and

The Five Things

a plain sheet of paper on which we were to draw a plan of the desks. On the plan, we were to write the name of the class member who sat in each place. We were told to write our own name on the exercise book, and *Class 3*. We were told what lessons would happen that day.

We had a little time to do this and talk with the others in our group, then the teacher said it was time to go to assembly. We had to stand in pairs and line up near the door. We could hear the children from the other classes being taken along the corridor to the hall. Soon it was our turn. We were last to file in, and now that we were Class 3, we made up the two back rows. Everyone stood in the wooden-floored hall where we would also have P.E. lessons on rainy days. It was used for all events, school plays, and jumble sales. In the middle of the day, it was one of the places where, if we chose, we could eat our packed lunch.

Miss Charlton and the other teachers sat on plastic seats, facing us, and Mrs. Marshall stood right in the middle, in front of all the pupils.

"Good morning, children," she began.

"Good morning, Mrs. Marshall," we all responded—apart from the youngest kids on their first ever day at school. It would take them a little while to get used to how it all worked.

"Please sit down." There was a long series of bumps and thuds as the whole school sat down cross-legged on the floor. "I'd like to begin by welcoming the new children," Mrs. Marshall said, looking down at the small, unsure faces in the front row. "Children, you are all welcome to Cherlton Primary. This is a very important day for you and one you will always remember. Some of you have brothers and sisters at the school, and some of you have cousins here, but I am also aware that some of you do not. Whichever of these applies to you, you will soon feel part of the school. You've met your teacher, Mrs. Allen, and in no time, you will get to know the others in your class and make new friends. Later this morning, I will come to your classroom and speak to each of you. I shall have to try to remember all of your names!" Some of the older pupils laughed, realizing this was one of Mrs. Marshall's jokes. "Children," she carried on, "I know that you are going to be very happy at Cherlton Primary." Next, she welcomed back the rest of the pupils. "...and I'd like to remind you that every one of us has moved on a year, and the new term will bring new challenges for us all. We will embrace these challenges! We should look forward to the new school year and everything that it holds."

Mrs. Marshall then told us to stand. Miss Charlton was at the piano, and she played the opening chord of the hymn, "All Things Bright and Beautiful." She waited a moment, then began to play it through, her hands bouncing up and down on the keys. We all sang. The words were written on large sheets of paper clipped to an easel at the front of the hall. Mr. Jenkins turned the pages. We sang three verses and three choruses.

Everyone sat down again. There were some announcements, and then Mrs. Marshall asked Mrs. Allen to take the new starters back to class. I knew the bit that was coming next was going to be difficult to listen to. She waited for the little ones to be at a safe distance along the corridor, and then she began to speak about Tommy. Tommy would have been moving up to the second class had he been at school that day. Her voice took on a different tone, and even the way she stood changed so that she portrayed the depth of the tragedy. I couldn't really listen to what she was saying. My ears were doing the humming thing again. I couldn't concentrate. Her voice was boomy; it was almost as if she was talking too slowly and that she would grind to a halt. I heard some of the words. I knew that she said it was very, very sad and that we would all miss Tommy, that he was a good and loved member of the school and the community. Tears began rolling down my cheeks, and I was trembling. Then the trembling became shaking. I felt Sam's hand take mine. His head was bowed. He took his big, white handkerchief from his trouser pocket and placed it on my knee. I picked it up and put it to my cheeks, first one, then the other, and I clung tightly on to Sam.

It was playtime straight after assembly. We went up onto the bank above the tarmac rectangle and just sat there. In the previous few days, the rawness of losing Tommy had subsided a little, but the school assembly had brought the feelings back to the surface.

"At least it's all said now," Sam told me. "Old Marshmallow had to say something about it."

We went back to class where we were to do maths until lunchtime. In the afternoon, we were going to do some reading.

****

I was still a little down when I reached home, and Mum had to get to the bottom of it. It took her no time at all.

"Were people talking about Tommy?" she asked.

"Yes, Marshmallow—I mean Mrs. Marshall—said something in assembly." I showed her the large, white hanky I had in my sleeve. "Sam gave me his hanky."

"He's such a kind boy. You're lucky to have a friend like Sam. And Marshmallow only means well, you know." She smiled gently, gave me a big hug, and told me that every so often I might feel tearful but that was quite normal and everyone understood. She suggested I change out of my dress and we'd feed Poppy together, then Philip would be home. Philip would have plenty to tell us, and she'd made one of our favorite meals because it was the first day back at school.

Over the coming weeks, my parents would gather me up, busy my mind, and push me forward into the future. My time would be taken up not only by schoolwork but by the sports and the music lessons I took part in after school hours. I would return to Brownies, where once a week I would also see Anna. Sam would return to Sea Scouts.

There was no funeral for Tommy, at least not in our village. He was taken to the village where he came from and where he still had grandparents. They held a small, private funeral. No one from Cherlton attended. The local paper briefly reported on it. Somehow a distance was developing. The event had happened, there had been consequences, but the aftermath had sort of moved away.

Philip arrived back full of news about the school, his curriculum, new pupils, new teachers, old teachers, other people's summer holidays, and so on. He could have talked for a week. It was just what we needed at that point. He changed out of his uniform, came to the kitchen, gathered a handful of cutlery, and began to set the table. He continued to recount the tales of the day as he found the salt and pepper pots and arranged the tablemats. He poured a glass of water for each of us while Mum checked on the contents of the boiling saucepans and the casserole dish she had perfecting in the oven. Soon Dad arrived and we all sat down, Philip still in full flow.

Chapter 14

It was a good thing that Brownies was on Wednesday nights because it was something to look forward to at the beginning of the week, and after that, it wasn't long until the weekend. I enjoyed going to Brownies, not least because it meant I would be seeing Anna.

At Brownies, the girls spent any time that wasn't organized running up and down the hall and jumping up onto the huge vaulting horse that lived at one end. It belonged to the scouts. We didn't use it in any official way; it just made a good game we never seemed to tire of. I was already sitting on the horse when Anna arrived and jumped up beside me.

"How's school?" she asked.

"Okay. The lessons are going to be harder this term, I think. How's yours?"

"Oh, fine. I have a new teacher. He's supposed to be fierce, but he doesn't seem too bad so far."

We jumped down, ran to the other end of the hall, touched the wall, ran back, and pulled ourselves back up onto the horse again. We smiled at each other. I would have to tell Anna about the school assembly later, as Brown Owl was just about to speak.

"Right! Girls!" She waited for the noise to subside. "Please all come and sit in a circle. We have two new members to enroll tonight, and I have some badges to give out."

I had quite a few badges: cook, crafts, cyclist, hostess, and I was about to receive gardener. The badges were made of cloth. They were small, brown, and triangular, and each one had a stitched on a motif in yellow. The gardener badge had a wheelbarrow on it. Mum would sew the new badge onto my sleeve, underneath the other ones, before the next meeting.

Later, before I brought up the subject, Anna asked me, "Did they talk about Tommy at your school?"

"Yes, they did. In assembly on the first day." I think she could tell by my face that it hadn't been easy for me.

"Is Naomi back at school?" she asked.

"No, she hasn't come back yet."

"Will I see you on Saturday?"

"I could meet you after tennis?"

"Yeah, come to my house."

****

On Saturday morning, I finished my lesson, strapped my tennis racquet across my back, and rode my bike to Anna's. She answered the door, and we went to her bedroom and sat on the candlewick bedspread. There was a lot to talk about.

When we met in term time, we would usually start by getting any grievances about school off our chests. I could say whatever I liked, blame whomever I wanted, portray myself as completely right and everyone else as completely wrong in any situation, and Anna would support me. It worked both ways; I would always be on Anna's side whatever the circumstance. It had helped us through various crises.

The first week back at school, though, hadn't been

beset with any of the usual kinds of difficulties and there was really only one thing to discuss, how my school had dealt with losing Tommy. We'd had a brief talk at Brownies, but we needed to go over it in more detail. I told Anna what had happened in assembly. I explained how the assembly had progressed, the singing of the hymn and the removal of the new starters, then the head mistress's statement and the gravity of it. I said that it had made me sad.

"Poor you. It must have been totally awful," Anna said. She could be sharp, even critical, but when she made a statement such as that, you knew she genuinely meant it. "So is Naomi still not back?"

"No. We've asked to leave a desk free for her."

Anna stretched out on the bed, she twisted the button of her top round and round between her finger and thumb. She was thinking. I looked at the familiar walls. There were animal posters and a framed drawing of a young girl sitting on an old kitchen chair. There was a calendar, also adorned with animal pictures; September's animal was a stoat.

"I wonder if she's at home?" Anna said.

"She must be, mustn't she?" I said.

Anna turned over and lay on her stomach. "We could cycle to the green and see if we can see anything? We don't have to call at the house."

"She might see us from the window."

"She could even be in the front garden."

We were suddenly full of optimism and thought Naomi would be pleased to see us. We set off using the back paths and reached the green in no time. We wheeled our bikes up onto the bank and lay them on the grass. We sat on the bench and studied the row of cottages opposite. There was no sign of Mr. Morris. In fact, there was no sign of anyone. At Lavender Cottage, the curtains were drawn almost right across the windows, the gate was closed, and it gave the impression that no one was there at all.

We sat for a while. A tractor passed, the trailer stacked with bales of golden straw. We waved to the driver, who was the son of the farmer from the farmhouse on the corner. It was nearly lunchtime and we both had to get home. We picked up the bikes and started to wheel them back over the green. As we approached the farmhouse, we saw Mr. Johnson working near the barn, Meg beside him. He looked up, mopped his brow, and gave us a wave. We'd not seen Mr. Johnson since he'd found Tommy. We waited, and as if pleased to have a break, he walked over. We bent down and made a fuss of Meg.

"Hello, girls," he said. "Back at school now, I suppose?"

"Yes," we answered.

"Have you seen Naomi, Mr. Johnson?" Anna asked, without prevarication.

Mr. Johnson paused, before saying he thought the family were away. They'd need time, he told us. He had sympathy in his eyes. He knew we were all grappling with something that wasn't easy to deal with.

"Naomi's not at school," I said.

Mr. Johnson said he wasn't surprised about that. Naomi had had a big shock. He asked if we'd come to look for her and we said that we had. He told us that when he saw her he would tell her that we'd been, and that we were looking forward to seeing her again.

"Thank you, Mr. Johnson," we both said. Then we

hopped onto our bikes and sped off back along the paths.

"I'm glad we went," Anna told me, as I left her on the road outside her house.

"Me too," I said. "I can't play tomorrow. Mum and Dad are taking us out somewhere."

"See you at Brownies then."

"Yeah, see you."

****

This term at school we were to have a project. We would work on it in pairs, and at the end of term, we would have to do a presentation to the rest of the class about our subject.

Sam and I would work together. I was hoping our subject might be hedgehogs. Miss Charlton came round to each group of desks with a list of topics. There was no choosing. Each pair was given a subject, and ours was to be fungi.

"Is that mushrooms?" I asked her.

"Mushrooms and toadstools in the main," she said. She could probably sense my disappointment and tried to compensate. "There are a lot of varieties. It will be a very interesting project to undertake," she assured me. She wrote our names next to *fungi* on the list. We felt a little hard done by. Some of the other subjects seemed better; *trees* was one, *moths* was another.

We would have to research and write about our topic and we would make a large scrapbook of items. We could include drawings and tracings, and we could cut pictures from magazines so long as we had asked for permission to do so. Miss Charlton was going to give us all a book or two on our subject to start us off, but she hoped we would also use the local library and any books we had at home to find out as much as we could.

"We have encyclopedias at home," I told Sam. I started to wonder if we could press a mushroom or whether it would be too thick.

"Now, I'd like you all to start thinking about your subject and how you're going to approach it," said Miss Charlton. "And Class, there is going to be a prize for the best project and two runners' up prizes for the ones that come second and third."

"Wooooh!" the class said as one.

Adam Smart put his hand up.

"Yes, Adam?"

"What are the prizes, Miss?" he asked.

"You will find out in due course," Miss Charlton told us with a cryptic smile.

****

The autumn term progressed. We settled into our new regime. The mornings became full of mist-covered spiders' webs, the wheat had all been harvested, and we never did go blackberrying. A new rhythm entered our lives as the summer moved further into the past.

We threw ourselves into the fungi project. We planned to have a number of sections. There would be definitions. We would look into the differences between mushrooms and toadstools, and into which species grew in our area and which grew farther afield. There would be a recipe section, we would include a lot of pictures, and Sam was keen on making some toadstool sculptures, perhaps from stones, which we could then paint. We were to spend two afternoons a week on our project, and we started to look forward to them.

At school, there was always a craze. The other girls

and I continued to collect and swap our jewels. We would also have a way of wearing our uniform that was the fashion. For the girls, the thing to do that term was to wear long socks but push them down so that they were bunched at our ankles. Sometimes one of the teachers would tell us to pull them up.

"Wendy, Charlotte Porter! Socks!" We'd push them down again at playtime or home time. There was a popular fortune-telling game, which involved folding a sheet of paper so that you made a structure that you would open and close with your forefingers and thumbs: choose a color, choose a number, and then you'd choose again and open a flap to reveal a consequence. We spent hours making and playing with those.

At home, I played jacks. I could be found sitting in the hall or the outhouse or the bathroom—anywhere with a smooth, hard floor surface—throwing a small ball up into the air and picking up the little metal pieces. Onesies: bounce, pick up one, catch, bounce, pick up one, until all were collected. Twosies: bounce, pick up two together, catch, bounce, pick up two together. Threesies, and so on. It was a game that I could happily play alone and was good on rainy days and dark evenings. The game was quite obsessive and staved off boredom.

Anna and I made two more trips to Lavender Cottage on our bikes, but there was still no sign of Naomi. Both times, the curtains at the windows were in the same position, partly drawn. We could tell they'd not been opened or closed since our first trip.

"It would be so nice to speak to Naomi," Anna said. "I'm beginning to think she's not coming back."

"She'll have to come back eventually," I said. "Everyone has to go to school."

"I suppose so. We'll keep making visits. That's all we can do."

****

I'd taken a book out of the library, *Mushrooms and Toadstools of the United Kingdom*, and was looking at a chapter on edible mushrooms that grow in the wild. There was a long list; I was amazed at how many there were. I viewed the pictures carefully: *the scarletina bolete, the glistening ink cap, the shaggy ink cap*. I tried to work out which ones I'd seen growing; I would concentrate on those. For each mushroom, there was a Latin name and a common name. I decided to make a note only of the common names, and then I would trace the pictures. I started with the first one, the horse mushroom; I was sure I'd seen one of those. Piggy and I were on the landing, Mum was downstairs, and no one else was home. I was kneeling on the floor and using it as my desk. Every now and then I had to get up, either because I had pins and needles in one of my feet, or because I felt dizzy due to my head being in a funny, low position. I traced the mushroom as best I could, but the resulting picture was a bit small. I thought it might be better to use a bigger sheet of paper and just draw a bigger mushroom, freehand. Then I decided I would do that at school because there wasn't really enough space on the landing.

I went into Philip's room and found the record player. I put two seven-inch singles in a stack. I turned the speed to forty-five and pulled the switch. The first record dropped down, the arm went over, and it started to play. I made Piggy dance to the song.

"You like this one, don't you, Piggy?"
Piggy nodded.
"I think it's my favorite too."

The second record dropped down. When that one finished, I turned both records over and played the B sides. Then I went downstairs.

"How is your project coming along?" Mum asked.

"Quite well. I'll soon know which mushrooms we can pick to eat and which ones are actually poisonous."

"That will be helpful. We'll have to go to the downs early one morning and see if we can find any. We used to find mushrooms up on the downs years ago. I'd like to go and see if they still grow there."

****

Sam had asked his granddad if he would help him bring some large stones back to the house. He'd find them on the beach and take them to the workshop. His granddad was going to let him use some of the paint he used for the boats, and we'd paint the stones so that they looked like mushrooms or toadstools. There would be plenty of paints to choose from; his granddad painted the boats all sorts of colors. The stems could be made from more stones, a different shape, or we might be able to find some pieces of wood that looked like stems. We were at Anna's, and I think she was starting to get fed up with the fungi project.

"Are you doing a project at your school?" Sam asked her.

"No. No one's said anything about it. What lesson do you do it in?"

Sam and I thought about that. We didn't really know what lesson it was, it was just the one when we did the project.

"We do it twice a week," Sam said.

"We have art twice a week," said Anna.

We told her there was going to be a prize, but we didn't know what the prize was to be. Anna thought it would be a book token because that's what school prizes always seemed to be. We were in the kitchen and Anna's dad came in to see us. He told us he was busy doing some marking in his study, but shortly he would finish up and come to talk to us.

"He's always doing marking," Anna informed us.

"Does your dad teach you?" asked Sam.

"Not at the moment," said Anna, "but next year he might."

"I think it would be nice to be taught by your dad," I said.

"Maybe, but I'm sure I'd get called teacher's pet. It doesn't happen at the moment, but I bet it would if he was teaching my class."

"If anyone teased you, you could tell your dad on them," said Sam.

"I don't think you'd be that bothered if they teased you anyway," I said.

Every term, our school played Anna's at netball. Anna and I were both in the school team, so we played against each other, and in the days that followed, whoever had won would be sure to make merciless fun of the other.

Chapter 15
The Five Things

It must have been two weeks since I'd seen Robbo, but at the weekend, when I was on the beach with Mum and Dad, I saw him coming along the wall. I went up the steps to greet him. I asked him about going to school in Porton and if he liked it. He said it was different, but he was enjoying it. There were more kids there. The days were longer; you had break times, not playtimes. You were in different classes for different lessons, so you could make a lot of new friends. He was in Peter Clay's class for most of the lessons and he was in Mo Taylor's for some as well. There were corridors full of classrooms. He would be having woodwork lessons and science lessons this term, and there was a special room for each of those. St. Mary's sounded huge. There was another room where all the art lessons were held.

I told him Naomi hadn't come back to start the new term, and he said that Mrs. Williams wasn't going back to work at the grocery shop. Susan's mum worked there too, and she'd been doing extra hours because Mrs. Williams had left.

I filled Sam in about Mrs. Williams at the playground the next morning. He said he'd start taking a detour so that he passed by the shop on his way home each day. If she started back, he'd see her.

"I think Robbo meant she wasn't going back. Not ever," I said.

"Can you come out after school tonight?" he asked.

"Yeah, for a little while."

"We could go down to Lavender Cottage. When did you last go with Anna?"

"A few days ago. We could have another look, I suppose, see if anyone's there."

In the late afternoon, I went home, changed into my shorts, a T-shirt, and a windcheater, took my bike, and rode to the green. Sam was to meet me there. I arrived before him and sat on the bench. I could already see that the curtains at Lavender Cottage hadn't moved. I waited for Sam. Mrs. Barclay, the woman with the two very young children, came along the road from the other direction. She had one child in a pram; the other stumbled along beside her, clinging on to the bottom of her jacket. She went into Myrtle Cottage. If I looked ahead, I could see fields rise up behind the row of houses, and in the distance beyond them, I could just see the tops of the trees of the wood. To the left, the fields reached toward the downs; to the right, the road curled round, and from it, the little paths that led back toward the center of the village splayed out across the land. Sam would approach from the path behind me, from the lower, older part of the village near the river estuary.

I heard him coming and turned to wave. He sat down beside me. His face was pink from the cycling; he'd had farther to go than me and he'd also ridden past the grocery store. Just as we thought, Mrs. Williams wasn't working, and he could see what I meant about the cottage, you could tell no one was there.

"I've been thinking," Sam said. "I reckon we should have another look up in the wood."

"Oh Sam, we should stay away from there!"

"But think about it. Remember what Constable Gordon asked you—about the other person in the field? We didn't hear any more about that. What if there was someone? What if they…"

"Had something to do with Tommy?"

"Yeah."

I didn't understand why we should look in the wood. Sam said that it seemed strange things happened there—and always to children: the birds, the rabbit, the screeching noises. Tommy was always talking about the fields. Sam thought there was a connection.

Somehow, I knew Sam hadn't completely given up on finding a link between Tommy's disappearance, the wood, and Bridges, so the conversation didn't altogether surprise me. Nevertheless, I wasn't sure I wanted to go there, and perhaps the best thing would be to accept that the whole awful event of the summer was over and done with, and that it was time let go.

****

I told Sam I wouldn't go to the wood or the fields unless Anna agreed to go too. When I saw her at Brownies, I let her know we'd gone again to Lavender Cottage, that I'd seen Robbo, and that Mrs. Williams wasn't going back to the grocery. We were sitting on top of the vaulting horse.

"So he wants to go to the wood?" she said.

"Yeah. He still thinks there's something going on there," I said. "Something that needs solving."

"What do you think?" she asked me.

"I suppose if anything was going on in the first

place it probably still is, because we didn't get anywhere with it in the summer," I said. "We didn't catch someone trying to scare us."

"If we did go," Anna said, "I would only go in the middle of the day, when it was bright and sunny."

I thought that made sense. "Okay, shall I tell him we might go on Saturday—if the weather's nice? It would have to be after tennis."

She nodded. "Yeah, all right. I'll be home. Call for me when you're ready."

We all knew we wouldn't be telling the adults we were planning to go to the fields. We didn't tell any of the other kids either. We kept it to ourselves.

****

Saturday arrived. Dad was working, Mum had invited her friend Maggie round to the house, and Philip was playing golf. No one would bother too much about me. I put on my tennis kit, took my racquet, and set off early. Barbara was already there and asked if I'd like a game. We took some balls from the clubhouse, went to the far court, and started to knock up. We practiced a few serves until we were both ready to play a set. Barbara said I could choose to serve or choose an end. I said I'd serve and started hammering down the balls. I was playing well. We played the set, six-two to me. I asked if she wanted to play another. She looked hot and wanted to get a drink, so we took a break.

On the way across the courts, my memory was jogged. I suddenly remembered the conversation I'd heard a few weeks earlier, when some of the grown-up players had been gathered together and had said something about "another boy." How could I have forgotten about it? I'd meant to tell Sam but it had totally slipped my mind. Now I couldn't wait to tell him. I was all but ready to go straight away and try to find him, but Barbara gulped down her last couple of mouthfuls of water and said she was ready to get her revenge. I couldn't refuse. We went back to the far court. I tried to focus on the tennis, but my mind was working on my plan for the rest of the morning. As soon as we finished, I'd rush home to change, then go straight to Anna's. Sam and I had already arranged to meet on the wheat fields at eleven thirty. This set was harder, but I was serving and returning well. Four-all. It was a beautiful day, warm and not too windy, perfect for tennis in fact. Five-four. I was leading, but I had to break Barbara's serve because I didn't want to go to three sets. I just needed one more game. Barbara was in position. *Thwack,* she hit the ball hard, and I returned into the net. Mr. Thornton arrived at the side of the court and began to observe. Barbara served again, but I returned this time, right into the corner.

"Good shot!" Mr. Thornton said. He started calling the score for us and gave a few instructions as well. "Throw the ball higher," he shouted to Barbara. *Thwack*—and again I returned into the net. I walked to the other side of the court. Barbara was bouncing the ball. She served. "Out!" shouted Mr. Thornton. He stooped to pick up the ball, and Barbara produced another from under her tennis dress. "Second service." A double fault. "Thirty-all!" called Mr. Thornton. I crouched down to receive. The ball arrived and—*wallop*—I hit a really good forehand, which flew over low and hard and won the point. "Thirty-forty!" I just needed one more point. I was ready, Barbara was bouncing, I was crouching, and then the ball was on its way. I moved round so that I could hit another forehand. She returned to my backhand. I used my double-handed backhand and thumped the ball over into the back corner. I'd won!

"Wendy's game!" Mr. Thornton shouted. "Game, set, and match Wendy, by two sets to love!" He congratulated us both on a good game.

I quickly said my goodbyes, thanked Barbara, and said it would be nice to play her again the following weekend. I rushed home and up to my room to change.

****

We were at the top of the wheat fields. They were plowed now and stretched away each side of us in long, immaculate rows of rich, red-brown soil. The three of us stood astride our bikes in the warm sun, looking over to the lower field, the upper field, and the wood.

"Come on then," said Anna.

We pushed off and hurtled down the track. We left the bikes at the gate, ran across the lower field, and strode up beside the hedge to the upper field. We collapsed on the grass out of breath. We knew we'd come to talk about Tommy, and I was first to speak.

"Right, before I forget again," I said to the others, "I've got something to tell you that you might think is interesting." Sam and Anna gave me their full attention. "One of the times I was at the tennis club, before they found Tommy, I overheard some people talking. What they said, I'm pretty sure, was 'not another boy.' I don't know what it meant, and I was going to tell you, but my head got all mixed up and I forgot."

Sam and Anna were staring at me, and I couldn't tell if they thought it was important or if they thought I was being ridiculous.

"Who said it?" Sam asked. "And when? What did you say?"

"It was just a group of players, grown-ups. They were talking to each other and one of them said it as I passed. After that, they lowered their voices as if they didn't want me to hear."

"Not another boy," said Anna. "Are you sure that's what they said?"

"I think it's what they said."

"But another boy wasn't missing," said Sam.

"I might have got it wrong," I said.

We lay back on the grass. No one spoke for a while, except for every now and then, when either Sam or Anna would say, "Not another boy…" as if they were trying to solve a clue in a crossword.

Even though everything was so different, it felt good to be in the fields again. The hedgerows had changed: there was old man's beard growing, there were berries on the hawthorn, and there were sloes.

Sam stood up and announced that he was going to walk through the wood. He wasn't gone long, and when he returned, he said that there was nothing to report. Then he took a small notebook from his pocket. It had a little pencil clasped to the side in a loop of elastic. He opened it up.

"A few weeks back, I made some notes," he said tentatively. "It was when Constable Gordon spoke to us."

"Let me see," I said. He handed me the notebook. I read what it said on the page.

Five things:
The birds

The Five Things

The rabbit
Naomi said Tommy was taken, not missing or run away or got lost
Ball (now solved)
The person in the field

Then I read them out loud. Sam looked at me with his big blue eyes wide open; he looked at Anna, he looked back at me, he waited for a reaction. I felt confused. I couldn't think straight, and I didn't know what to say. Anna said to pass the book to her, and she read over the list, made out in Sam's careful handwriting.

"So what you're saying," she said, "is that there were a number of questions that came up. The question about the ball was solved. Mr. Johnson found the ball Tommy was playing with when he went missing. But none of the other questions were solved...and they still haven't been solved?"

"I wrote those things down when the constable said to tell someone if we thought of anything that might help. I started writing things down."

"But then, when Mr. Johnson found Tommy, no one cared about the questions anymore?" Anna said.

"No...and now there's another question..." Sam added. "What did that mean, *the other missing boy?*"

We looked at one another again. This time a sense of anticipation seemed to be hanging in the air.

Finally, Anna said, "I don't know what we should do."

"What I think," said Sam, "is that we should try to find the answers to the questions. We don't have to tell anyone else, not Robbo or anyone. No one will listen to us anyway."

"But how will we find the answers?" I said.

"I'm not sure. But we should all start thinking."

"Okay," said Anna, "every week we should meet and go through the list to see if we've come up with anything."

"Yes," said Sam. I think he was relieved. That was the sort of outcome he'd wanted.

After that, Sam insisted we all walk through the wood and out the other side. Then we had to go home for lunch.

Chapter 16

In the week that followed our first meeting about the event, I didn't think much about the list of questions: I had a cold, I had to have two days off school, and I couldn't go to Brownies. Mum filled me with spoons of medicine and squeezed oranges for me. I spent a lot of time asleep in bed or downstairs in my dressing gown.

I spent some of the time lying in bed looking through encyclopedias. Mum brought in a couple of volumes and left them beside me on the counterpane. I couldn't concentrate on anything for long and ended up just turning the pages, looking at various photos and illustrations. I looked at pictures of snakes, maps of faraway places, old masters' paintings, photographs of African landscapes, and drawings of machinery used in factories. I had the radio on, the music station. I had a series of strange dreams, brought on by a combination of the encyclopedias, the pop songs, and the various potions Mum was providing for me.

I was back at school by Thursday, and on Friday, Sam and I made a plan to go to the fields on Saturday. I said I would give tennis a miss because I still had quite a bad cough.

On Saturday morning, I fed Poppy. I'd not spent much time with her for a week or so. I promised her I would let her have a good long run in the garden later in the day. I called for Anna. She'd also had the cold, but she didn't mind going to the fields. We decided to walk there for a change, and I left my bike at her house. As soon as the bottom gate came into view, we could see Sam waiting for us. It wasn't long before we were climbing the path to the upper field. It was a cooler day with a real hint of autumn. We took off our anoraks, laid them on the grass, and sat on them.

"So," said Anna, "I haven't seen either of you for a week. Has anything happened?"

I coughed and blew my nose. Sam took his notebook from his pocket and put it down so that we could all see it. He'd rewritten the list.

Five things (and one solved):
The birds
The rabbit
Naomi said Tommy was taken, not missing or run away or got lost
Ball (now solved)
The person in the field
Another missing boy

"Right," said Anna, "I say we go through them one at a time and see if anything's changed. I suppose Naomi hasn't come back to school or you'd have told me."

I realized I'd not thought about Naomi during the week. It must have been the first time she'd slipped from my mind.

"Also, before we start," Sam said seriously, "I think we need a code name for these meetings, so that we can talk about this stuff without anyone else knowing."

"Have you come up with one?" asked Anna. She obviously thought it was a good idea.

"The Five Things," said Sam.

Although, there were now six things on the list, one was solved, so five was a good description. We agreed unanimously on that.

"Right," Anna said again. "What do we know about the birds?"

"Nothing new," I said.

"The rabbit," said Anna. "Nothing new either. Naomi said Tommy was 'taken,' what do we know about that?"

"You are sure she said that?" Sam asked me.

"Yes, definitely, when she first told me," I said. "I can still remember it."

We discussed this question for a while. What had Naomi meant, and did she also say that he was "taken" to the constable? If she said "taken" to the constable, was that why he asked me if I'd seen anyone in the field, or did Naomi actually tell him she'd seen someone in the field? If she'd seen someone, she would surely have told us.

"If she'd seen Bridges in the field, that would have been the first thing she'd have said," I made clear.

"That's probably true. So maybe she saw someone else? Someone she wasn't that bothered about? She could have seen Mr. Johnson, or Mr. Morris…or the farmer from the farmhouse on the corner," said Anna. "That's his field, isn't it?"

Sam made a few notes about this. Then we agreed we'd already covered the next question, the person in the field. The last question was about the other missing boy.

"We'd have to ask someone about that," said Anna.

"You should ask someone, Wendy, because it was you that heard it," Sam stated.

"Who would I ask?"

"Don't ask straight out. We don't want people to know what we're doing," Anna warned.

Sam wrote a few more notes into the book, and I told him he was getting just like Constable Gordon. The meeting came to an end, and we went for the usual walk through the wood.

****

Mum had a big baking session in the week. I came home from school to find her surrounded by her cake tins, weighing scales, bowls, and ingredients. It wasn't unusual for this to happen, and I loved the atmosphere she created, the warmth of the room, and the smells that emanated from the delicacies she concocted. I quickly changed out of my school clothes and came back to sit and watch her. I could get away with sampling a few things. There were dates squashed into a block, like a brick, so I asked for one of those. It was soft, sticky, and tangy; I ate it slowly as I continued to enjoy the production. I helped myself to a teaspoonful of desiccated coconut, which released its sweet oiliness into my mouth as I chewed. Mum had already put two date and walnut cakes into the oven; she usually made cakes in pairs and was now making a pastry case for the coconut recipe. She was going to put a layer of her homemade plum jam on the pastry, and the coconut mixture would go on top. She told me that she had plenty of eggs, and she thought she might have enough time to make some meringues, too. Mum's meringues were the best thing in the world as far as I was concerned.

It came to me that it might be a good time to try a question about missing boys. I thought carefully about how to start.

"It's really unusual for someone to go missing isn't it, Mum? I mean like Tommy did."

"Yes, of course it is. Have you been worrying about it?"

"I was just thinking how unusual it was for a boy to go missing."

"I'd say it's very unusual for anyone to go missing, especially here in the countryside." She sprinkled flour onto the rolling pin. She asked me to fetch the eggs from the cupboard. I came back with them. "You mustn't worry," she said. "It was an accident, a nasty accident, that's all."

"Everyone says that."

"Poor Tommy." She turned to the oven to check on the date and walnut cakes.

I didn't think it was worth asking any other questions about it. Mum obviously hadn't heard about anyone else being missing.

"Can I make the odd bits of pastry into hedgehogs?" I asked.

"Yes, you can have all those now. Make some hedgehogs and we'll pop them in and bake them."

****

We had a routine in place by now. Each Friday, Sam and I would decide where the Saturday meeting would be and at what time. On Saturday, I would call for Anna and we'd meet Sam at the location. The meetings would take place in the fields so long as the weather stayed fine.

The weekend arrived, and we made our way to the upper field. Anna asked if there was anything new to report and we went over The Five Things. I said that I'd asked Mum about boys going missing. I said I'd been careful in the way I'd asked the question, but that I was sure by the way she'd answered that she didn't know anything about any other missing boys. I'd already informed Sam about quizzing Mum.

"Well," he said, "because of that, I've had a think about what we should do, and I reckon we could ask a few more careful questions. What about we go and see if we can find old Mr. Morris? He's sure to know if there have been any other missing boys."

Anna and I thought that was a good idea, and after walking through the wood, we set off to the green to see if we could track down Mr. Morris. As we cycled round the corner by the farmhouse, we could see something going on at Lavender Cottage. Mr. Morris was also at his gate. Anna and I stopped next to Mr. Morris and Sam carried on the few extra yards to Naomi's house.

"It's new people moving in," Mr. Morris told us.

"New people?" I said. It didn't seem possible.

"Yes, another family. I hope they'll have better fortune."

Sam returned. He'd seen the people but didn't recognize them. I think we all felt deflated.

"We really miss Naomi and Tommy," Anna told Mr. Morris.

"Everybody does," he replied, with a look of understanding.

Anna somehow pulled herself together. I think she'd remembered there were questions to be asked.

"We were with Naomi the day Tommy went missing," she said.

"I was away," said Mr. Morris. "I spent a couple of days with my sister, and it all went on while I was there."

"Did people tell you what happened?" asked Sam.

"Yes, but no one really wanted to talk much...I can understand that...and Gerry finding the little lad...he must've had such a shock."

"The constable asked us questions," said Sam, "when they were trying to find him."

"We think they thought he might have gone off with someone," Anna said.

"They always ask a lot of questions, just in case," Mr. Morris said.

We hadn't made the progress we'd hoped for, but none of us could think of anything else to say, and we'd promised not to ask straight out about anyone being in the field or other missing boys at that stage. We thought if Mr. Morris knew anything else he'd be bound to tell us, but he was a lot more serious than usual. He seemed really disturbed by the whole occurrence. We should have realized he'd feel that way. We said goodbye to him and went to sit on the bench on the green. The swallows were gathering and flying in huge cloud-like flocks. They were getting ready to fly off for the winter.

Later, I told Philip that new people were renting Lavender Cottage. He said maybe it was for the best. It might be easier for Naomi and her mum and dad to be back in the village where they came from, where Naomi's grandparents were still living, and away from the place where they would never be able to avoid the painful memories of the summer.

I had a talk with Piggy.

"I always thought I'd see Naomi again one day, Piggy. I care about her. I've practiced things I could say to her to try to make her feel better. Now, I know she's never coming back. Tommy's not coming back, and Naomi's not coming back."

I made myself cry.

Chapter 17

I took another book out of the library. It was descriptively titled *Fungi*. There is no scientific difference between a mushroom and a toadstool, it stated, though toadstool has come to mean a mushroom that is poisonous. Nevertheless, not all toadstools are poisonous, and in contrast, some mushrooms are. This was quite a revelation to me. The book also said that a good number of wild animals fed on mushrooms and toadstools. Apparently, rabbits ate them, as did mice, badgers, deer, squirrels, and also things like slugs and snails. All this information could go into our section on fungi as food.

Sam and I were at the playground, trying to find a quiet spot to sit because Sam wanted to talk about The Five Things.

"Let's face it, we're getting nowhere. Mr. Morris wasn't any help. Now we'll never be able to ask Naomi anything. We can't question Constable Gordon." Sam was frustrated.

"We could talk to Mr. Johnson? We could talk to the Barclays? They might know something. They might have seen something the day before or somewhen, you never know," I said.

"Who's going to tell us about the other missing boy?" he asked me. It was a rhetorical question. "I think Anna's getting fed up with the whole idea too," he said.

"She might want to give up on The Five Things altogether."

"We need a breakthrough," I said.

"What can we do about Bridges? I know he was behind the birds, the rabbit, and the screeching noises. I didn't even put the screeching noises in the notebook."

"So what do you really think?" I asked him. "Do you really think Bridges took Tommy?"

He went quiet, but I must have said something right because he then had another thought.

"We could make a list of all the things that might have happened and see what we come up with?" he said.

I encouraged his new spark of enthusiasm. "Right, we'll do that at the meeting on Saturday. I'll tell Anna that Saturday's meeting is going to be a very important one."

"Good idea! She's bound to be more interested if you say that."

****

There were beach huts near to where Sam's granddad hired out the boats. They had wooden decks to the front that were partly covered by the overhang of their roofs. It meant that outside of the summer season, they made a good place to sit and shelter if you found yourself on the beach in unfavorable conditions. We arranged to go there for Saturday's meeting, as the forecast was for wet and windy weather.

I called for Anna and we rode our bikes down the beach road and along the sea wall. Sam was on the pebbles, throwing stones into the waves. It was windy, but the rain hadn't yet started to fall. We joined him and also began throwing stones. We threw them as far as we could; we tried to throw farther than each other. The sea was roaring, and the wind blew our hair and buffeted us, so that we became like a part of the wild shoreline.

We went up to the huts and chose the one that was painted a pale green color. We sat on the wooden deck at the front, leaning our backs against the padlocked doors, beneath the shelter of the roof.

"How come the meeting is so important this week?" Anna asked straight away.

"We have a new tactic to explore," Sam said.

We explained to Anna that we were going to think of all the things that could have happened the day Tommy disappeared. She looked a little underwhelmed; she'd probably thought there was going to be some really big news. Even so, she joined in energetically as we started coming up with possibilities.

"Well, he must have gone into the field behind the house," I said.

"Then somehow he got to the track," said Anna.

"But why did he go to the quarry? It's a long way along that track to the quarry," Sam said.

We came up with a variety of explanations. Most of these threw up more questions and some were completely daft and made us laugh, even though the subject matter was extremely solemn. In fact, the possibilities were endless, but, after a long discussion involving some strong argument and intense disagreement, we settled on three main options. Sam produced the notebook, turned to a fresh page, and neatly wrote them down.

1—Tommy went off on his own. He went into the field behind the house and walked along to the track.

He lost the ball near the quarry and slipped in trying to find it. That was what the grown-ups said had happened.

2—Tommy went off on his own. He left the garden and set off for the wood. At some point, something or someone scared him, or chased him, and something bad happened. He tried to run away. He ended up in the quarry.

3—Tommy was in the garden and someone was in the field. He went into the field to talk to them. He was lured by them or taken by them along the track. They pushed him into the quarry.

"How likely do you think they all are?" said Anna. "How likely is the first one?"

We made a grid. We gave each option a score out of five.

Option 1 Option 2 Option 3
Anna 3 3 1
Wendy 2 3 2
Sam 1 4 3

The result was very interesting. Sam and I thought the second option was most likely. Anna thought it was just as likely as the first, and we hadn't ruled out the third. We were onto something.

"What now?" asked Anna.

****

It was the last week of school before half-term. Mum and Dad announced that they were taking Philip and me away for a few nights. We were going to stay in a hotel, visit a historic town, and go to a Roman archaeological site, which Philip had been talking about recently. We would also be doing some clothes shopping. Maggie said she'd feed Poppy, so I wouldn't have to worry about her.

I was telling Sam about our trip at the playground, but he wasn't paying attention. Some of the others were trying to involve us in a game of *it,* but Sam wanted another conversation about The Five Things.

Edward, one of the little ones from the first-year class, stood in front of us. "Can't catch me for a toffee flea," he sang.

"Move!" said Sam. "We're not playing!" Edward looked crestfallen.

"I think Linda wants to join in," I told Edward. I pointed her out.

We left the rest of them running round shouting and found an out of the way corner where we could talk. We sat down.

"I want to go to the field behind Lavender Cottage and walk to the quarry," Sam said.

"We can't," I said.

"Then I want to walk from the field behind the cottage to the wood, and from the wood to the quarry."

"We can't. We can't go into that field. Someone will see us and wonder what we're doing. We'll get into trouble."

That was the field that had the no trespassing signs, but it was true the locals didn't actually take much notice of them.

"I want to find out how long it takes to go straight to the quarry and see if Tommy would have done that."

As Tommy was a couple of years younger than us, Sam still thought it was unlikely he would have made that journey on his own. It wasn't something he'd done with us, and we were sure he hadn't done it with Naomi.

"He was quite adventurous," I said.

"I still think if he was going to go anywhere, he'd have gone to the wood. So perhaps he went from the wood to the quarry for some reason."

Sam said the best time to do all this walking was during the half-term break. I reminded him again that I would be away for most of the holiday.

"I'll do it on my own," he said. He didn't seem at all perturbed by that thought. In fact, it seemed to me that he quite liked the idea. "If anyone asks me what I'm doing, I'll say I'm looking for mushrooms, or toadstools. I'll say I'm sorry and that I didn't mean any harm."

It did seem a good plan; I couldn't imagine anyone being cross about Sam looking for mushrooms in a cow field.

Chapter 18

October 1969

Mum packed two suitcases for the half-term trip. She put my things in with her own and Philip's in with Dad's. I was to share a room with her at the hotel; Philip would share with Dad. We set off on Saturday morning in the car. It was cool and bright. I settled into my seat and stared out of the side window, watching the world pass by. Philip talked about Roman archaeology and the site we were going to visit. He'd been studying it at school and knew a good deal about it. He said we would be able to see things that had been dug up there, like jewelry and coins. Mum said we wouldn't need to rely on a guide; Philip would be able to show us around.

We arrived at the hotel in the late morning. It wasn't too early to collect our keys and put our cases in our rooms. Part of the hotel was very old, but they'd built on an additional section and the new part was very modern. We had one room in each part. Dad insisted Mum choose the one she'd like most and she chose the old one. I went with her to look at it. A member of the hotel staff helped us with our case. We made our way up several very narrow staircases. The steps went round and round and leaned more and more to one side. There was carpet in the middle, but you could see dark wood at the edges. There was a lot of dark, varnished wood everywhere, paneling, and beams; there was a very particular smell. Our room was Number Seven. The man opened the door and gave me the huge black metal key before leaving us to settle in.

"It's pongy in here," I said.

"It's just the smell of the wood and the polish," Mum said.

"I think the room's quite odd."

"It's lovely, so quaint."

There were two beds: a single and a four-poster. I had only ever seen a four-poster bed in a picture before now. I wasn't sure I liked it. The walls of the room were cream, there was more dark wood, and everything else was red: the carpet, the bedspreads, the curtains. The window was small. I had a look out. We were quite high up, and you could see right across the countryside to the town.

Dad couldn't wait to see the four-poster. He and Philip came in and had a lie down on the crimson cover. Their room was completely different they said. We would go and look it over, then drive into the town for lunch.

****

I liked the town. We spent a few hours there. I was enjoying simply walking around, exploring the ancient streets. There were lots of little shops, and I found plenty of things I wanted to buy. We had lunch in one cafe, and later we went to another for a cream tea.

We did some more driving and finally went back to the hotel rooms. I was to sleep in the single bed beside the window. I sat on it looking out. I could see the lights from the town sparkling, something I wasn't used to. I started thinking about Sam and wondered if he'd done any of the walking he'd been planning. I wished I'd told him not to go to the quarry on his own.

"Mum," I said, "you know that man Bridges?"

"The old farmer in that big house on the footpath?"

"I don't like him very much."

"Oh?" She came and sat down beside me. "What's made you think about him, all of a sudden?"

I couldn't think of an answer.

"Has something happened? Did you bump into him in the village?"

"No."

"You know the village children have never liked him. Even when I was growing up, people used to tell stories about him. But I don't think there's any need to worry. He seems to keep to himself."

****

We went to the Roman villa. Philip was extremely impressed. He told me that people had been working on it for years and that it took a really long time even to uncover a small area.

"They call it excavation. They've found a whole load of stuff."

"The jewelry and things?"

"Yes. You'll see. All sorts of items from when people lived here. They call them artifacts."

"Arty facts?"

"A-R-T-I-F-A-C-T," he spelled it out for me.

"Oh."

"I think it might be Latin."

As well as jewelry and coins, there were cooking pots and even parts of clothing. They came from a very long time ago, more than a thousand years ago—long before the old part of the hotel was built.

There were drawings that showed how the buildings would have looked when people lived there. The archaeologists could tell how people dressed, what they did all day, even what they ate. Poor people ate bread and porridge. Rich people ate figs and grapes and olives. They also ate sheep and pigs and leeks and beans. All of this seemed acceptable I supposed, but then I was told they sometimes ate dormice, and I wasn't sure I could forgive them for that.

"I'm going to buy one of these books," Philip said.

"Let me see."

"There are pictures of everything. We'll be able to look at it when we get back." He turned the pages for me, hoping I'd share his enthusiasm. "One day I'm going to be an archaeologist and work on places like this."

Back in the town, Mum helped me choose a winter coat and some new shoes, and Dad bought me a silver charm bracelet, which had tiny coins on it that were a bit like the Roman coins we'd seen at the villa.

****

I told Mum and Dad I'd really enjoyed the half-term holiday, and I'd learned a lot about history. Philip said it had been "ace" and that he couldn't wait to visit the villa again. We traveled home with our now heavier suitcases squeezed into the boot of the car.

As soon as we arrived, I dashed into the garden to see Poppy. Everything was unpacked and we found places to keep all the new items we'd purchased. The following day was Sunday. Dad and Philip would play golf, and Maggie would come round to hear about the trip. I wouldn't see Sam until school on Monday. I couldn't wait to hear what had happened while I'd been away.

****

Monday morning came and I put on my white shirt, my pinafore dress, and the new school cardigan Mum had finished knitting. Sam called for me and we set off for school.

"How was your trip?" he asked politely.

"It was good. But what about The Five Things?" I said.

"Okay, I'll tell you about that first. There's so much to tell you. Well, in one way there is, and in another way there isn't."

"You weren't caught, were you?"

Sam said he hadn't done anything until Tuesday because he didn't want his granddad to think he was doing anything unusual. He spent Monday helping him in the garden and assisting him in repairing some of the lobster pots. On Tuesday, he set off on his bike after breakfast. He decided it would be best to start at the wood and work back to the field behind Lavender Cottage. He went to the wood and walked the route. The easiest way was to follow the same route Naomi and Tommy usually took. He went to the tree stump that acted as our lookout post, climbed over the fence, and walked down to the cottage. It meant walking through two more fields, but it was easy to get under or over the barbed wire fencing that divided them. The journey took less than ten minutes. Sam thought Tommy could easily have walked the distance on his own.

"Naomi and Tommy always walked through those fields, even though they weren't supposed to," I said.

We arrived at school, and because we were discussing The Five Things, we had to be careful. We went to the playground and sat on the wall. Sam said that once he came to the fence behind Lavender Cottage, he started walking toward the track that ran along under the downs. Charlotte came over and Sam had to stop.

"Have you got your jewels with you?" she asked. "I've got some new ones."

"I have. Can I look later, though?" I said.

"Okay."

Charlotte seemed to get the hint and walked off to find someone else to show her jewels to. Sam carried on. He'd walked along at the back of the cottages. After the last cottage, the field continued, and the boundary was marked by a tall hedge. He walked beside the hedge to the end of the field. At that point, there was a gap that you could push yourself through, and then you'd find yourself out on the track. It was obvious people had been doing that because of the size of the gap. The track was very muddy, but it wouldn't have been at the time when Tommy went missing.

I knew the track. It was like a tunnel, the long-established trees and hedgerows that grew on either side almost met in the middle overhead. It ran between the fields and the downs, so on one side there was a steep incline, and on the other there was hedging with fields beyond. The ground was just bare earth. The track ran for miles in each direction. You could walk along it; the farmers would take animals along it from field to field, but in most places, it was too narrow and uneven for vehicles to use.

Sam turned left in the direction of the quarry. The

downs were on his right. We were familiar with the quarry, but it had never been a place we thought about or spent our time. It was one of several old chalk quarries in the area. Sam said it was more than five minutes' walk from the field, and on the way to it, there was nothing remarkable to report. At the point where you came to it, the track wound round to the left, and the quarry was there on your right, dug into the side of the downs. You couldn't really miss it, but there was nothing interesting about it. Shrubs and plants now grew all over the bottom of it and up the sides. It was hard to tell how deep it was. Sam worked out that it would take well over ten minutes to walk the full distance from Lavender Cottage.

I asked if he'd felt a little frightened. None of us had been anywhere near that part of the village since the event. Mr. Jenkins came into the playground and started ringing the bell that beckoned us to our classrooms. We were going to have to continue the conversation at playtime. Mondays started with maths, and we had to concentrate because there was going to be a test. It seemed a long time until midmorning. When playtime arrived, I made sure not to catch Charlotte's eye, and Sam and I went back to the wall.

Sam carried on divulging the exploits of his half-term. After reaching the quarry he'd turned back and walked a long way in the other direction to see if the track went anywhere near the wood. It was difficult to tell. He would have to check it out by starting from the upper field again. He'd been out for such a long time by that point that he had to suspend the operation, find a path that led him back to the road, and go and retrieve his bike.

On Wednesday, he helped his granddad with various things in the morning, and after lunch, he and Adam went to the beach. They saw some of the other kids, but he didn't say a word to anybody about The Five Things or the walking he was doing. On Thursday, he went to the wood for a second time and right to the back of the field. At the back, the hedge was thick, and beyond were tall trees. He walked to and fro trying to find a way to get through. He felt sure that if you found a way through the hedge, you'd be able to get to the track. As much as he looked, he couldn't find a way, but he'd had another idea. He'd have to tell me later because playtime was over, and we were going back to class to write about something we had done in the half-term holiday. That was going to be easy for me. Sam smiled, he told me not to worry, he was going to write about mending the lobster pots.

It turned out that Sam hadn't managed to get any further with the investigation during the holiday, but he'd had a good idea about how to find the way from the wood to the track. He said we should go to the upper field together, go to the back, and tie some bright colored cloth high up at the top of the hedge. Then we should go to the track and walk along to see if we could see the cloth from the other side. We'd soon find out if there was a way through.

Chapter 19

Because of half-term, we'd missed two meetings about The Five Things. The following Saturday, there would be a lot to get through.

Sam had found some red fabric and torn it into strips. We met on the wheat fields. We were on foot as the paths were now quite muddy and the bikes would only hinder our progress. We walked across the road and climbed the gate into the lower field. We were to have the meeting inside the wood and then tie the cloth pieces onto the hedge beyond.

We sat on the fallen tree in our waterproof jackets and leather winter shoes. Sam told again, for Anna's benefit, how he'd gone on the various walks, and how long each had taken. Anna listened.

"What does it prove, even if we find a way through from here to the track?" she asked when he finished speaking.

"It's more evidence," he explained. "I think we're making some progress."

As we sat, we became aware of someone else coming into the wood. We could hear them approaching, but we couldn't see them. We stopped talking and kept very still. Anna grabbed my forearm and held on to it so tightly it started to hurt. There wasn't time to run or hide. The sounds of the person walking toward us continued. They were getting closer and my heart was beating faster and faster. The person emerged a few yards from us. It was Adam Smart.

"What are you all doing here?" Adam said, his red hair contrasting with the muted tones of our surroundings. He smiled.

"Just having a meeting," I said. The others frowned at me. "About our fungi project," I added quickly.

"I'm looking for owls," he said. We knew he was quite an ornithologist. He spent time down by the river watching the kingfishers.

"We were wondering about something," Sam said. "Do you know if you can get from here to the track?"

Adam's mind was wholly concentrated on his bird watching.

"Yes, you can. There are all sorts of birds that live along the track there. I've seen whitethroats," he said. Then he seemed to stop as if he'd said something he shouldn't.

"What is it?" Sam asked him.

"Are you still thinking about Tommy?" he asked. "Look, I'm not sure if you know. I saw Tommy the day he disappeared, but I've no idea why he went to the track."

"You saw him?" Sam said. I don't think he could take in what he was hearing.

"Where was he?" I asked.

"I was talking to him in the morning. I was in the field behind Lavender Cottage and he was in the garden. I had a conversation with him, about woodpeckers and cuckoos. Then I left him."

I caught Sam's eye, then Anna's in disbelief.

"I wanted to tell you. I told Mum in the end. She made me tell Constable Gordon. She was furious. She said I must never go there again."

"There's *No Trespass* signs," I said. But Sam and I knew there might be another reason Adam's mum was keen to keep him away from the area. It wasn't far from the old black barn. We remembered that Adam had suddenly wanted nothing to do with the surveillance, or even to speak about it. Now it made sense. "What happened when you told Constable Gordon?" I asked.

"I told him I'd seen Tommy that day, early in the morning."

"What did he say?" asked Anna.

"Nothing really, just wrote it down. He didn't even tell me off. It was quite a bit later that Tommy disappeared."

Adam took us to the back of the field and along to the corner at the right-hand side. He pulled back a tree branch, climbed through the barbed wire fencing, and helped us across. There was a bank. It dropped down steeply, then leveled out. It was thick with shrubbery, but there was a way down that you could tell had sometimes been used as a path. We pushed our way on, to where the bank sloped away again, and there, in full view below us, was the track.

Being with Adam had been useful, but we had to postpone any more conversation about The Five Things. We couldn't include him. We went back to the wood with him and looked for owls. Later, we had an emergency meeting. We held it at Anna's in the late afternoon. Sam produced the notebook. He'd written The Five Things out again on a new page, but now with the update.

Five things (and two solved):

The birds
The rabbit
Naomi said Tommy was taken, not missing or run away or got lost
Ball (now solved)
The person in the field (now solved)
Another missing boy

The Five Things didn't make sense anymore; there were six things: four unanswered questions and two solved. Nevertheless, we continued with it, because it still made a good code name.

We needed to discuss the significance of Adam being the person in the field.

"It changes everything," Anna said. "If Adam was the person in the field, the person in the field had nothing to do with Tommy disappearing."

"Naomi must have seen Adam. She must have told the constable," I said. "But why did he ask me about it?"

"She can't have known it was Adam," Sam said.

"Or she thought he might get into trouble, so she didn't tell," said Anna.

"But she would have told me she'd seen him, and if she didn't know it was Adam, she would have surely told me she saw someone in the field?" I said.

"That's right," said Sam. "You know, I don't think she saw him at all. I think Adam told the constable he was there, and then the constable must have asked Naomi if she'd seen anyone in the field...and then he asked you if you'd seen anyone."

"That would explain it, except if she didn't see anyone in the field, why did she say Tommy had been taken?" I said. "Nothing makes sense anymore."

"Do you think Tommy followed Adam out of the field?" Sam asked.

We were coming up with more questions than answers.

"Maybe we won't be able to work it all out until we've answered the rest of the questions," said Anna.

****

Sam's mum was coming to visit again the next weekend, so there was to be no meeting. Sam was surprised she was making a second journey so soon. He hadn't seen her in ages, and now she was coming again after traveling over only a few weeks beforehand. Marcel wouldn't be accompanying her this time, and she would be staying with Sam and his granddad at the house.

****

I asked Mum if she could think of any good recipes involving mushrooms. She had shelves full of cookery books, and she said we could have a look through them together. There were salads that incorporated mushrooms, and they were an accompaniment in a lot of fried dishes and grilled dishes. They were popular in omelets and also as an ingredient in various pies. This was all very informative, but I wanted to find dishes where they were the key ingredient. There were two dishes that featured in several of the books: mushroom soup and mushroom tarts or flans. I picked the best recipes and wrote them out. I would take them to school and include them in the project. Mum remembered that we were supposed to be going to look for wild mushrooms but until we found time, she said, she'd buy some from the village, and we'd make the dishes I'd selected and try them.

****

The usual Guy Fawkes party was on that Friday on the playing field. It was another village event that everyone attended. There was always a giant bonfire. People would begin to take wood to the site a week or so beforehand. It would be stacked up, and as the days went by, we'd see the pile grow higher and higher into the sky. There would be fireworks: rockets, fountains, and Catherine wheels pinned to tall posts erected by the organizers. There would be a stall selling jacket potatoes and roasted corn, as well as ginger cake and toffee apples.

Mum, Dad, and I were going together. Mike had called for Philip, and they'd set off before us. The road was busy with other villagers making their way. We bustled along, looking forward to what the evening would have to offer.

There were lanterns burning at points around the field, but even so, it was hard to make people out. It was dark, and the flickering of the lanterns and the fire meant that people were just shadowy shapes, lit only occasionally by the flames.

Sam found me. He was with his granddad and also his mum, who'd arrived early so that she could come along. Mum and Dad greeted them, and Sam introduced me. His mum seemed nice. She was pretty and very fashionably dressed. She said that Sam had told her all about me. Dad asked her about the area in France where she was living and how she'd traveled. Philip and Mike came to join us. I couldn't see Anna, though I knew she must be there somewhere.

Dad went to buy hot potatoes for everyone and

arrived back just in time for the start of the show. It was a good display. We all shouted "wow" and whooped as the fireworks were let off. It was an occasion when you somehow felt like part of the village, even though you didn't see most people or speak to them. It was an occasion that bound us all together.

At the end of the night, people quickly dispersed. I took hold of Dad's hand and he as much as pulled me through the crowd to the exit. As we approached the gate, it was as if I felt someone looking at me. I turned and saw a man standing, his back to the fencing. He wore a long coat and a brimmed hat. I stared back. The lanterns were still burning and for a moment his face was lit up. It was Bridges. I turned and tried to see Sam, but Dad was walking purposefully, dragging me with him. I looked back again, but the light had changed, we'd moved past, and the man was now indistinguishable in the crowd.

His dress had been scruffy, his face pallid and puffy; his watery eyes had been fixed on me. He'd stood motionless; his big, gloveless hands hanging at his sides in fists. I shivered when I thought about him and the gaze that I'd felt directed toward me. I tried to think of other things as we spent the weekend making mushroom soup and raking up the fallen leaves in the garden.

Chapter 20

"How was the weekend with your mum?" I asked.

Sam and I were walking to school. "Okay. She was being really nice to me. It was hard to get any sleep, though. Mum and Granddad kept me awake talking until really late both nights."

"I suppose they had a lot to tell each other."

"They don't usually talk all night."

"I have something big to tell you," I said. I couldn't hold back any longer.

"What is it?" said Sam. At this point, we stopped and turned to face each other.

"Bridges was at the fireworks," I said.

"He couldn't have been," he said.

"He was. I'm absolutely sure of it. He was in that long coat and the hat he wears, with the brim. I know it was him, and he was looking straight at me."

"What did you do?"

"I lost sight of him then, there were so many people." We carried on walking.

"Maybe he was looking for the kids who go to the wood," said Sam.

****

There was no Brownies as there was maintenance work going on at the hall. That meant we had plenty of catching up to do at the next Saturday meeting. We met at the beach huts. We sat straight down to get on with business. The first thing to discuss was the sighting of Bridges.

Sam prompted me. "Wendy has something to tell us."

I was aware of a sense of expectation. "I saw Bridges at the fireworks...and it was as if he was looking at me," I said.

Anna seemed cautious. "I was at the fireworks, and I didn't see him."

"Well, I didn't see him either," said Sam, "but it was at the end when everyone was leaving all in a crowd, wasn't it?"

I explained to Anna what I'd seen. Once she'd heard me describe what happened I knew she believed me and that she thought it must have been him. I told them both I couldn't stop thinking about it afterward and that it had scared me.

"I've never seen him properly," Anna said. "Not up close."

"Me neither," said Sam.

"What's he like?" Anna asked.

"I'm not sure," I said.

"I think he's really fat," said Sam. "With a big, warty face."

"His hair is dirty. It's long and matted," said Anna. "And he's all beardy."

"His teeth are rotten...and I bet he smells," said Sam.

"Something like that," I said.

Even so, Anna told us we hadn't to forget that we now knew Adam, not Bridges, was the person in the field. Sam said he kept wondering if we should tell Adam about The Five Things. If Adam trusted us enough to tell us about seeing Tommy that day, maybe we should involve him. He might come up with something we hadn't thought of. I wasn't sure. Then Anna suggested we look at the grid again, reevaluate the findings, and see if we had changed our minds in any way. Sam opened the notebook at the appropriate page and Anna read out the three options we'd listed.

1—Tommy went off on his own. He went into the field behind the house and walked along to the track. He lost the ball near the quarry and slipped in trying to find it. (That was what the grown-ups said had happened.)

2—Tommy went off on his own. He left the garden and set off for the wood. At some point, something or someone scared him, or chased him, and something bad happened. He tried to run away. He ended up in the quarry.

3—Tommy was in the garden and someone was in the field. He went into the field to talk to them. He was lured by them or taken by them along the track. They pushed him into the quarry.

Then Anna said, "I think there's another option now." We agreed to include it.

4—Tommy watched Adam leave the field. Later, Tommy took the same path. He was looking for Adam, or for woodpeckers or for cuckoos. He fell into the quarry.

Old grid.
Option 1 Option 2 Option 3
Anna 3 3 1

Wendy 2 3 2
Sam 1 4 3

New grid.
Option 1 Option 2 Option 3 Option 4
Anna 3 2 0 3
Wendy 3 2 1 3
Sam 2 4 3 2

But I realized what we'd done. "Option 4 is really Option 1, only with us knowing about Adam being in the field. If you think about it, Constable Gordon knew about Option 4 all along."

Option 4 was a real possibility; we all agreed on that, but Sam still thought it most likely that someone had chased or even pushed Tommy.

"So you don't think it's more likely he followed Adam?" Anna put to him.

"No. I'm not sure. But after Wendy saw Bridges, it made me think he was looking for us kids. Why else would he be at the fireworks?" Sam said.

"So what does it all mean?" Anna asked. "It's making my brain ache."

No one spoke for a while. Anna lay back on the wooden decking. Sam sat with his back against the hut doors, studying his notes, and I sat cross-legged in front of them, gazing out to sea.

"I know," said Sam. "We'll set a trap for Bridges. I can be the bait."

"You're not serious?" Anna looked alarmed.

"Let's concentrate on the other missing boy," I suggested—mainly to change the subject. "I've asked my Mum. Why don't you ask your Mum or your Dad,

Anna, and you ask your granddad, Sam?"

We left the beach hut and walked along the wall to the road. We climbed the steps beside the hotel and walked back to the playing field. There were a few boys kicking a football at the far end, and I showed Anna and Sam where Bridges had been standing after the fireworks. We sat on the swings, just hanging. Sam noticed that Adam was one of the footballers. After a short while, Adam started walking toward us. He'd left the others still playing, taking it in turns to be in goal. He greeted us, then threw himself down on the grass in front of us.

Sam asked the question, "Adam, did you ever hear of anyone else going missing round here?"

Adam studied the three of us. He must have thought we did nothing but think about disaster and misfortune, and I was beginning to think that too. We didn't expect the answer that came.

"There's only that story about the boy in the boat," he said.

Sam sat up straight on the swing. "The boy in the boat?"

"Yes, they found a boy in a boat. I've heard people say it. I don't really know what happened. I think it was ages ago."

"I've never heard about any boy in a boat," said Sam, "and my life's full of boats."

"You could ask your granddad?" Adam suggested.

I think Adam saved us, at least temporarily, from discussing the setting of traps and the baiting of Bridges. Sam became absorbed with the boy in the boat, and how it was possible that he'd never heard anything about it before.

The Five Things

****

It was only two weeks until the end of term, and Sam and I had a lot to do to finish the fungi project and win first prize. We still didn't know what the prizes were to be, but Miss Charlton was encouraging Sam and me. She'd said that we might be rewarded if we kept up our good work.

Every pair had been given a large scrapbook with thick, black sugar paper pages. We'd put our project title on the cover along with our names. Our first section was the definitions. They were quite complicated, and Sam had done most of the work on that part. Next, we had a section on mushrooms with descriptions and pictures, mostly our own drawings. We'd listed the ones most common to the area where we lived. We'd done the same for toadstools. Following that there was the recipe section, which I'd put together by myself. Then there was a section called *Fungus Fun*. We'd included pictures we'd drawn of towns where all the houses were actually mushrooms with little windows and doors. We'd found a poem about a toadstool and an elf and that took up a double page. Our final section was on legends involving fungi, and in particular, fairy rings. At the weekend, Sam and I were going to finish the three toadstool sculptures he'd been making in his granddad's workshop. Dad was going to drive us to school in the car on the last Wednesday of term so that we could bring them with us. The presentations were to be on Wednesday, and on Thursday we would find out who had won.

At home, everyone was talking about Christmas: various parties, and preparations for the Christmas lunch. The mood was becoming festive, but just before

I went to sleep—in the dark when the water pipes made wailing sounds—I'd been having strange thoughts about Bridges and the birds. I put my head under the blankets. I tried to concentrate on the mushrooms. I attempted to learn the toadstool poem by heart, but the thoughts would always find a way back. I'd be in the wood. The sun would be low in the almost white sky, shining through the trees, throwing shafts of light across the mossy path. I'd see the birds, dangling and be about to run, but then I'd see Bridges standing in his long coat and his hat. I'd see his dark shape, but I could never make out his face. I'd see that he was holding a gun, a shotgun with a long double barrel, but the gun was hung over his arm, broken open. Next, I'd feel that I was spinning, and then I could see into the barrels, and it became clear that the gun wasn't loaded. The barrels were empty. I saw the same thing every night as I lay in my bed. I held on to piggy and tried to remember the poem over and over again.

Chapter 21

On Saturday, we met in the workshop at Sam's house. We'd roped Anna in to help us add the finishing touches to the toadstool sculptures. There were three, so we worked on one each. They needed a final coat of paint, and the top of one of them had fallen off its stalk, so Sam was trying to glue it back together. He said we'd just have to balance it on top if all else failed. Anna suggested she should come with us on Wednesday and sit on one of the toadstools dressed as a fairy during the presentation. We all started laughing, which made it difficult to paint. We were in high spirits, and Sam and I were expecting to win.

The toadstool Sam was working on was in fact like a typical fairy tale toadstool, with a shiny red top and white spots. Anna's was pink with white spots, and mine was all colors and stripy. Once we'd done all we could, we walked round and round them admiring our work. Then we went for a walk along the riverbank.

We sat on the wall near the little bridge and watched some swans that were swimming about on the water.

"Are we having a meeting today? I mean about The Five Things," Anna checked.

"Let's find Granddad and ask him about the boy in the boat," Sam said. "I was hoping to ask him when you were here, and he's not too busy today."

We found Sam's granddad making tea in the little kitchen in the cottage. He had a range-type cooker, and the kettle was whistling away on the hot plate. He said he would make a large pot. "Have you finished the toadstools?" he asked.

"Yes," said Sam.

"Let's drink this tea and then you can show me."

He went into the small pantry and emerged with a patterned tin and a wooden board with a round-shaped cheese on the top. He put them on the old wooden table, followed by four thick, white china plates and four thick, white china mugs. He opened the tin and cut a big slice of fruitcake for each of us, and then a good lump of cheese. He poured milk from the enamel jug into the mugs and strained tea into each. We sat on the benches around the table. The little window looked out toward the river. It was really cozy.

"Granddad," Sam began, "can you tell us about the boy in the boat?"

Sam's granddad held his mug; he took a sip of his tea, then put the mug down on the table.

"That's an old tale, from long ago," he said.

We couldn't think why we hadn't asked him before.

"What happened?" Anna asked.

"I've heard a few versions," he said. "It's supposed to have happened when I was very young, before I ever went to school. I'm not even sure that it's true."

We drank our tea and ate the sweet cake with the sharp-tasting cheese. We listened intently.

"It was a summer's evening," he said. "They were looking for a boy from the village."

"He'd gone missing?" Sam questioned.

The Five Things

"They say he'd gone off to hide," said Sam's granddad. "They looked high and low. The whole village became involved. Many hours later a fisherman was coming in with his catch. He said that as he came into the harbor, he thought he caught sight of a small boat out on the water in the bay. He couldn't be sure. It seemed odd at that time of the evening, and it was a long way out. Perhaps it had come loose from its mooring."

We were gripped.

"The people of the village went down to the shore with lanterns because by then it had become dark. They walked along the beach together, a large group of them, and then someone shouted, 'I see something!' Sure enough, when they looked, they could make out a boat, a rowing boat. It was rocking up and down far out to sea. Some of the men took off their jackets. They began to wade in. They swam toward the boat. Fortunately, it was a clement night; it was quite a swim. Those still onshore watched. They saw the men get slowly closer. The first man reached the vessel, put his hands over the side, and lifted himself up to look into it. He began to wave and shout. 'He's here, the boy is here!' They brought the boat in with the boy lying down inside."

"Who was it?" I asked.

"I don't know," said Sam's granddad. "A local boy. Now, drink up that tea, and let's go and have a look at those toadstools."

We'd solved another of The Five Things. We'd found out about the other missing boy, but it wasn't going to help much with our investigation; it was too long ago and there was one big difference. Later, Sam talked to his granddad again, and he found out that the boy in the boat was found alive. The boy had lost his oars or discarded them. He was exhausted, but he was rescued. He was very much alive.

****

It was Wednesday morning. Dad and I arrived at Sam's in the car, and Sam's granddad helped us load our toadstools onto the back seat. We drove to the school entrance and Dad gave us a hand to bring the sculptures into the classroom. We'd kept them a secret until Tuesday when Dad had said we'd better warn Miss Charlton we were bringing them in and ask her where we should display them. She'd put one of the gym mats on the floor in the corner near her desk, and we arranged them carefully on top. The mat was green—so it was perfect.

That morning, on Miss Charlton's desk, in the classroom now decorated with Christmas paper chains, there was a trophy. It was to be presented to the winners. The names of the winners would be engraved onto it, and they would retain the title for the year. The projects were to become an annual event.

Mrs. Marshall, the head teacher, came into the classroom. She was going to watch the presentations and help with the judging. The presentations began. We were fourth up. I felt very nervous and found it hard to watch the ones that went on before. It was soon our turn. We went to the front and stood beside our sculptures. To start with, I recited the poem about the toadstool and the elf, then Sam took over.

"Imagine this mat is the mossy forest floor and you are walking through the trees amongst the toadstools. What is the difference between a toadstool and a mushroom?"

He spoke for a time before I took over with my information about mushrooms that might be found locally and delicious dishes that could be made from them. Sam then took us to the land of legend and the fairy ring. I looked around the class and could see that everyone was absorbed. We tied everything up with our most amazing fact: that as long as there'd been people on the earth, there'd been fungi, and that types of fungus, such as mushrooms or toadstools, had provided food for all of our ancestors, not to mention the wildlife.

"Next time you're at home enjoying your fried breakfast and you look down at those little mushrooms on your plate, we hope you will fully appreciate how truly amazing they are," we concluded.

Everybody clapped. I sneaked a look at Old Marshmallow. She was also clapping, and she was smiling.

****

Late on Thursday morning, the children of Cherlton Primary gathered in the school hall along with some of the parents for the annual nativity play. It was put on by Class 2. It was entertaining, if short. At the end, as usual, a lot of fuss was made over those who'd taken part. There'd be a write-up in the local paper along with a photo.

Afterward, the parents who'd come for the play were invited to look at Class 3's projects. We'd all left our scrapbooks on top of our desks. Class 2 and Class 1 would be brought in during the afternoon to look at them, and we would go to their classrooms to see the pictures they'd painted during the term. The best pictures were now exhibited on the classroom walls.

Sam and I spent lunchtime in agony at the playground, waiting for the trophy to be awarded. We knew there were at least two other projects that were very good. Adam's was one of those. His partner had been James Low. Their subject matter was farm machinery, and their work was very detailed. Some of the drawings were good, too. We thought our presentation had been better, but they'd done well. They'd had a question and answer session at the end, and we wished we'd thought of that.

In the early afternoon, the school gathered in the hall for the final time that term. There were some announcements, we sang some carols, the teachers each read a Christmas related story or, in Miss Charlton's case, a poem. Then the moment arrived, and Mrs. Marshall walked to a table at the side of the hall where the trophy had been placed along with the other prizes. There were awards for each year. She began with Class 1. Three small, wrapped items were presented for good work. Everyone clapped. Then Class 2, again she presented three small items. There was more applause.

"Now," Mrs. Marshall began, "Class 3's projects have been judged. The standard is extremely high. All of the pupils in Class 3 have worked extraordinarily hard, and it has been very difficult for us to choose the winners." The time came. "In third place, we have Charlotte and Linda with their excellent project on moths. Well done, Charlotte and Linda."

Charlotte and Linda set off up to the table looking slightly embarrassed. Everyone was clapping again. They were given two small, wrapped prizes. I heard Sam take a deep breath.

"Second prize," said Mrs. Marshall, once the

clapping had subsided, "goes to…" There seemed to be a very long pause. "Wendy and Sam for their imaginative look at fungi. Well done!"

Sam led the way and I followed. I was disappointed, and I don't think I was smiling as Marshmallow shook my hand and awarded me a large oblong shape with a smaller oblong shape on the top. Sam was given the same, and we went back with them to our places. Adam and James were on their way up to receive the trophy. My name wasn't going to be carved onto it.

Later, in the classroom, we opened the items. I had a jigsaw of a country scene and Sam had a jigsaw of a steam train. We both had a set of colored pencils. Charlotte and Linda just had the pencils.

We went over to Adam's desk, and he handed me the trophy. "You're sure to win it next year," he said.

"What's in the envelope?" Sam asked.

Along with the trophy, Adam and James had each been given an envelope. Adam had already opened his. He passed it to Sam. I saw a smile come to Sam's face as he realized what it was. He turned it round and showed it to me. Of course, a book token!

Friday would be the last day of term. We wouldn't have to wear our uniforms, and we were allowed to bring games to play in the classroom. We would all bring Christmas cards to give out to each other, and at the end of the day, Dad was coming to pick us up—Sam, me, and the three award-winning toadstools.

****

On the last Saturday before Christmas, we were to have a meeting about The Five Things, and Sam had said to me that he thought it might be the last. I decided that was probably a good thing. What else could we discover? We'd found out about the person in the field and the other missing boy.

We all wanted to go to the wood for the last meeting. It seemed right. I'd decided to tell them about the thoughts I kept having about Bridges because I wanted to talk to someone about it, but I didn't want to tell Mum or Dad or Philip.

We wore our toughest shoes as we trudged up the side path and across the upper field. We walked to the fallen tree and sat on the trunk. The sun was low in the sky; it shone almost white, just as in my imagined scene.

"I want to tell you about this thought I keep having," I said. "About Bridges."

I told them what I was seeing before I went to sleep. I finished by telling them that Bridges had a gun, but that the gun wasn't loaded.

"It's a message," said Anna. "It means he didn't do anything wrong. He had a gun because he's a farmer. He laid traps because he's a farmer. The birds, the rabbit—they're all to do with him being a farmer. But he didn't really do anything wrong."

It made me feel better, which was what she'd intended.

Sam didn't join in. He waited until we'd finished and then he said, "I have something to tell you both as well." His voice was uneasy.

I felt tense again, thinking there was another twist, some more information about Adam in the field or the boy in the boat, or some new thing altogether.

"This has to be the last meeting, and I suppose it's a good way to finish. I will miss you both, and I'll never stop thinking about Tommy and Naomi."

Anna and I stayed quiet. We didn't understand what he meant.

"I'm moving to France," he said.

Chapter 22

1974

We carried on growing up. Our worlds moved on. Tommy's story became entwined in our lives; it remained with us, though rarely spoken of, something we'd been a part of and would always share.

It was the start of the summer holidays, and I was in my room checking out my wardrobe. So much happens at the beginning of the holidays, and I was working out what I might wear to the various upcoming functions. To begin with, there was the disco on Thursday evenings, then there'd be the village fete where it was always good to look presentable. There was the Taylors' party too, of course, though for that I would have to be in fancy dress. As usual, I had no idea what to go as.

"Laura's on the phone!" Mum shouted up to me from the hallway.

I rushed down to take the call. Laura asked if I could come round. Gail was to be there late morning and we could all have lunch at hers. I arranged to meet them, grabbed the bus timetable from the side table in the hall, and returned to my room to get ready.

Not long after, I stood waiting for the local bus that wound along the coast road joining up the villages and towns. My journey was less than five miles, but it could take the best part of half an hour by the time the bus had weaved in and out of the little streets and loaded up all the passengers. The service was especially busy in the summer and often ran late.

I could tell that most people on the bus were headed for the market in Porton. They were laden with baskets ready to buy weekly supplies of fruit and vegetables. We passed by the school. It was good to think I wouldn't need that stop for six whole weeks. My journey would take me on four more stops, to Binton.

I stepped down from the platform and walked down the hill until I came to Laura's house. Her Mum ran a cafe in the small town and the family lived on the premises. The cafe was popular and most of the outside tables were taken. I could see that there were a good few customers inside too. I waved to Sandra, who was waitressing, and went round to the side door. Laura came to greet me. Gail had already arrived, and we decided to have a walk before having something to eat. We walked on downhill to the seafront.

"Who's the DJ on Thursday?" Gail asked. "Is it Gary?"

"I think so," I said. The holiday camp where the disco was held was out on the cliff top, close to Cherlton. Because I lived nearest, I was supposed to know all the details.

"He's really good looking," Gail said.

"What time should we get there?" asked Laura.

"I'd say eight o'clock would be a good time," I suggested. "It'll be underway by then."

The camp was close enough for me to be able to walk, but Gail's Mum was going to give Gail and Laura a lift.

"We can wait for each other at the reception," I said.

"I hope Baz will be there," said Laura.

"I'm just going to find a seat and look at Gary all evening," Gail said.

****

Mum and Maggie were in the kitchen drinking tea.

"Do you think I'll be able to wear my new dress on Thursday?" I asked Mum. She was making a summer dress for me. It would be perfect for the disco if it was ready in time.

"I'll do my best," she said. "What are you going to wear to the Taylors'?"

"I've no idea. What's Philip wearing?"

Philip was home from university. He lived in halls in term time, but he'd been back for a few weeks now, for the summer break. He was currently on the golf course.

"He said he might go as a comic book character. I can't remember which one."

"I think I'll go as a Greek goddess, or a Roman goddess. Philip can tell me what they wore."

Philip was studying an honors course, Classical Archaeology and Ancient History.

"I do admire confidence in a young lady." Maggie laughed. Then she got thinking and told me she had a pair of strappy sandals she'd brought home from a holiday in Crete. "They'd be perfect for a goddess," she said. "They're flat soled and you wrap the laces round and round your legs. They'd look fabulous on you."

Philip came in looking hot. He greeted Maggie and went to the sink to pour himself a large glass of water.

"Philip, what would a Roman goddess wear?" Mum asked.

"Or a Greek goddess," I said. "I'm not fussy."

"It's for the do at the Taylors'," Maggie added.

Philip drank most of the water and refilled the glass. "Probably get away with wearing a sheet and a headband," he said.

"That's easy, then," said Mum. "I can knock up a white toga-type garment, and we'll find some material for a headband and a sash."

I was quite looking forward to becoming a goddess for an evening. The phone rang. Philip went to answer.

"Gail, for you!" he shouted.

****

On Thursday morning, Mum woke me. She'd come to my room with my new summer dress. She'd stayed up late to finish it.

"Thank you, Mum, so much," I said. I was delighted.

"Put it on when you get up, and I'll check it over one last time." She hung it on the handle of the cupboard and went to start preparing breakfast.

****

It was seven thirty when I set off from the house wearing my dress and carrying my small shoulder bag and my pale-yellow cardigan. I didn't want to be the first to arrive, but I didn't want to be late either, so I set off reasonably early, planning to walk relatively slowly. I walked to the main road and along until I came to the lane that led to the path along the cliff top. At the end of the lane, the holiday camp came into sight. There were chalets and caravans, which the holidaymakers would rent for a week or a two-week stay. It was popular. This was the type of holiday people liked now. The village hotel had closed down a few summers back.

The camp had a restaurant, a games room, a shop, and a few other facilities such as a laundry. Then there was the big building housing the hall and bar. That was where the disco would be held. The reception area was beside the entrance to the hall. There were a few outdoor tables and chairs close by. It was a good place to arrange to meet.

As I strolled along the cliff top path, I could already hear the music. This was the first disco of the summer. There would be one every week during the holidays. Some of our friends had summer jobs at the camp, and as I arrived, I saw Robbo and Max and they came to say hello.

"Bloody nice dress!" said Robbo.

"Thank you. It's new. Mum finished it just in time for tonight. Are you coming to the disco later?"

"I have some cleaning work to get done, worse luck, and I have to help move the deck chairs back inside. I'll come after, if I get finished in time."

"Same here," said Max.

I left them. I recognized the small, dark green car coming through the gates at the main entrance. I started walking over to the reception. The car pulled up. Gail and Laura emerged from the back seat and Gail's mum leaned out to greet me.

"Hello, Wendy," she said. "Pick you all up at eleven." With a wave, she began to turn the car and set off back toward the gates.

Gail was wearing a skirt and blouse, and Laura was in her wide trousers with a smart, short-sleeved top. They both looked so grown up, and very beautiful. I told them this and they enthused over my dress in return. The locals were welcome at the camp, and there was no charge to get in for the disco. We went inside and each bought a soft drink at the bar. We found a seat facing the stage, with a good view of Gary the DJ, and made ourselves comfortable.

The disco always seemed a little strange to begin with, when it was still light outside, but the atmosphere soon took over. There were already a few people dancing out on the floor.

By the time we'd bought our second drink, the hall was nearly full. We danced to "Rock Your Baby" and "When Will I See You Again." Gail kept an eye on Gary, and Laura looked out for Baz.

"When's your boyfriend coming over?" Gail asked.

"He's not my boyfriend!" I said.

Gail and Laura often teased me about Sam. They reminded me that the last time he'd visited, I seemed to spend all my time with him and forget about them altogether. I didn't get to see him that often. He only ever came back on his school holidays, and he'd not been able to get over at Easter. I hadn't seen him in months.

"He is coming, though?" Laura checked.

"Yeah, supposed to be. In a week or so," I said.

"Can we all go out together when he's here?" asked Gail. "Remember, we still haven't actually met him. We didn't set eyes on him last time."

"Once he's here, I'll arrange something. He'll want to spend time with his granddad too, so I'll need to find out what he's doing."

I caught sight of Mo Taylor, and he came to talk to me. He asked what I was going to wear to the party, but

I said I hadn't decided. He said he couldn't wait for everyone to see his costume.

"Baz just came in," Gail told us. She kept her hand over her mouth in case anyone overheard, although it would be almost impossible given how loud Gary was playing the records.

By the end of the evening, Baz and his brother Neil, Robbo, and Max had joined us at our table. Robbo had managed to get us all a cola on the house, and Max had danced with Gail. He was the only one of the four males who could be persuaded onto the dance floor.

Chapter 23

I sometimes thought Mum could get more excited about the Taylors' parties than Philip and I. We were in the kitchen. Philip was consulting with Mum on how to perfect his comic book character outfit. He was wearing the costume: a huge baggy sweater, a pair of shorts, and some old leather boots. Mum suggested his hair needed fixing and that he could do with some makeup. She had some very creative ideas, some of which Philip thought went a little too far.

"I don't want to look crazy!"

"Oh, is there someone you want to impress?" she asked. "Look at the pictures. He looks pretty disheveled!"

"I know, but I'll have to face people again the next day, don't forget."

They discussed options while Mum continued to ruffle his hair, attempting to perfect a messy but not overly messy style.

The phone rang and it was Anna. I'd not spoken to her for a while, so I knew we would be having a long conversation. I took my drink with me. Anna had also broken up from school, and her parents were taking her and Mal away to Spain, to the mountains, for a walking holiday. They would be camping most of the time and spending a few nights staying at hostels. It was the sort of thing Anna would love. Her dad was offered a really good teaching job a few years back. That meant the family home was now a couple of hours drive from us, and although we kept in touch with each other, we didn't meet that often. I asked if she could come to visit when she was back from the holiday, and she said she'd love to and that I should also go to stay with her during the summer. She asked after Sam and I told her he would be coming to the village, but I wasn't quite sure when. I told her I was going to the Taylors' dressed as a goddess, and she insisted I send her a photo of me wearing my outfit.

"Anna says hello," I told Mum and Philip, back in the kitchen.

"She took a while to say it," said Philip.

"She's invited me to stay with her when she gets back from holidays," I told them.

"I'll look forward to that," said Philip. "I could do with some peace and quiet."

I pinched him and then gave him the additional news. "She's going to come here as well. So you can have double noise and irritation as punishment."

"What am I being punished for?" he protested.

"Being so rude!" I said. "Mum, Anna can stay for a couple of nights, can't she?"

"Yes, of course," Mum said, smiling at Philip.

"I can't win with you two," he said.

Dad arrived home and started to laugh at Philip, who'd almost forgotten he was still dressed as the comic book character.

"It suits you," Dad told him.

"Don't you start, Dad. I'm getting enough grief from these two."

Dad said we were going to make a right pair, a

The Five Things

scruffy urchin, and a goddess dressed in a sheet.
****

The day of the party came, and I tried on my outfit in the morning. Mum had made a toga from white cotton, and we'd found some gold material in her cupboard and made a sash and a headband. I'd borrowed bangles from everyone I could think of, and Maggie'd lent me her sandals. She was right about them; they were perfect. I found my old bracelet with the Roman coin charms and put that on too. I still wasn't sure if I was Roman or Greek, but hopefully, no one would ask. I looked at myself in the full-length mirror and was satisfied.

I went downstairs, now in my jeans, and had breakfast with Philip. He asked if I wanted to walk over to the Taylors' house with him in the evening so that we wouldn't feel so daft in our strange clothing. "Safety in numbers," he said. We agreed on a time before Philip went off to spend another day on the golf course.

I had no plans. Mum was gardening and Dad was at work, so I went to the lounge and played records. Then I went upstairs and read magazines. Later, I went to find Mum who was in the garden, busy sowing lettuce. She always had a list of garden jobs she wanted to get done, and she never tired of doing them. She probably had a little more time for herself when Philip was away, but I knew she was happier when he was home, and she had to cram everything in. We had lunch together: some homegrown new potatoes and salad vegetables. We ate them with some cheese.

Mum made Philip up in the early evening, tousling his hair and making him look generally grubby by adding dirty marks to his face and clothes. She did me next, applying a large amount of dark eye makeup. We arrived at the party soon after eight. Philip had brought flowers for Mrs. Taylor. We found her at the front door, and he presented them to her. She ushered us in. As was usual at the Taylors' parties, the house was very dark. We made for the garden to begin with. A lot of effort had gone into all the outfits. Mo was dressed as a city gent in a bowler hat. He came over to greet us with his furled umbrella and his briefcase.

"You look glamorous," he told me, from beneath his false mustache.

"Oh thanks," I said, "...or did you mean Philip?"

He laughed. "Come and get something to drink," he suggested.

We followed him into the house. The kitchen was full of party food, but we headed for the huge bowl of fruit punch. Mo ladled out a glassful for each of us.

"There's no alcohol in it, I'm afraid," he said. "But Philip, you're old enough to drink beer. Jonathan is allowed to hand out a few bottles to the adults amongst us."

I never knew many of the guests at the Taylors' parties. I continued to be one of the youngest invited, but they asked me every year and I always felt welcome. I looked around. I'd known Robbo was coming, and I spotted him across the lawn. He was with Peter Clay and Max, and I could see Judy and Susan as well. Susan came over.

"You look wonderful," she told me.

"I think you do, too," I said.

I wasn't sure what she'd come as, but she looked like a film star. She informed me she was dressed as a Twenties flapper. She asked if I'd like to go the room with the music, and I went with her. The room had been decorated with giant posters of pop stars, and there were large floor cushions but no other furniture. We found Judy and danced to "Metal Guru."

After more punch, we returned to the garden and I went over to talk to Robbo. He'd come as a French onion man. It reminded me to tell him about Sam.

"Sam's coming over, Robbo."

"Bloody good news. When?"

"I'm not sure exactly. You should see him, though. I hope he'll be able to come to the disco." We found some seats at a table and sat down, and for a while, we costume spotted. "Can Max actually play that guitar?" I asked. Max was across the lawn, strumming quite tunefully.

"Yeah. He's good. Have you never heard him?" He'd come as a pop singer.

Mr. and Mrs. Taylor circulated toward us. They offered us food from large plates. I took a *vol au vent* and Robbo selected a deviled egg. Mo came and sat with us. He identified some of the other guests for us, but there were a few that even he didn't know.

We went back to the music room, which was busier now, and sat down on the cushions. We watched some of the older guests dancing. Some were really good, like dancers we'd seen on the pop programs on TV. There was also some kissing going on.

Toward the end of the evening, I went to look for Philip. He was sitting at a table with Jonathan Taylor and a few others. They were drinking glasses of beer.

We went home very late, and I couldn't help wondering if Philip might be just a little bit drunk.

****

A couple of days later, I was on the phone to Gail, telling her about the party, but although she said she wanted to hear about it, she was really only interested in who was there.

"Robbo was there," I said. "He was dressed as a French onion man. Mo Taylor was dressed as a city gent."

"I don't think I know anybody called Taylor," she said.

"Do you know Susan Jones and Judy Ball? They hang about with Robbo at school."

"I'm not sure."

"Well, they were there. I spent some time dancing with them. One room in the house was just for playing records and dancing."

"I wish I'd been invited to a big party. I never get invited anywhere," she said.

"Anyway, are we meeting up? What shall we do?" I said.

Gail wanted to go to Porton and look in the shops. She'd already spoken to Laura, but she was waitressing at the cafe until after lunch. We decided we should meet in Porton and then go and find Laura when she finished.

"Let's bring our bathing suits, then we can go to the beach later," I suggested.

"Yes, okay," Gail agreed. "I'll bring the coconut oil."

Gail and Laura weren't that keen on swimming but they both liked sunbathing. We could go to the beach in Binton in the afternoon.

There were some larger shops in the more modern part of the town but parts of Porton were older and

The Five Things

more characterful, with narrow streets and passageways. In the old part, there were little shops that sold all kinds of wares: clothing and jewelry, books and stationery, items for the home. There were gift shops and sweet shops. There was a good hairdressing salon. The older streets were beguiling; some of them were cobbled. The passageways were winding, and it could be hard to find your way around unless you knew the town well.

We met at eleven thirty at the bus station and pottered around the shops. Gail was already looking forward to the next disco at the holiday camp, and I think she had that in mind when she tried on a new skirt in one of the more fashionable boutiques.

"You know, that's quite expensive," I pointed out.

"I know. But I still have some birthday money left, and I'd rather buy something a bit different."

"Well, you look fantastic in it."

"It'll go with the top my sister bought. I hope she'll let me borrow it!"

There was a record I wanted, so we walked over to the store on the main high street. It was out of stock but I ordered it.

"I've never heard of it," said Gail. "Is it one of those hippy songs you like?"

"I don't! It is sort of folky, I suppose."

"I just love my soul music now." She sang me a medley.

"Soul is good to dance to," I said.

We went to the chemist's and looked at the makeup. Gail bought a new mascara, and I bought a blue eye shadow. We sat on the green for a few minutes, then decided to go for a cup of tea at The

Lounge cafe. That meant going back to the old area.

"Don't tell Laura," said Gail. "She'll say we could have had a free cup at her place. She wouldn't like the thought of us going somewhere else."

"We could always force another one down at Laura's," I said.

We sat in the tiny cafe. People from all over the area came to Porton and there was always a businesslike buzz. The atmosphere was vibrant. Even in the cafe, people had a sense of urgency, whether they were taking a break from work, or like us, from a busy shopping schedule. We finished our tea and returned to the station, stopping to look in a few more shops on the way. We waited for the next bus to Binton.

We were soon at Laura's cafe, and we did indeed sit and have another cup of tea while she finished off.

"We've brought our bathing suits," I told her when she eventually joined us, looking in dire need of a plunge in the sea.

"Oh great! Shall we change upstairs?" she said. "Have you eaten anything?"

"No," said Gail. "Not a thing since breakfast."

"I'll get us some rolls and we can take them with us. We can make a cold drink and bring it in a flask."

So we put our suits on under our summer dresses and took the food and the flask down to the beach. Binton's beach was very pretty and traditional. It attracted hordes of holidaymakers. We walked along the front past the cafes, bars, and ice cream kiosks, beyond the striped beach huts, and on until we found a quiet section. We spread out our towels and lay down on them.

"Why did they invent school?" said Gail. "I could

do this every day."

"Are you two coming in with me?" I asked.

"Not yet," said Gail. "Not until I'm baked."

"I will," said Laura. "I feel as if I've been in an oven all morning."

We ran into the water and got under straight away. It felt icy, but we soon became used to it. We swam a little and then Gail joined us, after all.

When we were back lying on our towels, I told them more about the party, and we talked about the previous week's disco and the coming week's disco. It looked as though we were in for a good summer.

Chapter 24

"Sam! I can't wait to see you. When can we meet up?"

Sam was on the phone. He'd arrived at his granddad's. He would spend the morning at the cottage but could call up to see me in the afternoon.

"I'll be at home," I said. "Come over whenever you're ready."

I was looking forward to seeing him so much I couldn't settle into doing anything else, and when Laura phoned, she picked up on the fact that Sam was the only thing on my mind.

"I'm not even going to ask if I'll see you today," she said, "or tomorrow come to that."

"I'm hoping we can all meet up," I said.

"How long is he here for? Do you think he'll want to come to the disco on Thursday?"

"I don't know, but I'll ask him," I said.

****

It was just before three when I opened the door to find a taller, more tanned version of the Sam I remembered. He wore a smart pair of olive-green shorts, a white short-sleeved shirt, and a pair of deck shoes. We gave each other a hug, and I took him to the kitchen to chat with Mum before leading him into the garden where we sat on the reclining chairs on the lawn. For a few minutes, we didn't really know what to

The Five Things

say, we just kept looking at each other and dissolving into laughter.

"It's hard to believe I'm finally here...sitting in the garden with you," said Sam.

"You look different," I said.

"So do you." He laughed.

"Do I? How?"

"Taller, slimmer, more girly."

"Really?" I said. "More girly?" That surprised me.

"Yeah," he confirmed, and then we laughed again.

Neither of us knew where to start, but during the next couple of hours, we got through a lot of catching up, our conversation darting from one subject to another. Sam was going to stay for two weeks. His mum wasn't coming over. She and Marcel were running a little restaurant now, and they couldn't spare the time to take a holiday. Sam had traveled to England with a friend of Marcel's who was coming to work in a hotel in the city for the summer. I asked after Sam's granddad; I'd hardly seen anything of him. He was well, Sam told me. Of course, there were no longer boats for hire on the beach, but he still had his lobster pots, and he did some work painting and repairing boats for people. He'd sort of retired but kept busy with things like that.

Sam lived on the west coast in a small harbor town. He always said it was similar to Cherlton in a way. He told me snippets about his life there and his French friends. I told him things about school and about Laura and Gail and what we'd been getting up to. I filled him in about Anna being away on holiday and about how I still saw Robbo fairly often.

"Laura and Gail are dying to meet you," I said.

"I'm sure I'm going to like them…and I'm looking forward to speaking English for a few days. I almost forget my English sometimes."

"It sounds so glamorous, being able to speak French," I said.

"Not really. I'd be lonely otherwise!"

I missed Sam like crazy when he first went away, and I could tell he was having a tough time. He hadn't wanted to go. His granddad was the most important person in his life, and all of a sudden, he'd been wrenched from him and taken against his will to another place where he knew no one and couldn't even speak the language. He used to write to me, short letters in his immaculate handwriting, that tried to send a positive message. But I knew him, and I could tell he was struggling. It seemed to take him a long time to make new friends. I don't suppose he tried very hard at first. It must have been painful for Mr. Wells, too. His life had come to revolve around Sam. I'm sure it wasn't easy to let him go. I don't know the background. Perhaps it had been agreed from the start that once Sam's mum properly found her feet, she'd come back for him, and in the long term, even with all the upheaval and trial, it was probably the best thing for Sam.

Sam didn't want to spend much time away from his granddad on his first day back in Cherlton. I walked through the village with him so we could carry on talking. On the way, Sam spotted things that had changed since his last visit: there was a new shop, one of the huge oak trees had been taken down. We arrived at the beginning of Sam's lane, and I said I would leave him there; I'd come in to see his granddad the next

The Five Things

time. Sam was to call for me again the following afternoon. We'd go down to the bay and go swimming.

****

In the morning, I went through the chest of drawers and found an old pair of jeans. I borrowed Mum's dressmaking scissors and a tape measure and cut the legs off them. I selected a fuchsia-pink-colored T-shirt, then sorted out my pumps and picked my favorite pair. I dressed and had a look in the mirror. I didn't mind looking girly, but I still preferred my shorts and T-shirt look for the beach.

I went downstairs and found Philip. He was reading and watching television at the same time. He asked me if I wanted to take him on at putting and we went outside and had a contest. He'd created a new course on the lawn and Dad held the current record. It wasn't that easy. There were eight holes and Dad had done the course in twelve shots.

Philip said he'd like to see Sam at some point. He was meeting Jonathan later and said they might come to find us. Jonathan now had a car. Like Philip, he was home from university for the summer. He had a holiday job delivering groceries for one of the local shops but he was off that afternoon. He was due to call for Philip, and they were going for a drive.

When Sam arrived, he was on a bike. He'd bumped into Adam Smart and Adam had lent it to him. I went to the shed and found mine. The tires needed pumping, but it was soon up and running, and Sam and I were on our way to the beach.

"This is just like when we were kids!" I yelled over my shoulder as we sped down the hill.

"Sure is," Sam shouted back. He was standing on

the pedals, freewheeling, with a big smile on his face.

We pushed the bikes along the sea wall, deciding on the ideal place to sit. It was a warm day, with a light breeze. There was a scatter of holidaymakers, but since the hotel closed, the numbers had dwindled. It was easy to find a good spot. We left the bikes on the wall and went down the steps, kicked off our shoes, and walked across the sand to the water.

"You'd miss the boats, wouldn't you?" said Sam.

"Yeah. The beach has changed a lot," I said.

The row of huts was still there, but few were being used, and they looked less well maintained.

"I have a dingy in France now," Sam told me. "A sailing dingy. I have a friend who has one too...Luc. We sail together all the time. I love it."

"You'll have to teach me one day," I said.

"I will...when you come over to visit."

"Do you still go to the jazz? Is that with Sofiane?"

"Yep. It's his dad who plays. We go and watch him on a Friday or a Saturday evening usually. He played at a street festival last weekend."

We changed and went into the sea. Sam had become a strong swimmer and swam out into the bay. I swam after him and we stayed out in the deeper water, talking. Sam suddenly ducked beneath the surface. He hadn't forgotten the games we used to play. He came up beside me and tried to push me under. I fought back.

"Stop, Sam! You're gonna drown me! Stop!"

"I'll have to tell everyone you're no fun anymore!"

I found a lump of seaweed floating beside me and slung it at him. It hit him right in the face.

"That's done it!" he shouted, and he made a lunge toward me.

I set off back to the shore, swimming as fast as I could. He followed, trying to grab my ankles. I reached the point where I could stand and tried to wade quickly through the shallow water to the sand. I made it and stood panting, hands on knees.

"You're like an eel these days," Sam said, arriving just after me. "It's a compliment!" he added after seeing my face.

"I've been called nicer things!"

The tide was on the way in, and we had to gather our clothes and move them, or everything would have been soaked.

Philip, Jonathan, and Mike appeared on the steps and came to join us. Sam shook hands with them, and we sat and chatted for a while. Philip tried out some of his French and Sam assured him he was very good.

"What happens in France?" Jonathan asked Sam. "Is it bad like here? We had the three-day week thing, and there were power cuts all the time. The election's made everything worse."

"There have been strikes," Sam said. "Some of my friends' parents were on strike. Not Mum and Marcel, of course. Those two never stop working!"

"Don't people go to work really early in the morning?" said Philip. "When I was there, they seemed to…and by lunchtime, they were all in the cafes drinking cognac!"

"Some do. School starts earlier."

"What about the World Cup?" said Mike. "Who did you support?"

"France weren't in it," said Sam.

"England neither," Mike confirmed.

Jonathan threw himself into the sea. Later, the

three of them left us. They were driving over to Binton to meet up with some other friends. We lay on our towels and soaked up the sun.

****

"Wendy, Gail's on the phone!" Mum called up to me.

I came downstairs to speak to her.

"Are you going to the disco tonight? We've heard nothing from you," she said.

"I'm sorry," I said. "I've been spending time with Sam, but I was going to call you. He wants to come."

"Brilliant! We're doing the same as usual. Mum's dropping Laura and me off at eight, so shall we see you up there?"

"Yeah, that's perfect. We'll meet you at the reception."

I wasn't sure what to wear. I had a long look in the wardrobe, even though I knew everything that was in there. Eventually, I picked the pastel blue skirt and a mauve colored top with short sleeves. I picked out the white canvas shoes that were quite smart. I had a little white shoulder bag that would match them, and I would wear my Roman coins bracelet. I'd forgotten about the bracelet before taking it out for the Taylors' party; I was pleased to rediscover it. I decided the outfit would be okay but that I might have to go on another shopping trip to Porton before long, if our social life was to remain this busy. I went to talk to Mum.

"Mum, can I get some more clothes?"

"What about your new dress?"

"I absolutely love the dress, honestly, but I wore it to the disco last week. I can't wear it again."

"You have lots of things in your wardrobe," she

told me.

"I'm going to wear my blue skirt this evening, but it would be nice to have another skirt for the summer...and perhaps another top."

"We'll have to see."

"Thanks, Mum," I said. *We'll have to see* generally meant I'd get my own way if I persisted. I'd have another discussion with her later.

I phoned Sam and told him we were meeting the others at eight. He was going fishing with his granddad in the afternoon. I suggested he should call for me at seven thirty. Afterward, I went to find Philip to check what stories he had to tell me after his evening out in Binton.

****

Sam was at the door. He was wearing white trousers, a blue and white check shirt, and smart—obviously French—shoes, not the sort the local boys were likely to be wearing. He said hello to Dad, and they had a chat about sailing. We set off for the disco. Sam hadn't been to the holiday camp before. When he lived in Cherlton everything went on at the hotel; we couldn't remember much happening up at the camp back then. We took the route along the cliff path, the sea still glistening below us in the evening sun. We arrived at the reception area before Gail and Laura, sat on the outdoor seats, and waited. Then we heard a familiar shout.

"Oi!" It was Robbo. He came toward us with a wide smile. Sam stood up.

"Bloody hell, look at you!" said Robbo. He gave Sam a huge hug. "You're so much taller. You're as tall as me, mate!"

"You're looking good, Robbo," Sam said, "and you've changed a little too!"

"Yeah, and I've nearly finished school. One more year. I can't bloody wait!"

I left the two of them to chat while I met Gail and Laura. The green car was coming through the gates at the entrance. It arrived beside me and the girls scrambled out, Gail in her new skirt and Laura in a lemon-colored summer dress. I greeted Gail's mum, and we turned to walk toward the hall.

"Where is he?" Gail asked straight away. "Where's Sam?"

"He couldn't make it," I joked. For a moment they looked disappointed. "I'm kidding. He's the one over there, with Robbo."

We'd soon joined up and Sam was giving the girls a kiss on each cheek. Robbo excused himself; he said he'd find us later. We went into the hall. Dad had given me some money to buy drinks. We found a table, and I went to the bar to order them.

Laura and Gail had forgotten about Gary and Baz for a moment and were concentrating on Sam. They asked him a lot of questions: how long had he lived in France; was it better living there than living in England; did he go to discos in France; could he dance; had he eaten frogs legs? Sam tried to answer the questions accurately and asked Laura and Gail a few things too.

There was a temporary pause in the interrogation, and Gail began to drink her cola. She'd asked for a bottle of cola with a straw. Next, she wanted to dance. Laura went with her, and Sam and I were left at the table.

"You are doing well. It's not easy to survive being

cross-examined by my friends!"

"They're making me laugh. I really like them."

"They're good fun." I drank some of my ginger ale. "Do you recognize Max? Look, he's over there."

"No way! His hair's longer than Robbo's!" Sam went over to speak to him. Gail and Laura returned to the table.

"Sam's so nice," said Laura.

"And extremely handsome," said Gail. "Let me sit next to him, so I can make everyone jealous!"

The evening progressed. Everyone seemed to be having a good time. Gail wanted to find out about the charts in France. "Who's number one?" she asked.

"Oh wow, I'm not sure. A French song," said Sam. "I don't know if "Waterloo" ever made number one, but it's always on the radio."

"Yeah? Here too," said Gail. "Shall I ask Gary if he'll put it on?" She stood up, trying to work out the best way to get to the DJ through the crowded hall.

"Any excuse to go and speak to Gary," I said.

"So do you have to work in the restaurant sometimes?" Laura asked. "I work in the cafe in the holidays."

"Yeah. I get paid, though," said Sam.

"Me too…are you a waiter?"

"No. I work in the kitchen mostly—help with the food prep and stuff. I often go to the market with Mum or Marcel. They buy nearly everything from the local markets. Marcel says he can't wait for me to get my driving license."

"I can see you running that restaurant in a few years' time," I said.

"Then you can give us all a summer job!" said

Laura.

Gail's mum would soon arrive, but no one was ready to think about leaving. Gail and Max were dancing again, Laura was sampling Robbo's cider, and Sam and I were chatting away as if we'd never been apart.

Chapter 25

I called Anna the day she arrived home from her holiday. I asked if she could come to stay while Sam was in Cherlton. She was keen to come and said she'd check with her parents and call me back.

She called back five minutes later to say she could come on Sunday, if that was all right. She'd have to go home on Wednesday because she was going to a classical concert with Mal and her mum and dad in the evening. That all sounded fine and meant we'd have two whole days together, and three nights. Mum said we'd get the foldaway bed out and put it beside mine in my room. It wouldn't be any trouble, and it would be lovely to see Anna.

"How's she getting here?" Mum asked. "She might need a lift from the station."

"I'll find out," I said.

I phoned Sam with the news. "Anna's coming on Sunday; she's staying for three nights."

"That's great! I've said I'll help Granddad tomorrow, but he won't need me on Sunday. I can meet you both when she gets here."

"I'll check what time she's arriving and call you."

Sam started laughing. "Granddad's showing me his disco dancing," he said.

****

Anna's dad had agreed to drive Anna to Cherlton

on Sunday afternoon. She'd arrive in time for tea. Her dad wouldn't stay long. On Wednesday, my dad would take her to the station in Porton, and she'd catch the train back. Anna's mum would meet her at the other end.

Sam called me on Saturday evening. I was expecting him to be checking in about meeting up the following day, but there was something else.

"Something happened this morning. When can you come over?"

"What do you mean? What's happened?"

"I'll tell you when I see you."

"Sam! Why can't you tell me on the phone?"

"Well…" he went silent for a moment. I thought he was about to tell me, but then he said, "It's about The Five Things."

I couldn't believe what I was hearing. We'd not spoken about The Five Things for years. The Five Things were a thing of the past. I didn't expect them to come back into our lives. Even so, my mind had a Five Things type of response.

"Is it urgent? Anna will be here tomorrow afternoon. Shall we wait until she's with us?"

"What time is she arriving? It'll be no good if it's dark."

"We're not going to the fields, are we?"

"No, no. I'll tell you everything as soon as I see you. What time is she getting to you?"

"Late afternoon. I suppose we could be at yours by six."

"Right then," said Sam. "See you at six."

****

Anna and I spoke regularly on the phone and we

met up every few months; we were still very close. As we were walking over to the old part of the village, she was telling me about her holiday: how it was hard at first, but each day they found themselves hiking a longer and longer distance, and the views were amazing, and the food was so nice, really different, and so on and so on. Sam was waiting for us at the top of the lane. Anna was in mid-flow, animated, gesticulating, and then she set eyes on him and she stopped.

"Is that Sam? No!" She left me and ran to throw her arms around him. "I can't believe it's you!" she said.

"I can't believe it's you, either!" said Sam.

The two of them spent a few minutes getting used to each other, but in the way that close friends can, they'd soon progressed beyond any formality and were exchanging trivial conversation, completely at ease. We carried on along the lane.

"So," Anna said, "what's happened? What's all this about The Five Things?"

Sam pushed his fingers through his hair and began to tell us.

"It was yesterday morning…early. I woke up. I'm not sure what woke me. I opened the curtains and looked out across the river, and then toward the church. And who do you think I saw?" We stopped walking. He stood, waiting for suggestions.

"Who?" asked Anna.

"Who, Sam?" I said.

"You'll never guess," he admitted.

"So come on, tell us!" we pleaded.

"A certain old farmer."

"You don't mean Bridges?" said Anna.

"Bridges. And I could see he was carrying flowers. I pulled on some clothes and shoes and ran downstairs and out and down the lane. I could see him in the churchyard. I had to find out what he was up to."

"Did he see you?" I asked.

"No. Once I reached the church I walked slowly and went in quietly through the gate. I went round to the other side of the building. He was farther on, getting water from the tap. He had a white jug. He had no idea I was there."

"Did you stay there?"

"Yeah. I stayed and watched him. I kept my distance. I saw him walking over toward the far side of the churchyard. I didn't follow him."

"Is that it then?"

"No, there's more. I waited for quite a long time. I thought he must have gone out some other way, but then I heard footsteps and he was coming back along the path."

"Are you sure it was him?"

"Yes, and I have something to show you."

Anna and I couldn't wait to find out what Sam was going to reveal. All the catching up and the social arrangements we were planning to discuss would have to wait because we were having a meeting; we were having an important meeting about The Five Things.

The three of us set off purposefully. We reached the church. There'd been a service but the last few members of the congregation were heading home, and the door of the church had been closed. We walked along the path, past the water tap and on. We came to an area with a number of graves that we could tell were very old. They all faced the same way. Some were quite grown over. There were various headstones; a few were hard to read, the weather had all but worn away the carved lettering. Sam then drew our attention to one grave in particular.

"Look, you see those flowers there? There, in the white jug. Read the inscription on the gravestone."

Anna and I looked. The jug held a spray of delicate blue, yellow, and white flowers. There was a small carved headstone, and we could easily read what it said.

Isaac Bridges
Son of Edith and John
7 November 1912—10 August 1919
Jesus blesses the children
Mark 10.13

A lump came into my throat. I knelt down beside the little grave. Anna crouched down next to me, and Sam stood behind us.

"This child was only six years old," I said. All sorts of thoughts came into my head. How did he die? Was he Bridges' son? But what I said next was, "These are wildflowers, it must have taken a long time to gather them. They're beautiful."

"And yesterday was the tenth," said Sam.

We stayed for a minute or two, then Anna stood up.

"Come on," she said. "Let's go and sit by the river."

We didn't speak on the way to the river. Close friends don't always need to speak. We walked to the bridge and sat on the wall. We looked like friends: Sam in his dark blue shirt and olive shorts, Anna in red shorts and a white T-shirt, and me in my cutoff jeans and yellow top. We sat for a little while, thinking.

"So who was he?" Anna said, finally.

"He died in 1919," Sam said. "It was a long time ago."

"How old do you think Bridges is?" I asked.

"Older than Granddad, anyway," said Sam. "Granddad was sixty this year. He was born in 1914, the year the war broke out."

"Isaac must have been Bridges' brother," I said.

"He could have been a cousin," said Sam.

"If he was born in 1912," said Anna, "perhaps your granddad knew him?"

"But Granddad would have been so young, I'm not sure he'd even remember."

We fell silent again and watched the river flowing under the bridge.

Anna then had a thought. "Do you still have the notebook, Sam?"

"I wonder if it's still there? I used to keep it behind the drawer of the chest in my bedroom. The chest's still there."

We went to the house and up to Sam's room. The chest of drawers was in the corner, two small drawers over three large drawers. Sam pulled back the small drawer on the left. He pulled it right out and peered into the space where it had been. A smile came to his face and he reached in and dislodged the little notebook, which had been waiting there all this time. We went to the kitchen and sat around the table on the benches.

"Let's look at the questions again," said Anna.

Sam hadn't updated it.

The Five Things

Five things (and two solved):
The birds
The rabbit
Naomi said Tommy was taken, not missing or run away or got lost
Ball (now solved)
The person in the field (now solved)
Another missing boy

"We've solved the missing boy," I said.

Anna had already moved on. "Are you thinking what I'm thinking?" she said.

"What?" I asked.

"Isaac was the missing boy!"

For a moment, we were all excited by the thought, then Sam remembered something. "But Granddad said the missing boy was found alive," he said.

The catch of the door clicked, and Granddad was standing in front of us. There was quite a commotion as he set eyes on Anna and me; we couldn't have been more delighted to see each other. He soon had the kettle on and was producing fruitcake and chocolate biscuits from the pantry.

"Granddad," said Sam, "we have something to ask you."

"Go ahead," said Granddad.

"Who was Isaac Bridges?"

"Isaac Bridges, Isaac Bridges..." said Sam's granddad as if trying to tap into his memory. "I'm not sure I know," he said, eventually.

"He's something to do with Bridges, the old farmer," said Sam. "He's buried in the churchyard here."

"Well, it's not his father, and his father and mother would be buried together."

"Isaac died when he was six," I said. "We've seen the dates on his grave."

"Could he have been the boy in the boat?" asked Anna.

Sam's granddad was trying to take it all in. He didn't ask how we'd come to be analyzing graves in the churchyard.

"When did he die?" he asked.

"1919," I said.

Sam's granddad thought some more. "I think that could be around the date the boy was found in the boat...but I'm sure that boy was older. He'd been out rowing. They said he'd gone off to hide from something. I always had the impression he'd done something wrong, upset his parents or something like that. I always had the impression he was an older boy."

"Six is too young to row out to sea," said Sam.

His granddad poured the tea. Then he continued. "To die at six years old back then wasn't as unusual as it would be now, you know. Children sometimes died from things like the flu, back then. The boy may have been ill. What does it say on the gravestone?"

"It just says he was the son of Edith and John," I said.

"Well I never," said Sam's granddad. "That would make him Bridges' brother. Bridges' name is Joe, you know. Joseph. And he'd have been a brother to Isaac, I'm pretty sure."

We were intrigued. Later, we decided that we should sleep on our new findings and meet in the morning for another discussion.

The Five Things

****

"Did we get Bridges wrong?" Anna asked.

I didn't answer. I'd given her my bed and was lying on the fold-up one, which meant I might not be going to have the most comfortable of nights. We'd done nothing but talk about Isaac and Bridges the whole evening. I was pretty sure Anna had finally gone to sleep, so the question hung in the air in the dark, and carried on going around in my head.

We woke early and had breakfast with Mum and Philip. Dad had gone to work. Anna had to fill Philip in on Mal and how he was getting on, and we heard more about the holiday in Spain. We had a game of putting. Still, no one could beat Dad's record.

Later in the morning, we took my bike, Anna borrowed Philip's, and we cycled over to meet Sam. He brought us into the kitchen, and we sat around the table. He said he'd had a long conversation with his granddad after we'd left him. Sam couldn't work out why no one had ever talked about Isaac, why no one had ever really talked about Bridges. His granddad had said he needed to remember that times had changed. Nineteen nineteen was soon after the end of the First World War. Death wasn't the same then. There'd been a lot of loss, a lot of pain, and people probably dealt with things in a different way at that time. He'd always regarded Bridges as a solitary man and perhaps a sad man. Sam's granddad said he thought there had been loss in Bridges' family, but there'd been loss for many families.

"Do you think Bridges dislikes children because he lost a brother?" said Sam.

"Perhaps he doesn't dislike children," I said. "Anna

thinks we may have got the wrong idea about him."

"I'm not sure what I think," said Anna.

"I keep picturing the bouquet," I said. "He must have cared a lot to gather those flowers and bring them to the grave."

"So we think he's a good guy now?" said Sam.

"Well, not necessarily a good guy, but maybe not such a bad guy after all," I said.

Sam took out the notebook. "What about the birds? Wendy, you saw them. You said they were truly horrible, really frightening. Did a good guy do that to them?"

"I don't know," I said.

Sam's granddad came in. He'd been in the workshop.

"I was telling Wendy and Anna what you said about Bridges," Sam told him.

"The poor old fellow. I knew the family'd had bad luck. But in all the years, I swear, I've never heard anything about Isaac. I suppose it could be why the old man is the way he is."

"Granddad," said Sam, "did you ever hear of anyone hanging dead birds up for any reason?"

"Well, they hang fowl after shooting them, but you don't mean that?"

"No, I mean crows."

His granddad took his time before answering; he turned on the tap and poured himself a glass of water.

"I think perhaps they used to hang them to frighten other birds, to sort of do the job of a scarecrow...a long time ago." He looked at Sam. "Are we still talking about Bridges?"

"To scare birds? So they'd hang them where there

was a crop, or a vegetable patch?"

Sam's granddad left us again. He was in the middle of some painting work.

"It doesn't make sense to hang them in a wood," said Sam.

"We should go swimming," I said. "It will help us think."

It was a beautiful day and windy; the waves would be high. We cycled to the house. Philip was in the garden with Jonathan and Mike. They were putting, of course.

Philip announced us. "Look out, it's the terrifying trio."

"That's a bit mean," I said.

"The terrific trio?" suggested Jonathan, attempting a long, ambitious shot.

We joined them and watched the round, cheering them on, oohing and ahhing.

"Let's ask them about Bridges," Sam said.

They soon took a break. We were sitting on the outdoor seating, drinking homemade lemonade. It seemed a good moment.

"We have a question for you," I said to Philip and the others. "What do you know about Bridges?"

"Bridges?" said Philip. "The old farmer chap? I'm not sure I know anything much about him…nothing that you don't know already."

"How do you mean?" said Mike

"I just mean generally," I said.

"His past," said Sam.

Jonathan joined in. "Something happened to his family, a long time ago, I think."

"We found a grave," said Anna.

"A grave?" said Mike. "Where?"

"Oh, it was in the cemetery," Anna said, realizing Mike probably thought it was up in the fields.

"He had a brother who died really young," said Sam. "I saw Bridges leaving flowers for him, in the churchyard down near Granddad's house."

Philip and the others were quite interested. We exchanged a few stories. Everyone had played in the wood when they were younger; everyone had thought Bridges was an ogre and had heard all sorts of tales about him.

"What I really think," said Philip, "is he's just a recluse."

"That might be why. If he had a brother who died young. Perhaps he withdrew from the world," said Jonathan.

"His mum died young too, I think," said Mike. "I remember people saying it was just him and his father living on that old farm for years. When the father died, they thought he might do some work on the land, bring it up to date and things, but he just got worse."

"So you don't think he's an ogre?" I asked.

"No," Mike said. Philip and Jonathan shook their heads.

"Will you come to the beach with us?" I suggested.

"Why not?" said Jonathan, without consulting Philip and Mike. "I might be able to squeeze us all in the car!"

****

The next day flew by. We made a picnic and rode the bikes around the coast for a few miles to where there was a little bay we knew of, but that few people visited. It was hard to reach; you had to clamber down the cliff. There was a makeshift rope handrail, probably put there by a fisherman; even so, it wasn't that easy to get down to the shore.

We were the only ones. That was usually the case. The beach had no man-made additions. It wasn't much more than a strip of shingle that fell away sharply into the sea. The water was immediately deep. We swam, sunbathed, and ate our picnic. We took refuge under our towels or back in the sea when the sun became too much. We talked about discos, and France and Spain, and about our friendship and how strong it was. We didn't talk much about The Five Things. There wasn't a lot more to say.

Anna would soon be leaving again. I would go to stay with her in two weeks' time and by then Sam would be back in France. Sam said we must try to visit him the following summer. We should start working on our parents and see if we could manage to arrange it. Anna said the three of us could do anything if we set our minds to it.

****

Not long after Sam went back to France, I went to the wood. I went alone. It seemed I needed to go there to sort out my thoughts. I'd been thinking about The Five Things all over again and trying to work out if all the questions had been answered. The way I saw it was that Bridges had been hurt by the death of his brother. His parents had been hurt too. The family had pretty much given up on life. It led to his mum dying young. He put birds in trees and trapped rabbits because he was an old farmer who was stuck in the past and only knew the old ways.

Tommy had become bored the day his parents went

to the hospital. He didn't want to read or watch TV. He was full of energy and liked to be outdoors. He took his ball and went to play in the garden. He saw Adam and chatted to him. Adam seemed happy, and free, and independent. Later, Tommy went into the field, perhaps initially to retrieve the ball. Once in the field, he kicked the ball a few times. He ended up near the track, and being inquisitive, he stepped through the gap in the hedge. He heard something: perhaps the screech of an owl, perhaps the howl of a fox, and followed it. He heard the sound again, coming from the quarry. He put the ball down and went to look. He could have been looking up into the trees; he could have been peering down to the bottom of the quarry, obscured by the thick foliage; he may have tried to climb one of the trees for a better view. He lost his footing.

What was Bridges doing at the fireworks? Perhaps he wanted to be reminded of Isaac. Perhaps he wanted to see the children from the village enjoying themselves. Could he have yearned to be included but have been unable to communicate that to the rest of the village?

Then I remembered the strange thoughts that used to keep me awake at night. In my thoughts, Bridges had a gun but it wasn't loaded. Why did I have those thoughts? Was there something I understood about him deep inside my head, that he wasn't evil or mean, he was just old and a captive in a world he couldn't understand?

Chapter 26

2019

Every now and then, over the years, I grappled again with memories of Tommy. I wondered if the others still thought about him too.

I consider how this all came about. It began with a conversation.

"Sometimes I wish it'd been me who'd been made redundant," Roger said.

"You love your job," I pointed out.

"I could do with a change," he told me.

"I've never heard you say that before," I said. It was Sunday evening, and I could tell he was tired after a good weekend, tired in a way that was brought about by knowing you have to get up early the next day, dress correctly, travel on crowded transport, and slot into the working week you are so used to but love to hate. "I would happily go to work tomorrow," I said. "I don't enjoy being a free woman."

Roger picked up his mug and peered at the contents. He put it back on the low table in front of us. We were sitting on the sofa, in the front room with the big bay window. It was where we'd been sitting on and off for the past ten years. "What about," he said, with a sudden inspired spark in his eyes, "we do what we always said we'd do? I mean now?"

I wasn't sure what he was talking about. "What did we say we'd do? You mean drive to southern Italy and stay for the whole winter?"

"No. Though I'd still like to do that one day. I mean move out of the city."

"Did we say that?"

"You know we did. I'm sure it was your idea. You said you couldn't live in the city indefinitely. We said when work allowed, we'd move away. You know we did."

"You're still working though. You're not going to give up your job."

"But I have a different role nowadays. I've already been thinking about it, to be honest. I'm sure I could work from home a couple of days a week. I could set up an office in the house. How about we move out a bit? I could commute on the other days. It would be something different."

I gazed at the magazines on the table, the countryside magazines I've always bought because I find the glossy images calming. "Perhaps," I said. "But I'm sort of used to it here now."

****

A few months on and I'm turning things out, looking through the mountains of stuff we've accumulated over the years. I come across some old photographs in one of the desk drawers. There are even some from the '60s. I find an old school photo of me, taken at the primary school. There are a few that were taken on the beach: me with Mum, me with Mum and Philip. There's a picture of Anna. She's beaming. I think she would have been about ten at the time.

Another picture shows her in a gymnastic pose. It's a good photo; it depicts her well. She was what you might call wiry. She was always absolutely bursting with energy and here you can see it. Then I find a shot of Sam and me in the garden with the white rabbit.

Why ever have we kept all these magazines and newspapers? There are various piles in various places all over the house. Surely most people throw them straight out. When a new one arrives, it should take the place of the previous one. We have no discipline, Roger and I. I need to get rid of them. At least the recycling gets collected every week now. I carry them all to the dining room and arrange them on the table. I start looking through them, of course. There are lots of the rural lifestyle mags. They're entertaining; I enjoy them but they're nothing to do with the countryside. They show beautiful houses, beautiful gardens; beautiful people wearing perfectly tailored, outdoor-style clothing; angelic children running through immaculate fields of barley. I wonder if Roger is expecting life to be like this when we move. Perhaps he thinks I will be weaving willow baskets and getting up early to forage for his breakfast.

"If anyone moves out of town based on this, they will have a rude awakening," I tell myself.

I hear the door and Roger comes in, swirling round—a cup of tea, a quick sandwich, a change of shoes.

"What are you doing with your day?" he shouts. He puts his head round the door.

"Sorting out," I answer.

"Is there much to sort?"

"Well, just a houseful!"

He stares at the contents of the table. "Just chuck it all away," he says. Then he's off out again to deal with some other pressing task. It's the city way. He may be the one who's instigated the move, but I'm not sure he'll take to the easygoing pace of the coast.

****

The loft will have to be cleared. I open the hatch and pull down the ladder. I climb up and view the task that lies ahead. Everything will have to go. There are rolls of carpet, old suitcases, old board games. I see the once much-loved stereo unit and some odd bits of furniture that fell out of favor. Then there's an army of cardboard boxes. I groan. I go over and start to open them up: books and more books, forgotten Christmas decorations, some aged linen.

I start to move things toward the hatch and clamber precariously back down the ladder with a few items. I think about just dropping some of the stuff down, but know I should wait for Roger to come back and help me.

I soon find myself sitting on the boarded flooring at the back of the loft where there's a roof light, reading. There are factual books, mostly out of date, and lots and lots of novels, all of which I've read at some point in the past. I can remember the storylines but not always in great detail. I read the back cover of a few of them to remind myself what happens. I become totally engrossed in an Irish novel I recall absolutely loving the first time around.

I come to my senses, put the book back on top of the pile, and open up more boxes. Soon I find one I've carefully stored, but not looked out for years. It's a box full of things I've kept from when I was a child. It's not particularly large; it contains a collection of small ornaments, a tiny watercolor painting someone once gave me, my ragged old gonk.

"Hello, Piggy," I say.

There's also an old tin that I used to hide away under my bed. It was where I kept my most precious possessions. At the bottom of the box, I find my diaries. I was always given a diary for Christmas when I was young. I pick one up and flip through the pages. On some days there are entries, and on others there are gaps. I read a few of the entries and they make me laugh, simple records of my day, what I'd done, reminders about people's birthdays, and other key events. There are also some earnest entries, containing my thoughts on how to put the world to rights.

There's one diary that's almost shouting at me to be found. I dig deeper into the box. I find it: a large journal with a brightly colored cover. Each page is illustrated with a cartoon character and the day and month written in large print, still leaving plenty of room for each day's entry. The diary is from the year 1969. I flick quickly to August 24th, a Sunday, but there's no entry. I replace the diary, half wanting to spend more time looking through its pages and half wanting to throw it out with the newspapers. I close the box up again, take the thick, black felt-tipped pen I have in my pocket and write *KEEP* on the side. Then I write it on the top as well, just to make sure.

****

"So how did you get on with the sorting?" Roger asks in the evening.

"I made a start."

"I can't wait to move, you know."

"I can't either."

"We'll have to visit all your old haunts once we get settled, too."

"I'd like to find some new haunts."

Roger goes over to the shelves and comes back to the sofa with the road atlas. It's old; the corners are turned up and some of the pages fall out as he opens it.

"No wonder they invented the sat nav," he says. He reassembles it and finds the area we're moving to.

"It's at least thirty miles from Cherlton," I tell him.

"More like fifteen I'd say," he replies.

We're buying a house in Sherbury West. In fact, Sherbury is not as far west as the area where I grew up, but it's also on the south coast and a very pretty area. We went to view the house three times before we made the offer, though I think Roger was ready to buy it as soon as he set eyes on it. The property is vacant at the moment and has been for nearly a year. The garden's been allowed to go a little wild; it will take a good bit of work to get it back into some sort of shape. On the third visit, I saw a pair of robins taking short flights between the bushes and perching on the fencing. I watched them for a time. They seemed very much at home. I think it was probably the robins that finally sold the house to me rather than the agent, who babbled on endlessly and got right on my nerves. There are a few old tumbledown sheds, and the house itself is in need of a little care and attention. It couldn't be described as spacious, but I think it will work out for us. It's along a lane with fields to either side. There are footpaths aplenty. The beach is a couple of quiet, leafy roads away—walkable in little more than a few minutes.

Roger puts on the television, the news channel.

"I've thrown out so many old newspapers," I tell him. "Why do we need papers these days anyway, when you can see it all twenty-four hours a day on the TV?"

"But it's not proper news, this," he says. "It's just events. Event after event, things that might be happening anywhere in the world, reported within minutes."

"You're right. They're reporting it before they really know what's happening."

"Everyone's disaster is shared by all of us now. We get other peoples' storms and wildfire. We share our knife crime and terror…and Brexit."

"Please don't mention that!"

We change the channel and watch an episode from an old detective series.

"Shall we have a cup of tea," Roger says before it finishes. He soon returns to the sofa with two mugs and a plate of fattening-looking biscuits.

"I was just thinking about the news again," I say.

"Why, what's happened now?"

"I mean the news in general. When we lived in the village, we only cared about the local news. It was like a currency in a way. It was valuable. You could exchange it."

"Don't they call that gossip?"

My mind wanders back to the road with the row of little semi-detached brick cottages, typical of the older countryside housing, with hollyhocks and sweet peas growing in the gardens, clipped hedges, and well-tended vegetable patches. Primrose Cottage. Myrtle Cottage. Lavender Cottage. I think about the old fellow who would seemingly always be leaning on his garden gate and would speak to every passerby; how he always had news for you and how he eagerly extracted yours with his expert line in questioning. News would spread. The neighbors, the shopkeepers, too, passed on anything and everything, and soon everyone was in the know. But, once in a while in that little village, they might also stop the news. If there was good reason, for the sake of the village or the villagers, information could be withheld or shared only sparingly. Nods, winks, and utterances would warn off any further repetition or discussion; the local news channel would close down.

Chapter 27

"Shall we have a go at getting those boxes down?" Roger suggests.

"Okay," I say.

We climb the stairs, pull down the ladder, and set about the task in a business-like manner.

"Pass me another," he says, his head popping up through the loft hatch.

I slide the next box to the edge of the boarding and he receives it, stepping back down the ladder and placing it with the others on the landing.

"It's so much easier with two of us."

"We're not taking all this stuff with us to Sherbury?" he says.

"No. Most of it can be dumped."

"Let's dump as much as we can. We're having a fresh start, aren't we?"

"There's just the odd thing…"

"We hardly ever go into the loft. We haven't looked at any of this old rubbish for years. We're hardly going to miss it." Roger is right and he can be quite persuasive. "Any more?" he shouts.

"No. That's it."

"Thank God."

I smile down through the hatch at him. I start to climb back down and pause to admire my work. The loft space is empty, but for the one box I have vowed to keep. Roger doesn't need to know about that one.

"Are you definitely away next week?" I ask him.

"Yes. Confirmed. It'll be useful, I suppose…and I can get to know the new guy a bit better…buy him a drink or two."

"What's it about anyway, the conference?"

"Materials. You know, new materials and the advantages of using them and so on."

"Sounds riveting." Roger gives me a resigned look. "Well, I've been thinking. I've packed everything I can pack. I've cleaned everything I can clean. I think I might take a trip to Sherbury, have another look around, maybe even stay a night at a nice hotel."

"Why don't you. It's a good idea, unless you want to sit here in the house amongst all these boxes."

"I might even look for a job while I'm there."

****

Although I grew up only ten or twenty miles from Sherbury, I don't know it well. It wasn't a place we visited, and when my parents eventually moved from Cherlton, they moved farther west, in the opposite direction altogether.

I book a couple of nights at what they call a country hotel and surprise myself by how much I'm looking forward to my trip. There are a couple of people I could have asked to come with me, but I've decided I want to go on my own. I can have a good look around and then, once I am an expert on the area, people can visit and I'll be able to show them the highlights. As much as anything, I'm looking forward to lying between beautiful white sheets that someone else will launder and eating irresistible food that someone else will prepare. It's late spring, and I'm hoping the weather will be good. The evenings are stretching out, so there will be plenty of time for long walks and sightseeing. I'll get on the internet later and do some research.

****

The following day, I pack a bag. I remember to bring my swimsuit. I've often thought about how the things I was introduced to as a child, and that I enjoyed as a child, remain things I always derive pleasure from. I ponder on why that is. Did I learn to enjoy them in a sort of non-intellectual way? Do I enjoy them in an almost primal manner, able to tune back into some kind of basic, unsophisticated feeling? When it comes to certain pastimes and situations, I seem able to temporarily switch off my brain, switch off the debate, the worry, and the caution, and simply take pleasure in them with a childlike sense of freedom. I love being out in a field on a wild, windy day, the distinctive smells of the coast and the woodland. Swimming, playing tennis, and working in the garden are all pursuits I adore. I will surely be able to spend more time doing the things I delight in once we move.

There's another thing I want to take with me. I pull down the ladder to the loft and go up to find the box I marked *KEEP*. I open it and pull out a few items. I take the large diary, from 1969, and go back down the ladder. I will pack it with my swimsuit and bring it with me on my long weekend.

****

The hotel is perfect. I'm looking forward to exploring the facilities and acquainting myself with the surroundings. I drop off my bag, and almost straight away, go back to the car and drive to the sea path. I walk to the shore. The sun's still out, and there's a strong southwesterly blowing. I'd swear that the salt-infused air is nutritious. The sea is rough; it's that striking blue-green or green-gray color I love but can never describe, the color the producers of expensive house paint try to replicate. My clothes flap around me noisily. The waves crash in and draw back in loud repetitive motion; at their tips, the light shines through the water making it translucent.

My hotel room is big and airy with high ceilings, beautifully decorated with a view right out over the gardens. I open the window, unpack the few things I've brought with me, and hang a couple of items in the wardrobe. I go to the bathroom and wash my face and hands. I take the diary out of my bag, go, and lie on the king-size bed. I open the book and my thoughts begin to take me back to the summer of '69 and the group of young children who were tied up in events they couldn't control. I remember the Sunday morning when I was told of Tommy's death. He was found in one of the disused quarries at the foot of the downs. He'd fallen, it seemed, and hit his head. Mr. Johnson, a neighbor of Naomi's, found him. He'd been out early in the morning with his dog. The dog found a ball, a blue ball, and Mr. Johnson realized that it was the color of the ball Tommy had been reported to have been playing with when he went missing. Mr. Johnson picked it up; he was intending to take it to the police, but as he was near to the quarry, he thought he should take a look. He found the boy's body among the bushes that had grown up there. The sides of the quarry were steep. It looked as though the boy had slipped and fallen headfirst. He was facedown. Mr. Johnson turned him over. At first, he thought the boy was unhurt, he looked perfect. But Mr. Johnson found that he wasn't breathing and had no pulse. Later, he was told that the boy's neck was broken.

There was a colossal search. The police and the rescue services were out night and day, and a large number of volunteers took part. It was as if the whole village was under a dark cloud. I read about it afterward; some of the reports I read several years on, because even though I was very much involved, I was very young. Like the other children, I was kept away from the harshest realities of the situation. So much was going on, but we were too young to take a lot of it in, and our parents continued to make sure we only had to deal with those things that were necessary. Even so, that summer, I can divide my life into the before and the after. The before was idyllic, and the after…it's hard to describe, but I think I developed an awareness that I hadn't had before. Perhaps it was the loss of innocence. Maybe it was just about growing up; I'm sure my friends and I had to grow up a little more quickly than we otherwise would have. Another thing I realize about that summer, and have realized several times over the years, is that I still find it hard to remember some things about it. I wonder if it's my mind trying to protect me from the trauma. This isn't the first time I've looked at the diary, but I find it hard to recall what's in it. It's not the first time I've gone over what happened, but I still have to think long and hard to take myself back there, especially to remember any details. In one way I have a vivid memory, but it's hard to bring the facts to the surface of my consciousness. It's a little like waking from a dream;

you think you can remember it, but try as you might you can't. Sometimes you can bring it to mind, but minutes later, it's gone.

There was an inquest. The verdict was accidental death. However, Sam, for some reason, remained convinced that the man we knew as Bridges was to blame. He just wouldn't let it go. All summer he'd been ready to accuse the old farmer of something. It had been Sam's idea to watch for him, then he and Robbo wanted to follow him, and when Tommy disappeared that was it, Sam was determined Bridges was involved. For my part, I'm sure at the time I didn't think all that watching and following was anything much more than a game. I'd say Anna felt the same. I look for entries about it in the diary, but there's nothing.

****

I've driven past the house a few times, the house that will soon be our home. The next morning, I plan to drive there again, park up, and have a walk around. It's uninhabited; there's nobody to disturb. I set off toward the village, approach the house, and find a section of the road where it seems wide enough to leave the car without causing a problem for another passing vehicle, should there happen to be one. I walk along, and instead of going through the usual entrance, I walk round the outside of the wall to another gate we've noticed at the back of the property. The path runs between the house and the farmland beyond. I come to the gate but I can't open it; it's stuck fast. I walk a little farther along the path and then return. As I come back, I try to pull away some of the ivy growing on the old gate posts. They are stone, like the wall, and would look lovely if they were only cleaned up a little. I pull away enough of the ivy to reveal the tops of both posts and then notice that one of them has some letters carved into it a little way down. I drag at the ivy again until I can make out what's written. It's surely the name of the house. We know the property as The Haven, a name I'm not particularly keen on, but the letters read *Mead Cottage*. That must be what the house was originally called; I'm delighted with the alternative name, it suits the place so well, and it surely must date back to when it was first built. I go back to the main entrance feeling pleased with myself, then walk round the house, peering in through the windows as I go. I suppose I could have picked up the key, but I don't mind that I can't go inside; in fact, the garden is almost of more interest to me. It's been a long time since I've lived anywhere with a good size garden, and though overgrown, I know that a few weeks of hard work will soon improve it. My plan is to rescue the existing trees and plants and resurrect the lawns and the vegetable plot, certainly not to take away any of the charm. I'll keep the garden ornaments and paraphernalia that have been left behind. The ramshackle sheds might need to be replaced, but there's a usable greenhouse that I don't think I'd properly taken note of before.

It's quiet in the garden. I sit on a lichen-encrusted stone seat and listen. I can hear a light wind whispering in the trees and the conversations of the wood pigeons. I wonder if, on a wilder day, it might be possible to hear the sea. It's not far off. I also think the church bells will be audible when they're ringing—I can see the steeple across the fields. The longer I sit, the more I look forward to moving in, and just when I'm about to drag myself away, I hear another sound from farther along the lane. It's unmistakable. Nothing could be better; what more could I wish for. I can hear the sound of tennis being played.

I'm drawn in the direction of the sound of racquets hitting balls, and sure enough, on the other side of a tall hedge are two tennis courts, and playing on one of them are two women, both of a similar age to me. I can't leave without speaking to them. I find the gateway in the hedge and let myself in. I wait for a break in play. Both women look over to me.

"Hello," I say. "I hope you don't mind me interrupting. I used to play tennis regularly, some years ago now…and I'm about to move to Sherbury. Is there a local club?"

"Yes and no, I suppose," replies one of the women, heading toward me with a beaming smile. "There's a sort of loose arrangement whereby people who play have each others' phone numbers, and we just call each other up and plan games."

"I imagine we should be more organized, but it seems to work," says the second woman, who's followed her opponent over.

"We're always looking for more players," adds the first woman.

"There are these two courts, and there's another on the other side of the village. When are you moving?" asks the second.

"Well, quite soon. In a few weeks' time," I say. "I'm Wendy."

The women hold their hands out to be shaken. "I'm Helena."

"And I'm May."

We chat some more and decide the best thing is for

The Five Things

me to get in touch once I've moved in, and we'll arrange to play. They tell me if I don't find them on the courts, whoever else is playing will have their numbers and will put us in touch. I thank them and say I will definitely contact them. I watch them go back, then leave them to their game and return to the car.

****

As I head back to the city, I drive past Mead Cottage one more time and on toward the beach. I leave the car and go down to the water to swim. It's still early in the season and the sea is cold, but for me, some of the most enjoyable swims are had in cold temperatures. More effort is required but the reward is greater. Once I'm out and dressed I know I will feel rejuvenated, and so proud of my achievement.

Being beside the sea again may throw up some unwanted memories, but I'll just have to deal with them. I feel that I'm doing the right thing and at the right time.

****

Roger is home. He has his mind on work. I make tea, call him to the sofa, and begin to tell him about my stay in Sherbury. I'm not too hopeful he'll take much interest, but to my surprise, he seems to visibly relax and soon becomes involved in discussing our plans. He's intrigued to hear about the name I discovered on the old gatepost, and we take the decision, original name or not, we will call our little house Mead Cottage. It will be fun looking into its history and it can mark a new start for us all, Roger, me, and the neglected little property.

"And did you find a job?" he asks.

"Er, no. I didn't even think about it."

"Great! That means the house will be tidy and the garden will be immaculate."

"Ha, ha," I say. "I might start my own business. By all accounts if I do that, you'll never see me and the whole place will be a tip."

I've never before thought about starting my own business but Roger is immediately engaged.

"Own business? That's a brilliant idea! What would it be?"

"Oh, I don't know. Perhaps I could make wedding dresses or something. I'm no good at sewing, though."

"You could grow vegetables. There's plenty of room for that."

"Or I could start a cleaning agency. There are a lot of holiday lets in the area that must need frequent attention."

"Make a list. That always puts you in a good mood. Start at A and go through everything. You're bound to come up with a bright idea."

Chapter 28

June 16th, 2019

It's less than a week until the move. Everything is packed. I've been cleaning diligently. It's a long time since I last moved home. I'm not sure of the etiquette, but I suppose I need to make sure every room is spotless. No one will be making Mead Cottage spic and span for us, however, that will be my job too. All in, I'm likely to spend a good part of my time in the coming days in the company of my mops and dusters.

Roger is upstairs on the phone. He doesn't have much time to spare, so everything will be down to me. When we finally get to Sherbury, he will be extra busy. He'll have to set up his new office space, and he'll have to get used to commuting a day or so each week. I call up to him to see if he wants tea. I'm not sure why I call because he never refuses tea, whatever the time, whatever the frequency. The kitchen is bare but for the kettle, the toaster, two saucepans, and a minimal amount of crockery and cutlery. Everything else is in boxes. I've tried to be methodical, give each box a number, and make a list of what's inside. I'm trying not to keep opening them back up, but every so often I give in. It's harder when it comes to my clothes. The minute something is washed and packed I get the urge to wear it.

Roger appears in the doorway. He's taken a break

and come down to drink the tea. We go to sit on the sofa in the room that has nothing on the bookshelves or the mantelpiece.

"So where have you got to with the list?" he enquires.

"L. L is for Laundry," I say.

"You're going to take in washing?"

"I'm not saying I'm going to. It's just on the list."

"M might be better," he suggests. "Mechanic."

"What about Meringues?" I counter. "Did you ever have one of my mum's? She makes stupendous meringues."

"Those ones they sell at Nelly's are good," he says.

"Yeah, and huge," I say.

"I like the raspberry ones best, by the way," he tells me. "You could make a note of that."

****

June 19th, 2019

The boxes the removal men are due to pick up are stacked in the lounge. They'll take them with the furniture early in the morning the day after tomorrow. We've made a list of the things we'll transport in the car. The reality of what we're doing sometimes hits me. I hope we're doing the right thing.

****

June 21st, 2019

It's the day of the move, and Roger has suddenly realized that we are leaving and doesn't seem to remember anything I've told him. He asks a multitude of questions. We did forward the post, didn't we? Did I pack his golf clubs? Have I read the meters? What about the water meter? I remind him we don't have a water meter, never did.

We load the last few things into the car. We lock the door of the house. I have an envelope ready, and I put the keys into it. We've agreed to drop them through the estate agent's door because it's too early for them to be open. We walk away and I get a sinking feeling. I'm expecting the feeling, but it's still not pleasant. I look at Roger. He puts an arm round me and squeezes. He tells me not to be daft, that we know what we're doing, and then he ruins it by saying it's too late for us to change our minds now in any case. After that, he asks if I'm sure I cleared everything out of the loft.

We stop at the motorway service station. We're almost exactly halfway between our old home in the city and our new home in the country. I feel better. I'm full of enthusiasm now. I tell Roger I think I'm about to reinvent myself. I have that tingly feeling of anticipation, the way I usually feel when I'm setting off on holiday. Roger is in an exuberant mood as well. I think we must be talking too loudly as the man at the next table is giving me disapproving looks. We eat the expensive, rubbery-cooked breakfast and drink the giant cups of tepid coffee without complaint, knowing that tonight we will be in our rural idyll and our new adventure will be about to begin.

****

Roger is driving and I'm navigating. We've left the motorway and we're on the B roads headed toward the coast, then we'll veer westwards. We have the radio on, and we're singing along to the music. We're like a couple of let loose teenagers who've only recently learnt to drive. The removal men are due at Mead Cottage at midday. We've remembered to tell them the house is actually called The Haven, and that the best route to take is the one straight through the village, then carry on in the direction of the beach.

****

We've picked up the keys, and we're here at Mead Cottage. We've opened the doors and the windows to allow some fresh air to circulate. We've made sure the gas and electricity supplies are up and running and the water's turned on. We're sitting in the garden waiting for the removal truck. As soon as it arrives, I'll find the box marked *Kitchen 1* and make everyone a cup of tea.

"Imagine all this in a year from now," says Roger.

"There's a lot to do."

"I'm looking forward to it."

"Yep, me too."

"And you'll have your business up and running."

"Of course, my cafe."

"Or your expensive cushion-making concern."

"Or I'll have retrained and I'll be running a little garage from over there in the shed."

"Mending classic cars."

"Yes, or lawnmowers!"

We laugh. The moving process has brought us close again.

****

We're inside Mead Cottage, sitting on our trusty old sofa, surrounded by boxes, but happy. Most of the furniture is in the wrong place, but at least our bed is in the bedroom and we've made it up. We've found some towels and our toothbrushes. Although I was methodical about listing what I'd packed into each box, I keep putting the list down and forgetting where I've left it. Roger is doing the same with his reading glasses.

We decide we've done enough for the day. We're

exhausted and starving. We don't feel able to make ourselves presentable enough to go out to eat, who knows where all our clothes are. We decide to walk into the village, buy some takeaway food, and go and have supper on the beach.

I come across the diary again as I'm unpacking—the one from 1969. It falls open on a date in late September and I see that there's a reference to Bridges. I think about Bridges, as I have done so many times before. Everyone called him Bridges, the adults and the children. He was never Mr. Bridges or Farmer Bridges, let alone Joe or Joseph. He was known only as Bridges. He lived on his own in that dark, old house, overgrown with trees. It's no wonder the children didn't trust him. You could believe any grim story you heard about him, and the adults, in the main, didn't seem to make any attempt to counter them. Calling him Bridges, it was as if no one had any respect for him. Cherlton had been a friendly village. People were generally falling over themselves to be welcoming, to ask you in, to offer you tea, or just to pass the time of day. But no one seemed to speak to Bridges or include him in any of the pastimes that the villagers enjoyed.

****

June 23rd, 2019

We've realized we don't know how to go about changing the name of the cottage, but Roger thinks we must do it straight away or it will only become more complicated. We know we can't simply remove the sign that says *The Haven* and put up a new one. Roger will do some research when he's in his office in the city next week. He says he'll try to check when and why the name was changed, too, in case there's a reason that might affect our decision. What if something terrible happened at Mead Cottage?

I ask in the shop where I buy the newspaper if they know how long the house has been called The Haven. They say they've lived in Sherbury for thirty years and they can't remember it ever having any other name.

I can't help thinking the paper shop will be a little like the village shops back when I was growing up in Cherlton. I'll bet most of the village will soon be informed that new people have moved into The Haven. I suppose we should announce ourselves in some way. As soon as we have properly unpacked and are in a position to welcome visitors, I think we should have some sort of housewarming party. I haven't forgotten about Helena and May, and I resolve to make sure they're the first to be invited.

****

June 26th, 2019

Roger has found out that we need to contact the Highways Division at the council and tell them we plan to change the name of the house. They will check if there are any other properties with the same name in the area, and so long as nothing comes up, they will inform the Royal Mail. We will need to register the new name at the Land Registry, then it will be a case of letting all the suppliers know. He hasn't been able to find out much about the property, but he thinks Mead Cottage was the original name and that it may once have been the place where local children were taught. This surprises us as it doesn't seem big enough. Roger says the original cottage dates back at least to the mid-nineteenth century and that it was an estate cottage at that time. It was enlarged later, but hardly to the size of a school.

Whatever the history, it is a very appealing cottage. I love the lounge area. There's a flagstone floor and a large open fireplace with a wide stone hearth and a little bread oven to the side. The ceiling is boarded; the beams are exposed. We'll brighten everything up, clean the stonework, strip the beams back, and paint the ceilings white. I'm determined not to develop a snooty, towny attitude, but I do want to transform the cottage into the kind of place you might find in one of my *living in the country* magazines. I want to preserve and restore the old, and add modern comforts, and plenty of contemporary furnishings.

****

July 1st, 2019

We've been in Sherbury for just over a week and we're already making progress with the cottage. I've hired a gardener to help with some of the heavier work, and between us, we've cut the long grass and disposed of the larger weeds that had taken hold. It's made the outside area look a good deal bigger. There are quite a few trees on the land, silver birch and oak, some apple trees, and a flowering cherry. We've removed a lot of the ivy and cleaned up the old patio area where weeds had also taken over, growing up brazenly between the stone slabs. We often see the robins; they hop around so close to us that it's almost as if they are tame.

I shout to Paul, the gardener, to let him know it's time for a break. I head inside to get some drinks. On my way in, I hear players on the tennis courts. I'll get these drinks together, then walk over to see them.

I find Helena and May just finishing a game. They know Paul, and I ask them to come and have a glass of lemon squash and a digestive biscuit with us. I tell them I hope to be able to offer something a little more enticing if they come again, but they seem delighted. We pull the garden seats onto the patio and sit down. Everyone is disheveled and perspiring, so we feel at ease together. Neither Helena nor May has ever been to the cottage before. I tell them we're in the process of changing the name back to what we believe to be the original. They like the old name. They admire the garden, even though it's at quite an early stage. I tell them what I'm planning. I tell them we're hoping to have a housewarming party and that they will be first on my list of invitees—Paul too of course. I go to find a notepad, write down their numbers, and tell them that as soon as we are connected, I'll call them with our landline details. Mobile signals are far from reliable here. It's a sacrifice we're going to have to accept.

There's a plumber and an electrician working inside today, so Helena and May say they will look around the cottage on their next visit.

****

July 3rd, 2019

We've had the phone connected, and we're on the internet at last. I can't believe how awkward life had become without it. We also have television; I think I'll take a break from gardening and spend the day watching the news channel.

****

July 6th, 2019

"What have you doodled on the phone pad?" Roger calls to me. "It looks like *The Fish Fingers*." He's in the hall and I'm in the kitchen preparing coffee.

"The Five Things!" I shout back.

The Five Things

He comes into the room carrying the pad. "Has it got something to do with the party?"

"No, it's nothing to do with the party." I've been looking at my old diary again and I must have doodled it absentmindedly. "It's to do with Tommy Williams."

Roger knows about Tommy, of course. I've talked about him before. He knows the basic facts about what happened to him.

Roger asks me several times to tell him about The Five Things. "Come on, what are they?"

"I'm not supposed to talk about them."

He thinks I'm joking. "Perhaps you could just tell me one thing…to start with?"

Later he asks if he can have a look at my old diary. I tell him he can, but not at the moment. He still finds it hard to work me out on occasion.

****

July 7th, 2019

I've trapped Roger on the sofa, and we're going through the list of invitees for the housewarming. There are about fifteen names: May and Helena, Paul, the four men who've been working on various aspects of the house, and some additional members of the tennis club I've been introduced to. We've also invited our nearest neighbors on each side. We've let everyone know they're welcome to bring a plus one. We think we'll cater for around three dozen to be on the safe side. Roger is in charge of drinks and I'm in charge of food. It will be a casual affair; we'll tell everyone to drop in whenever suits them. We'll lay out a buffet in the kitchen, and with luck, it will be fine enough to use the garden as the main place to mingle; otherwise, we'll all have to squash into the lounge. Roger will make sure we have music, and I will attempt to rig some outdoor lighting.

****

July 20th, 2019

It's the day of the party, and luckily the weather forecast is suggesting a mild evening with no rain. They don't always get it right, but I've decided to base the preparations on that outcome and cross my fingers.

Roger's gone to the off-license for wine and beer and I'm working on the nibbles. The cottage is looking good. We've by no means finished all the work we plan to do, but we're happy that we've done enough to celebrate our first occasion here. I think we should be pleased with ourselves. We've taken the plunge, given up our urban life, nothing's gone woefully wrong, and neither of us is in a state of deep regret over our decision.

The phone rings. It's Philip.

"Hey, how are you, stranger?" I greet him.

"Busy...but coming to the party!"

"Brilliant! I had a feeling you were going to let me down."

Philip is working all hours at the university; there are deadlines coming up and some of his students are resitting exams.

"No. Would I? And Jayne's dying to see how you're getting on."

"Can you stay the night?"

"No, we'll have to get back. Too much on at the moment."

I go to the utility room and find the box marked *Kitchen 3*. We still haven't unpacked everything. With luck, the glasses should be inside. I hope we have enough. I'll get them out and give them a good wash. We'll have to go into the village again if we think we need more.

Roger is back and he's brought a few bits and pieces from the farm shop: some cheese, some magnificent local tomatoes, and some freshly baked bread. We make a simple lunch.

"Want to taste the wine?" he asks.

"No. I'll pass on that. Otherwise, I'll be snoozing on the sofa by the time the guests start arriving!"

Roger is studying the label of one of the bottles longingly. "I'll make coffee instead," he says stoically. We're soon back to the preparations. "Right, I'll get the fridge loaded," he announces. He puts as many bottles of beer as he can into the fridge and stacks the rest in the corner of the room. Then he has to start again because he's forgotten about chilling the wine. We check we have enough ice in the freezer and arrange the soft drinks on the work top. Most of the food will be cold but I have a few things to pop into the oven. They can go in as soon as the first people get here.

I'm enjoying myself. We've not had a party of our own for some time. Roger and I are planning to dress up in our evening wear and try to make a good impression. Perhaps we'll be invited to some other events during the summer if we play our cards right.

We have plenty of time to prepare; even so, we end up spending the early evening adding finishing touches, wondering if we should put out more nibbles, and rummaging through the storage boxes for extra plates. Finally, Roger opens a bottle of Chablis, pours us each a glass, and suggests we go and sit on the patio. We've put on some music and the outdoor lights are glowing, though it's not yet dark. We can light the candles later.

It's beautiful in the garden: the birds are singing and the air is scented; around the patio, there's rosemary and lavender, and the honeysuckle's in bloom.

"Hello-o," we hear a voice and the click of shoe heels on the path. It's May and Brian, Helena and Charles. I'm pleased they're the first to arrive. We go to welcome them, and soon we're all in the kitchen pouring drinks and telling stories. Paul appears at the door with Sally and joins us. In no time we have a houseful, and our guests begin to spill out onto the patio and the lawn.

"Come and have a look round the cottage," I say to May and Helena, and take them off leaving Roger to open bottles, restock the fridge, and generally play the perfect host.

Our carpenter, Norman, has taken over the music and turned it up a little in the process. "You can't go wrong with this track," he tells me.

I return to the patio and begin to introduce myself to the other halves. There's a tap on my shoulder and it's Philip. He gives me a hug.

"Well, look at this for a crowd!" he says.

Jayne is with Roger. They've brought us a housewarming gift: a pear tree. There couldn't have been a better present. Philip is soon mingling. He's very engaging, and in no time, he's laughing and joking with my neighbors, Rose and Larry. I've hardly met them. Bernard is our other close neighbor. He's retired and lives alone. I'm dying to chat to him, but I can see he's currently in deep conversation with Paul and Sally. Roger has worked his way over to me.

"There's no need to worry about anyone," he says. "They're all having a good time. They'd be comfortable socializing with each other whether we were here or not!"

"There's such a nice buzz," I say. I find Jayne and take her on the tour of the cottage before introducing her to May. "My sister-in-law. She doesn't play tennis. Nevertheless, she's very nice."

I return to the kitchen to help a few guests top up their glasses before generously replenishing my own. Norman has put "Sorrow" on, and I almost feel like dancing.

Bernard is incredibly interesting. He knows a lot about local history, and I tell him we'll have to meet up again soon, and he can fill us in. He knows a little about Mead Cottage and says he's pleased we're opting to use the old name. He's also a bit of a gardener I find out.

"That time already!" Philip is leaving. I tell him it seems as though he's only just arrived. He goes on ahead to fetch the car and I walk to the gate with Jayne. She says she thinks we've made a good decision in moving here to Sherbury.

I wave them off, and as I walk back inside, I realize it's much later than I thought. The sky is dark but clear, and the moon and stars are shining. I feel a wave of pleasure as I go back to the garden. May and Brian, Helena and Charles have gathered on the patio and I join them. I ask how long they've lived locally and find out that May grew up only a few miles from the village and has always lived in and around the area. We begin talking about school. I tell her I was at school in Cherlton. I tell her when I was there and when I left, how long we've spent in the city. She and I are a similar age, and although we wouldn't have crossed paths, we do begin to wonder if we might have had any friends in common. She says she knows one or two people who went to school in Porton. Roger arrives with a bottle of red and a bottle of white. He does some topping up and sits down with us.

It's probably another hour or so before our guests start to tire and begin to totter off into the night. Paul's van is outside; he tells me he'll pick it up in the morning. Everyone else seems to have walked, which is a good thing, taking into account the amount of empty bottles and glasses that seem to have accumulated.

Roger and I are alone on the patio. He puts an arm around me. He says that maybe Mead Cottage has just seen the beginning of a new annual event.

"It's been a fabulous evening," he says, with perhaps just a hint of surprise.

I wholeheartedly agree.

****

July 24th, 2019
We discuss the party for days. We keep remembering stories and bits and pieces of conversations we had and recounting them to each other. We try to remember the names of everyone who came. Between us, we can remember most of them. I say I'll ask May or Helena to help with the others or it will be embarrassing if we bump into them in the village. We were given a few *good luck in your new home* cards, the names might be inside, but it's not always easy to read the writing.

****

July 25th, 2019
Roger's just in from work. He already has the

commute off to a tee. He can travel from the cottage to the office in just over an hour and he doesn't find the journey too awful. He walks to the station, changes trains once, and takes the tube five stops at the other end. He says that when he finishes, the thought of coming back to the cottage makes his journey easy to tolerate. He generally only needs to go to the city twice a week and we've made the tiny third bedroom into a study-come-office, so he's able to do a lot of his work from home.

I've spent more time cutting grass and weeding, planted the pear tree, and properly revealed the gate at the far end of the plot. Once Norman has fixed it, we'll be able to go out at the back and walk across the field to the shops. I've uncovered some lovely old paving slabs in various parts of the garden that form little walkways. We've decided we can save one of the old sheds and we can definitely repair the greenhouse. Paul is going to take down the second shed; it's too far gone. We'll have a think about what we want to put in its place.

****

July 26th, 2019

I'm walking round the garden with Bernard. He's a mine of information. I've decided to make the garden insect friendly. I want to fill it with bees and butterflies. Bernard is advising me on various plants that would attract them. It would be nice to encourage hedgehogs, too, or at least not do anything to discourage them. It's such a long time since I've seen a hedgehog.

There are some good garden centers in the area. I'll enjoy a few visits to them in the coming months. Bernard tells me which he thinks are best. He's also keen for me to come and have a look around his own plot. He says he's found most things out through trial and error over the years—what grows and what doesn't. He says our gardens will have similar growing conditions; he's sure that if he passes on his findings, he'll save me a lot of wasted effort.

****

July 29th, 2019

I'm playing singles on the nearby courts with May. To say I'm feeling rusty is a definite understatement. She's beating me hands down. At least I can get my serve in and I can get the ball back some of the time, so hopefully, it's not so one-sided that she can't enjoy the game.

After two sets of humiliation, I ask May if she'll come back to the cottage for a drink. We make coffee and sit on the patio. She says I will improve every time we play and that she is thoroughly enjoying the morning. She also suggests doubles might be a good idea. She wants to know if Roger plays because then she could team up with him, and I could play with Brian. As he is more of a golfer, she thinks we should arrange a ladies' game. Helena will be up for that, and she feels sure she can round up another female.

May suddenly remembers she has something to ask me. She wonders if there was a girl called Naomi at school with me. She says she was thinking after the party and remembered the time when Naomi came to her school. She remembered that Naomi had previously been at school in Cherlton, before the awful thing with her brother happened. I tell her yes, I knew Naomi. She was a friend. We'd expected her back at our school and it had quite upset me when she hadn't returned. I didn't tell her that over the years I'd often wished Naomi hadn't chosen me to ask for help the day Tommy went missing. Perhaps things would have been easier if I hadn't been so involved.

May says she didn't get to know Naomi but recollects she was a girl who never seemed too happy. She was quiet and her level of attendance was on the low side. I ask what has become of her, if she's living somewhere nearby. But May says not. She says Naomi and her family moved away again. She doesn't know where to. I make us some more coffee.

****

July 30th, 2019

I tell Bernard how much I like magnolias, and his eyes light up. I adore the magnolia, the large tree that spends the year without drawing your attention, and then for perhaps just one or two weeks, becomes the most beautiful tree you have ever seen, with its huge oval flowers that burst and then fall so rapidly.

We walk out of our back gate and left along the path. In a minute or two, we are at Bernard's back gate and he leads me through it. Here, near the wall, is the vegetable plot. It's well stocked and immaculately tended. There's a hedge that helps provide shelter and separates it from the other areas. We walk along the brickwork path to the terrace that runs all along the back of the property. We walk up the steps and turn to look. From here I can see the entire garden, and it's quite breathtaking. There are the most wonderful lawns and beds, clusters of shrubbery, little seated areas, and located on the far side, in pride of place, a magnolia. Bernard tells me it took a good few seasons to become established, but now it flowers magnificently every year.

He takes me through the doors that lead directly into his lounge and shows me how the tree is framed in the view from the room. He says that in the spring it never fails to give him pleasure to see the buds emerge, and he looks forward to the day that they open and the tree is in flower in all its glory. He often spends time just sitting here in the room, admiring it.

****

August 4th, 2019

We've started playing tennis regularly. Today I've played singles with May and singles with Helena. We're planning to persuade Helena's sister, Ruby, to play doubles with us. I'm slowly improving. I see May most often as she has more free time than the others. We get on well; she just drops in now. It's nice to have made a friend like May so quickly, someone who feels comfortable enough to stop by any time, and of course, she expects me to do the same.

Soon after May spoke to me about Naomi, I asked her if she knew where Tommy was buried. I suppose it's something I could have looked up, but I've never done so. She told me Naomi's family lived in an area known as Whaylee, to the east, inland from Sherbury. Whaylee has a church with a large cemetery, she said. She thought it the most likely place to find Tommy's grave.

****

August 5th, 2019

The chimney is being swept, so I'm going over to visit Bernard. I'll keep out of the way for an hour or so. Bernard is always pleased to see me, and he knows how to lift my spirits. He generally has something to tell me and his conversation is very entertaining. He'll make me a cup of tea, and we'll sit in the living room with the doors open, looking out over the garden.

"Hello, Bernard."

"Good morning, Wendy. Come in, come in."

He asks again where I used to live, and I tell him, Cherlton. He doesn't know it that well. I'm aware that local history is of great interest to him, and I can tell he's becoming curious about Cherlton simply because it's managed to evade him until now. I don't think he'll be able to resist doing a little research into the village and its past.

"You'd probably find reference to a boy called Tommy Williams," I say. "He died when he was very young. He was at school with me. We think he's buried in Whaylee… If you happened to find anything about a man called Bridges—Joseph Bridges—it would be interesting." We talk about the garden and a nearby horticultural show that is coming up. Then I realize I'd better get back to the chimney sweep.

****

August 9th 2019

Bernard is on the phone. He's never phoned me before. He usually just appears in the garden or at the back door. He has something he wants to show me, he says. I'm eager to find out what it is. Perhaps a toad or a bird's nest. Perhaps a new plant or tree.

I head out across the garden to the back gate and am soon with Bernard in his living room. He's been beavering away, looking into the archives of the local newspapers and local records. I believe he does all this online in the evenings. He's not sure, he tells me, if it's of any significance, but he's found reference to a Bridges back in 1919.

The Mid Southern Chronicle—Friday, 15th August, 1919

The search for a local boy reported missing in Cherlton came to a positive conclusion when the child was found floating in a rowing boat in the bay. Joseph Bridges, aged 13, was said to be exhausted but otherwise in good health. His disappearance followed the recent death of his younger brother, Isaac, in a tree fall.

I'm completely lost for words.

****

August 9th 2019, Evening

I realize I now need to share everything with Roger. I prepare some food, and as soon as he arrives home, I near enough push him to the sofa.

"I need to talk about The Five Things," I tell him. "The boy in the boat was Bridges. I'll have to talk to you about it. There's no one else I can tell."

Roger's not sure what's so urgent; he's not sure why I'm so agitated. He wants to change out of his work clothes, so I go with him and begin to tell him what's on my mind. He listens attentively. He knows about the main event of the summer of 1969. He knows that Tommy died, he knows other things about it in fragments, but I've never spelled out The Five Things to him.

Roger realizes it was a difficult for me and my peer group, at such a young age, to deal with what happened to Tommy. He's listened before when, out of the blue, I've suddenly been struck by a thought about it. He knows that coming here to Sherbury and rereading my old diary has stirred up some memories. We sit back on the sofa and I bring the food and we talk and eat and question and debate, and it helps me.

"The boy in the boat was Bridges," I say again. I don't know how many times I've said it. I'm really just telling myself. "I see it all now," I say. "Joseph Bridges, *Bridges*, was tortured by the thought of his little brother falling from a tree. That's why he hung those birds up, that's why he left that rabbit. He was trying to scare us away from the wood. But he was trying to scare us for all the right reasons. To keep us safe, to look after us."

Roger says perhaps he was looking out for us more than we thought.

"He could have been there watching over you, a wily old farmer who knew how to stay hidden amongst the vegetation." I listened while Roger's mind worked away at the questions. "I think The Five Things helped you, as young children, to deal with such a big issue. It meant you could reflect on it, talk about it, and work it out for yourselves in your own time."

"I've never thought about it like that."

"We should go to Whaylee and find Tommy's grave, and go to Cherlton, with the new knowledge about Isaac, and pay our respects."

****

August 11th, 2019

Sunday turns into a pleasurable day out in many ways. Bernard had told me before about a local business where they grow wildflowers. You can buy them in bunches, and they are popular for weddings.

I went yesterday and bought four lovely bouquets: understated, not big or showy, but very beautiful. I place them carefully in a cardboard box and load it into the boot of the car. I have some old earthenware jars and I pack those into a separate box and put it in beside the flowers.

Roger is driving. Neither of us knows Whaylee, but it's not far. We travel through the village and on. The roads get narrower and the hedges taller. There are very few houses. We come to a bend in the road where a lane turns off to the left, and I spot the sign for Whaylee. I point and shout, "This way, this way," and Roger turns into the lane. He drives slowly along, and the church appears in front of us. It's Sunday but there doesn't appear to be a service, and no one seems to be in evidence. Roger parks in a lay-by close to the hedge.

We get out, walk back to the gate, and go through. There's a notice saying that services are carried out here on the last Sunday of the month. It also says where the services are held on the other Sundays. Today is one of those other Sundays. The church buildings share their congregations and clergymen now.

I begin to walk methodically around the graveyard. It reaches to the church on the far side and then stretches away beyond. I can already see that many of the graves date back to the 19th century or earlier. There are yew trees and oaks growing. It's a restful spot, silent but for the intermittent birdsong. I look to see if I can detect any newer gravestones. Roger takes a different route and also begins to search.

It crosses my mind that there's something about being in a churchyard and amongst the graves that is profound and peaceful, rather than depressing or sad. I suppose that wouldn't be the case immediately after a bereavement, but today I feel at ease. I am doing the right thing for Tommy, and for myself.

I can't rush past any grave; every one represents a lifetime, long or short. It takes at least half an hour to locate Tommy's, but now I'm standing in front of it. The inscription is simple, names and dates, no more. It's not well kept. I imagine Naomi must have moved too far away to tend to it. I crouch down and speak to Tommy. I have an intense feeling that I can't describe, it's neither happiness nor sadness; all I can say is it's not a negative feeling. Roger has come to join me.

"So here he is, the little man," he says. He's found water and brought the flowers. We place them on the grave. There's a seat nearby. We stay for a while before it seems the time has come to leave. I don't feel goodbye is the right thing to say.

"I'll come again, Tommy," I promise.

We return to the car and drive back the way we came. We're quiet as we drive, wrapped up in our thoughts. We get onto the A road for a few miles. There's little other traffic. We drive toward Cherlton and in no time start to reach the area so familiar to me. I've not visited since we moved to Sherbury; I haven't visited for some time. We travel through Porton, past a voluminous, untidy car boot sale. We head on into Cherlton, to the old part of the village and the church. It will be between services here. I don't want to bump into anyone I know. I bring the box containing the flowers, Roger brings the jars, and we go straight to Isaac's grave. I see immediately that there's another grave beside it. It's Joseph's. Joseph John Bridges. He died in 1985. I imagine since then, nothing's been left on Isaac's grave. Roger passes our offerings to me, two jars of such delicate wildflowers. I didn't gather them myself in the countryside, but I give them from my heart. The emotion I feel is guilt. I've wondered before and will wonder again why no one rescued Bridges from himself, why I didn't go to visit him years back when we worked out the truth. I must have said it out loud because Roger tells me not to give myself a hard time.

"I wasn't up to you," he says. "You can't solve all the problems of the world. People must have tried, but he rejected them. If you keep on rejecting people, they give up in the end."

There's another grave I need to find. Bert Wells died in 2003. I didn't get to the funeral. Sam came over, of course, but I was away working, and I couldn't make it. We place flowers on Granddad's grave and I feel sadness this time.

"Come on," says Roger. "We need a walk. Let's leave the car."

We walk and gradually my mood lifts. We wend our way through the path to the green. I show Roger Lavender Cottage. We walk on toward Bridges' house and I wonder who lives there now. As we take the turn on the path, we see it. It certainly is a large property, and it looks magnificent. The plot's been opened right up, the pines and oaks are almost all gone, the new fencing is low, and the house looks recently renovated. There are horses in the adjacent field, and a French bulldog runs over to see us grunting and snorting. A man near the door, a grand looking entrance that I've never before set eyes on, gives us a wave. I've no idea who he is. One day, perhaps I'll start up a conversation with him.

At the top of the village, the tall trees of the wood still stand, unchanging but for the transformations of the seasons. I know the village so well, but there's also a difference about it. It's a strange experience.

The Five Things

"Some of your old friends must still live here. They can't all have moved away," Roger tells me. But I'm not ready to see anyone just at the moment. Not yet. Give me time.

****

August 14th, 2019

I go to the beach. I walk a good way along the bay and find a rock to sit on. I watch the long strands of brown seaweed flowing backward and forward with the motion of the water. They remind me of a person's hair.

For the last few days, I've thought a lot about Tommy, and Bridges, and Isaac. I can't help wondering what was going on in Bridges' head when he went off out to sea in that rowing boat. Had he tried to run away from his parents or from his own thoughts? He can't have cared if he lived or died. I hope he found some sort of peace, eventually.

I have to admit it feels good to have shared everything with Roger, though there's one thought I still keep to myself. I knew Naomi better than the others knew her, better than Sam and better than Anna; but did anyone really know Naomi? There would always be the question that we couldn't ask her. Could someone else have been involved? Mr. Morris—was he really away at the time that it happened? Mr. Johnson—how did he come to find the ball? What about Mr. Williams himself—perhaps he didn't go to the hospital at all? Naomi said Tommy was "taken," not missing or run away or got lost. Why did she say it? And whenever I think about that, there's one more nagging question that comes to me: I don't want to ask it, I hope I'm wrong, but it always comes back. Did Naomi try to mislead us in some way? Did she know a little more than she ever let on?

For a moment, I'm taken up with the thoughts again, but I tell myself to stop. I'm determined to put it behind me now. I've been reunited with Tommy, but I no longer yearn to find his sister. I will concentrate on Roger and Mead Cottage, on Philip and Jayne, on May and Helena and Bernard.

I find a few flat stones along the shore and skim them expertly, making them jump across the water.

Epilogue

2042

We lived uneventful lives in the main. Time passed by, some things changed, some things stayed the same.

Childhood memories remain magical: family outings and shopping trips, visits to relatives. Summer holidays were the best times of all. We were expected home at mealtimes but allowed to make plans with our friends and spend long hours with them: at each others' houses, out in the countryside, along the beaches, and in all the various places that made up our spacious green playground. We had the time of our lives. There were tracks and paths, downland, woods, and cliffs. There were old, ruined buildings, abandoned caravans, and beach huts, we knew them all. We dared each other and challenged each other. We stuck up for each other and teased each other. We knew who would give us drinks and who would chase us off their land. We swapped stories about some of the old villagers and some of the old houses. Some stories were passed down through the generations. We were children in a village where people's lives stretched right back to the wars; some of the wars' ways and lessons were still in evidence, yet our own futures would reach into a vastly different world, where communication was mostly done without ever meeting, and games were played on screens.

For those who grow old, the end of life can be much like the beginning.

"It's funny," I said to Roger, years ago when we first moved to Sherbury. "If they ever make the country hotel into a rest home, that's where I'd like to end my days." Ten years on, it happened. The country hotel was bought by a group that already owned other rest homes in the area. It was soon up and running and had a good reputation. In fact, it's more of a nursing home now, with staff able to care for those with greater needs. When Roger became too ill to be at the cottage, we looked into The Grange, as it's known, and we got him in. I don't think we could have found anywhere better.

When I was visiting him, I used to say to the staff, "I hope there's a place here for me when my time comes." I told them, "Make sure that lovely room that overlooks the garden is available." My time came sooner than I thought.

It was six months ago that I moved in. The staff are so nice. On the day I arrived, they brought me up to the room and opened the door, and sure enough, the room I'd stayed in on my first visit, many years before when it was still a hotel, was to be mine. It's so lovely to sit beside the window and look out over the grounds. They've used some of the land to build on a new block, but they've kept the gardens well. Once in a while, in good weather, I've even been able to sit out on a bench seat for a little while.

They really look after me, all the people who work here. They bring me food; they bring tea all day long. Someone's here in a moment if I call. There are a lot of different members of staff, and if they've been off duty for a few days, they come back with such stories to tell about how they've been spending their time.

One of the women brought her young son to see me the other day. He was on his school holidays and had come to meet her. She thought I'd like to say hello to him, so she brought him to my room for a few minutes before they left for home. He reminded me so much of Tommy.

I still think about Tommy, Naomi, Anna, Sam, and the days we spent together all that time ago. I've always thought about them now and then, my whole life. I suppose the events of that summer made a mark on our lives that would always remain. I don't think I was badly affected, and when you think about it, plenty of young people lose friends. Even so, that summer has always been there somewhere in the back of my thoughts. I never had nightmares, though I know some of the others suffered them. I couldn't even remember having dreams about those times until just recently.

I was sitting in my chair—I must have drifted off—and there he was in front of me. Tommy. He looked the same as ever, smiling, full of mischief. I think the others were somewhere in the background...and perhaps there was another little lad too.

"Count to a hundred," he said, "then come to find me." And he ran.

I heard one of the staff in the room, "Wendy, are you all right? Nurse, nurse, it's Wendy, she's not responding!"

I didn't want to be a nuisance. That poor girl. I should speak to her, tell her I'm perfectly fine. But I so wanted to go with Tommy and the others, and spend one more afternoon playing in those fields.

Beth Merwood

More about the characters (2019)

Robert "Robbo" Green became a motor mechanic and was for years a valuable volunteer member of the lifeboat crew.

Peter Clay did not become a footballer, but a very good plumber. He's fitted a lot of new boilers.

Adam Smart is the manager of a dairy herd.

Max Leigh became a landscape gardener—and there are a good number of Mini Maxes running around in Cherlton.

Philip is a university lecturer. He was born to be one.

Anna is a physiotherapist and her brother a teacher, like his father before him. We still exchange Christmas cards and promise visits that never materialize.

Sam moved to Canada and made a good career for himself with a forestry company. We're friends on social media.

The Taylors became a lawyer, a doctor, a carpenter (Mo), and two cafe owners (the same cafe). Three of the siblings still live in Cherlton.

Beth Merwood

The Five Things

Wendy's Poem:

Poor, Poor Birds

Poor, poor birds, I feel so sorry for you and hope that you are now free
Your lives were too short
Why did you have to leave?
I love to see you fly
I love to hear you sing
Did someone hurt you? Did you cry?
Are you now flying somewhere far up in the sky
Away from the badness here on the ground?
One day I will see you again
One day we will fly together to a better land.

A list of important dates

Joseph John Bridges — "*Bridges*" & family
1884 - John Bridges born
1886 - Edith Bridges, nee Palmer, born
1906 - "Bridges" Joseph John Bridges born
1912 - Isaac born
1919 - Isaac dies
1926 - Edith Bridges dies
1951 - John Bridges dies
1969 - Bridges is sixty-three
1985 - Joseph John Bridges dies

Albert "Bert" Wells (Granddad) & family
1914 - Bert Wells born
1919 - Millicent Wells, nee Morris, born
1942 - Sam's Mum born
1962 - Millicent Wells dies
1969 - Granddad is fifty-five
2003 - Bert Wells dies

A word about the author…

Beth Merwood is a writer from the south of England. *The Five Things* is her debut novel.

Thank you for purchasing
this publication of The Wild Rose Press, Inc.

For questions or more information
contact us at
info@thewildrosepress.com.

The Wild Rose Press, Inc.
www.thewildrosepress.com